WHAT SWALLOWS THE LIGHT

ALIEN HORROR NOVELLAS

JOHN DURGIN, GAGE GREENWOOD, ANDREW VAN WEY

BOOK 19 IN CRYSTAL LAKE'S DARK TIDE SERIES

Let the world know:
#IGotMyCLPBook!

Crystal Lake Publishing
www.CrystalLakePub.com

Copyright 2025 Crystal Lake Publishing

Join the Crystal Lake community today on our newsletter and
Patreon! https://linktr.ee/CrystalLakePublishing

Download our latest catalog here. https://geni.us/CLPCatalog

All Rights Reserved

ISBN: 978-1-964398-68-6

Cover art:
Ben Baldwin—http://www.benbaldwin.co.uk

Layout:
Lori Michelle—www.theauthorsalley.com

Edited and proofed by:
Paula Limbaugh, Victoria Kiszka, Janis Botha, Charlene du Toit,
and Theresa Derwin

**Follow us on
Amazon:**

WELCOME
TO ANOTHER

CRYSTAL LAKE PUBLISHING
CREATION

Join today at www.crystallakepub.com & www.patreon.com/CLP

SUFFOCATING SKIES

JOHN DURGIN

CHAPTER 1

ARRIE RICHARDSON STARED back at her reflection in the bathroom mirror inspecting the black eye and bruised cheek that her boyfriend, Reed, had gifted her the previous night. She hoped that nobody else would come into the workplace bathroom before she applied more makeup, desperate to cover up as much as she could before the rest of the office saw her. She would have done the cover-up at home, but she packed a bag and left the house soon after Reed assaulted her, sleeping in her car in the parking lot. She'd had enough. Today was originally supposed to be a day off, considering it was Thanksgiving, but at the last minute their department was requested to come into the office to work overtime. While most people were pissed, she was relieved, happy to have an excuse to not go back home.

She carefully applied concealer around the bruise, wincing at the pain. Each touch was a reminder of her shitty situation, but what choice did she have besides pushing forward? To be the fighter she watched her mother never be when she was in relationships just like this throughout all of Carrie's childhood. The apple didn't fall too far from the tree. Her therapist told her why she was attracted to men exactly like the ones her mom had dated, but that didn't make the habit any easier to break.

The bathroom door opened, and Carrie tried to quickly turn away but it was too late.

"Oh my. . .I told you to leave that son of a bitch," Sally Rhodes, an older woman from the office, said. "Let me see that, hon. What did that bastard do to you?"

"I'll be fine. Please don't let anyone else in the office know, Sal. It's fucking embarrassing."

"Girl, I won't have to say a word. They'll all see it with their own eyes."

"It's that bad, huh?" Carrie asked.

"Uh, yeah. I don't know how many times I gotta tell you, come stay with me. It's just me and my felines. No abusive assholes in sight," Sally said as she approached the sink.

"I appreciate it, really. But I packed a bag and have no plans on going back to Reed. This was the last time he put his hands on me."

"Mm-hmm. I've heard that before. Let me have a look, I can help."

Sally took the makeup and gently applied some. She was so motherly, far more than anything Carrie had experienced growing up. After a few minutes of applying, Sally backed off.

"You're beautiful, you know that? Okay, have a look. I think we did good," she said with a sympathetic smile.

The bruising was barely visible now, and someone would have to look long and hard to see it. A sense of relief filled Carrie and she took a deep breath, then hugged Sally.

"Thank you. Not just for this, but for always being there for me. It means the world."

"Don't thank me. I'd have to be a terrible person to not try and help. Now let's get out there for the morning meeting before Dominic bitches us out for being late on Thanksgiving. Ass."

They both chuckled and went to exit the bathroom as the door pushed in. The janitor, Amelia Henderson, almost bumped into them with the large yellow trash bin on wheels. Carrie sensed the janitor staring at her cheek, but she hoped it was just in her head. Amelia was nice enough but typically didn't talk much to the workers, as if she thought she was below them.

"Sorry," she muttered, then backed out of the way for the women to leave.

One thing abundantly clear was that nobody was thrilled to be working on a holiday besides Carrie. She just wished she could shake the feeling that Reed was waiting around every corner hoping to finish the job he'd started.

CHAPTER 2

FTER FILLING THE toilet paper dispensers, Amelia wiped down the sinks and left the bathroom. She needed a damn smoke. She cursed at herself for craving a cigarette this early in the morning, but the holidays stressed her out. Ever since she lost her son, Hayden, to an overdose a few years back, the joy she once felt this time of year vanished. Instead of prepping a nice meal for Thanksgiving or planning a trip to the mall for some Black Friday shopping, she spent all of November and December depressed and on the verge of drinking herself to death. It didn't help that her husband blamed her for the OD. There was no logic to his reasoning, but in times of grief, some people needed a culprit. Fair or not, that was her.

So, when she got the call to come in to work, she accepted it on the spot. Anything she could do to keep her mind occupied. It was better to be around other people right now even if those people didn't give a damn about her. She saw the way they looked at her. Like she was part of some inferior species just because she had a low-paying job and cleaned shit stains off toilets for a living. They didn't know that before her son died, she had a real career. Amelia worked for a hedge fund on Wall Street in her past life, slaving over her job and putting her family second. She wasn't there for Hayden, missing all the early signs of his drug use. After he died she lost her drive, finding it difficult to even show up to work let alone put in the time needed to perform at a high level. And one thing she learned early on was that the stock market didn't care about your personal life. It didn't take long for her to lose her job, and then she found herself wallowing in self-pity, moping around the house, and trying to find a reason to continue living.

Eventually she was forced to look for work elsewhere if there was any hope of keeping their home. Her husband didn't even speak with her anymore, but they still lived together, unable to afford the costs of an actual divorce.

She walked to the stairwell in the hallway, deciding to sneak a smoke break on the roof instead of out front in the gazebo designated for smokers. She could avoid talking to anyone on the roof, and that's what she wanted right now. Her steps echoed on the way up, even though she attempted to walk quietly so she wouldn't get caught going out. After climbing all eight stories, she reached the roof. She propped the door open with a broom handle that she kept leaning against the railing for occurrences just like this one.

The early morning breeze felt nice, refreshing in a way. Amelia inhaled a lungful of frigid air and looked around at the light snowfall starting to pick up. This was her quiet space, and she needed it right now more than ever. She pulled out her pack of Marlboro Reds and fetched a cigarette. After lighting it, she took a big drag, erasing the fresh air she'd breathed in seconds prior. She continued to think about her son and all that she could have done differently. The warning signs were there, but she was too damn busy to notice them. She closed her eyes and leaned against the wall, inhaling more nicotine. A chill overcame her, so she opened her eyes.

Amelia looked at the sky and gasped. It was as if a dark blanket had been placed over the surrounding area like a solar eclipse reaching complete totality. It was still early, but sunrise had come a few hours prior. She scanned the space directly above her and almost fell backward as the sky shimmered like an obsidian kaleidoscope. Amelia blinked and opened her eyes wide, hoping it was just her contacts shifting on her corneas. But there it was again, movement like a pack of slithering snakes, filling the entirety of the void above. And then she heard the sounds. Whispers of someone saying things she couldn't make out. Until a single voice made itself perfectly clear. It was Hayden.

"It's all your fault. You weren't there for me. . ."

"What the hell?"

The words of her dead son were met with a pulsating sensation buzzing through her head. And then she smelled the drugs. The strange medicinal smell of meth mixed with a sweet smoke. It was the exact scent she breathed in when she found Hayden in his room just moments after he'd overdosed.

SUFFOCATING SKIES

Amelia looked to the sky one more time, sensing that whatever was creating this dark cloud was also the culprit bringing her dead son to her. The center of the darkness widened, followed by a piercing whistle sound. The meth scent blew across the rooftop with a strong gust, swirling around her. She had seen enough. She turned and ran back through the open door, slamming it shut behind her as her ears continued to buzz, blocking out most sounds. *Most* sounds. But as she sprinted down the stairwell, she continued to hear one thing very clearly.

"It's all your fault. You weren't there for me. . ."

CHAPTER 3

CARRIE SAT IN her cubicle and booted up her computer. The rest of her team had all shuffled in while she was busy in the bathroom, hiding her shame. She looked at Sally, who responded with a slight smile as if to say, "We got this. It stays between you and me."

To Carrie's left sat all six foot six of Trent Nobile. He was one of the nicest guys Carrie had ever met, but she couldn't help being annoyed by him. Behind his glasses sat a pair of jittery eyes, always flitting around the office like they were looking for a gang of bikers to show up and beat the shit out of him. After she got to know him, Carrie realized that Trent was just a severe introvert. He was extremely intelligent and always willing to help her when she was confused by something, but any attempt to get a laugh out of him was a lost cause. The closest thing she'd ever had to a real conversation with him was when he overheard her talking with Sally about watching *The Mandalorian* and he couldn't help but jump into the chat to give his opinion.

Next to Trent, the beautiful Vanessa Kelly was busy checking herself on her phone's camera to make sure she looked good. Vanessa's biggest issue—besides trying to fuck her way to the top— was that she wasn't only beautiful, she knew it and leveraged it opportunistically. She was a narrow-minded, self-absorbed bitch. The only time Carrie ever interacted with her was when she was forced to during team meetings and mandatory training. It made Carrie sick to see the way Vanessa used her beauty to her advantage. She was single-handedly regressing feminism by fifty years, minimum.

There were a few more team members, but they were either running late or somehow managed to keep the holiday off. Carrie was okay with that. The less people she had to deal with today, the better. As if he could read her thoughts, her manager, Dominic Santoro, exited his office with a smug look on his face. A short but fit Italian man with a buzzed head, he presented himself like he was the most important person in the world, and there was a good chance he really believed he was. Sinclair Pharmaceuticals was one of the fastest-growing pharma corps in the world, and Dominic managed one of the top sales teams in the entire United States. The joke around the office was that if you cut him open, he'd bleed orange on account of Sinclair's logo being an orange circle with a capital SP in the middle. As he approached, Carrie brought her attention to her monitor in the hopes she'd look too busy to talk with him.

"Okay, folks. Thanks for coming in on Thanksgiving. The company can't thank you enough," he said.

"As if they gave us any choice," Sally muttered. A few laughs followed.

"Hey now, come on. You guys are the top-performing team on-site for a reason, and Mr. Sinclair has taken notice. We just have this one final push before the holidays to cement that top spot for the year. We wouldn't ask you to come in otherwise. And I wanted to have a flash meeting for a minute before the day started. As a thank you for coming in, they've opened the cafeteria. But not just the usual food, no sir. They'll be serving us a full Thanksgiving meal. Turkey, mashed potatoes, biscuits, you name it."

"I hope I get my glass of red wine with it," Sally said, getting another laugh from the team.

"Very funny, Sally. That brings me to my next topic. Mr. Sinclair is in the building today, so I expect you all to be on your best behavior. That means no jokes that go against HR policy," he said while glaring at Sally.

"Of course he's here today of all days. Does that man even have a family?" Carrie asked.

"Please, guys. Try not to embarrass me. We may not even see him, but there's always a chance he makes his rounds to see who decided to show up today and put in the extra effort."

"You know you don't have to worry about me," Vanessa said, fluttering her eyelashes.

Ugh. I hate her so much, Carrie thought.

Dominic cleared his throat. "Yes, I know that. And that goes for the rest of you too. This wasn't a mandatory day, but you're here earning time and a half, so we expect you to be working like you normally would. Meet down in the caf at eleven for an early lunch. I'll give you a few minutes back in your morning before we get started. Happy Thanksgiving, team."

With that, he was gone, and they were left to go about their business. Sally rolled her chair close to Carrie so she could talk quietly.

"Ten bucks says Vanessa's fucking him."

"Eww. Can we not? I got enough horrible images going through my head," Carrie said.

"Sorry, hon. I'm serious about coming to stay at my place tonight. We can get drunk on wine and watch a Christmas movie."

"I might take you up on that."

Satisfied with the answer, Sally rolled back to her cubicle and got to work. Over the next few hours, the only sounds in the office were the *click-click-click* of fingers on keyboards. Carrie paused a moment to stretch, and as she did, her screen glitched briefly. A spiraling symbol flashed over her spreadsheet, and she had a momentary panic, worried she'd lost all the work from the morning. Sally was always telling her to save her files regularly, not to trust the cloud. The concern proved all for nothing as the spreadsheet returned to normal. She took a deep breath and looked at the clock, seeing it was close enough to lunchtime to head down to the cafeteria.

"You ready to—" she started, turning to Sally, only to find her coworker with her eyes rolled back in her head, facing her monitor in a stoic position. Carrie jumped up, ran to her friend, and shook her.

"Sal! Sally, are you okay?"

Sally shook her head, her eyes returning to normal.

"Wha. . .what the hell just happened?" she mumbled.

Carrie didn't answer. Instead, she couldn't take her eyes off Sally's monitor. The same spiral symbol made its way down the center of the screen, frozen in place.

CHAPTER 4

ALBERT SINCLAIR SAT behind his mahogany desk, reading the financial pages *of The New York Times.* While he had a computer sitting in front of him and knew that actual physical newspapers were an endangered species, he still preferred to read them the old-fashioned way. It reminded him of his dad growing up, always trying to learn, back when the world had far fewer distractions. Distractions were bad for business. Which is why no matter what time of the day, he always had the curtains drawn. It was a requirement out on the floor, as well, for all teams. Even the cafeteria had tinted windows.

In the corner of the room, his head of security, Ed Rayner, sat in a chair quietly. He was a massive brute dressed in all black, his hair pulled back tightly in a ponytail, his dense beard hiding his chiseled jawline. Albert had considered making him chop off the tail, but he figured Ed was intimidating as is, so no need to change his appearance. The best part about Ed was he only spoke when spoken to. He'd sit the entire day in complete silence if Albert didn't start up a conversation.

"Ed. You getting hungry?"

"I can eat whenever, Mr. Sinclair. Are you ready for lunch? I can call it in from a place in the city, so you don't have to eat the shitty cafeteria food."

"No, no. I'm fine. I appreciate you working today. I hadn't planned on flying in until after the holidays, but duty calls."

The truth was, he didn't really appreciate Ed working, he *expected* him to. And he was paying good money to have him work. Albert had regular security at the office twenty-four seven, but Ed was his personal security, traveling with Albert wherever he went. While many likely considered the extra protection overkill, they weren't the ones worth billions of dollars. And it wasn't just his wealth that he wanted safeguarded, but also the relics and artifacts he collected.

Albert Sinclair wasn't only a titan in the pharmaceutical world, he was one of the globe's most infamous collectors. Not only did he have a house in the islands designated for storing many of his valuables, but each of the five regional offices for Sinclair Pharmaceuticals had a secret room where he kept some of his rarest items. His thought was simple: it was best to spread them out so if—God forbid—there was ever a break-in or raid, his treasures would be spread around the continent.

Only three people knew of these secret rooms, and two of them were already in the office. One of whom, Ed, willingly signed an NDA when hired. The third was Albert's ex-wife, who he forced to sign an NDA upon their divorce.

Albert stood from his desk and walked over to his wall-to-wall bookshelves, sliding his fingers along the spines until he reached his copy of *Way of the Wolf*.

"You know, Santoro making his team come in today throws a wrench in my plans. I expected to have the place to myself all day."

"Do you want me to have them leave, sir?" Ed asked.

"No, it's okay. I appreciate his hustle. We just need to make sure nobody comes up to this floor while I'm back here. Watch the door, please."

Ed got up from his seat and lumbered to the office door, standing guard. When Albert saw him in position, he pulled the book from the shelf, revealing a security pad. He flipped it open and pressed his index finger to the screen, then waited as the bookshelf parted down the center, sliding hydraulic doors opening slowly as they glided into the walls on each side, creating access to another room.

"This. . . This, my friend, is far more valuable than any amount of money I could attain. I know that sounds hypocritical, seeing as how I slave over the success of this company. But Ed, I do it all for *this*," Albert said, extending his hand out to the newly revealed space.

He entered, knowing that Ed would stay behind by the office door until told otherwise. The room was filled with glass displays, all of which contained a powerful security system, making sure that if anyone had the balls to try and break in, they wouldn't make it very far before they had multiple guns aimed at them. And considering that this room needed to remain hidden, no thieves would live to see the outside world.

Albert pulled a small box wrapped in cloth from his pocket, then typed in an access code to open the glass display in front of him. Before setting the box inside the display, he opened it to get one last look at its contents. A small obsidian stone sat inside, glistening as the fluorescent light above shone down. According to his contacts, this stone trapped a demon inside, and just a simple command would release it upon the world. Albert never planned to do such a thing but holding that power in his hand sent a tingling thrill through his entire body. The box was the reason he had to come to the office today. He needed to make sure it was secure, and like clockwork, he alternated which location each treasure would reside in.

"I could release you and make you do whatever the hell I wanted," he whispered to the stone.

Once he got his fix, he shut the box, sealing the demon once more, and set it in the display case. He locked the glass door before doing his customary lap around the room, admiring the countless objects that held more power than most humans would ever obtain in their lives. The Eye of Ra was a mystical artifact from ancient Egypt that apparently granted its possessor visions of the future and unparalleled insight. According to the legend, it was forged by the sun god, Ra, and held the power to see into the souls of mortals. Next, he came to the Wandering Compass, which was said to always point in the direction of the most powerful source of magic in its vicinity. Then the Whispering Skull, which contained intricate carvings on each side derived from an unknown civilization. Legend said that if you held it to your ear, it would whisper secrets of the past, present, and future.

Finally, Albert came to his most prized possession: the Epochal Tempora. A cube that some scientists believed could control time and even dimensions. Albert landed a deal with a powerful arms dealer who had ransacked the home of a famed historian while seeking out a specific weapon. The object was of no use to the dealer, but like many powerful and influential individuals on the black market, the dealer knew of Albert Sinclair and his obsession with such items.

As much as he wanted to admire his collection for longer, the security system in the room was set up in such a way to automatically seal the doors shut after remaining open for five minutes. He knew the code to get back out, but the extra layer of security prevented the doors from being unlocked again for another hour and he had no desire to be stuck in there for that long. So, he made sure everything was locked up then exited back into the main office where Ed remained at the ready with his firm posture and intimidating stare.

"Well, Ed, I'd say I've worked up quite the appetite. Let's hit the road, shall we?"

Ed nodded and without another word, they headed to the elevator.

CHAPTER 5

CARRIE AND SALLY entered the cafeteria, and the inviting smell of a perfect Thanksgiving dinner permeated the air. As they entered the main dining hall, it was easy to see why. Fred, who in Carrie's opinion was the best chef the place employed, worked rigorously, moving behind the counter with confidence. He was alone, but that didn't stop him from preparing a full-course meal for team Santoro. Even on a day Fred was supposed to have off, he worked with a smile on his face, with his white chef's hat planted on top of his salt-and-pepper hair.

"Fred! This smells amazing!" Carrie said as she walked up to the counter.

It was odd hearing her voice so clearly in the cafeteria, as normally there were hundreds of people scurrying around, trying to get their lunch in before it was time to get back to work. Today it was just their team and Fred. Countless tables remained unoccupied in the background with the lights off. It was actually a bit creepy, reminding Carrie of a food court in a run-down mall that was fighting to stay alive.

"Only the best for you, Carrie," he grinned.

"I feel bad they made you come in to work today just to feed us sorry bunch of misfits," Sally said.

"Oh, stop it. If I wasn't here doing it, I'd be at home doing it for myself. I'd rather others get to enjoy my cooking."

"I'm sure the extra pay doesn't hurt either," Sally shot back and winked.

Fred laughed, then said, "The food's ready to be served. And seeing as how it's just you guys here, I'll bring it all out and serve you directly today."

"Wow, five-star service."

The team sat at a table Fred had prepared ahead of time, even using placemats and real silverware, which wasn't the norm for the cafeteria. Sally sat next to Carrie, Vanessa sat next to Dominic, and Trent sat at the far end of the table by himself. Carrie also noticed the janitor lady sitting in the back of the cafeteria by herself, eating her packed lunch and staring toward the window as if she were looking for someone or something. She considered inviting Amelia over but didn't feel it was her place to do so. *What is she looking at out there?*

The cafeteria windows were tinted, but even so, Carrie thought it looked a bit darker outside than normal for this time of day. Snow continued to come down, so maybe the storm clouds were just really dark, giving the illusion of nightfall.

"Guys, we really wanted to pull out all stops and thank you for your dedication today. We're the top team on-site for a reason. You guys bust your asses here. It doesn't go unnoticed," Dominic said.

Fred walked to the table with a large metal tray with a dome cover. He set it in the center of the table, still smiling. He loved his job and it clearly showed. Carrie couldn't believe how Fred remembered everyone's regular orders when he fed so many people each day. For today, though, he only had to serve one meal to all. He removed the cover, revealing a browned turkey, the skin glistening. He didn't even have to cut into it for Carrie to know it was cooked to perfection.

"Oh, Fred, you've outdone yourself," Sally said.

He tipped his hat and retreated to the kitchen while the team continued their small talk. Once all the side dishes were in place, he carved the bird and went around filling everyone's plate. Even Trent was talkative, which rarely happened.

"Trent, what are you up to this weekend?" Carrie asked, trying to get him to open up a bit. His cheeks burned red, and she couldn't help but feel sorry for him.

"Not much. I'm supposed to attend a book event on Saturday, so I'm hoping the storm is cleared up by then."

"Book event? What type of books do you read?" Carrie asked.

"I. . . Well, I write horror novels on the side, under a pen name."

"Shut up! Seriously? This whole time we've been sitting next to Stephen fucking King?" Sally joshed.

"I wouldn't go that far, but I do well. Enough to make my car payment and live comfortably, at least," he said with a hint of pride.

"No kidding. That's great, Trent," Dominic said.

"So," Vanessa began, "what sort of stuff do you write? If you don't mind me asking."

"All over the place, really, but I write a lot of slasher stuff. It's pretty big right now, so it's a great market to target."

They all sat quietly, and Carrie noticed Trent getting uncomfortable again, so she said the first thing that came to her mind, which probably didn't help.

"So when you're not here taking apart computers, you're at home taking apart bodies, is that what you're saying?" She immediately realized how that sounded and quickly added, "I'm sorry, I didn't mean it like that. Bad joke. I think it's great. You'll have to send me a link to your stuff. I'll gladly support you."

"Same, send it in the team chat when we get back," Dominic said.

Once Fred had served everyone, the group convinced him to sit and enjoy some of the food. He initially refused, but Sally pulled up a seat next to her and eventually, he gave in.

"You're always so busy serving us, Fred. Tell us about yourself. Have you always been a chef?" Sally asked.

"Oh, no. I've always enjoyed cooking, sure, but in my past career, I was far from a chef. I'm a retired police officer. I did that for almost thirty years before calling it quits. Then I decided to enroll in Culinary Arts school and here I am."

"Did you picture working at a cafeteria for a bunch of office geeks?" Carrie asked.

"I wouldn't have it any other way. Less stress, benefits, and I'm out of here after lunchtime most days."

"Did you ever shoot anyone?" Vanessa asked.

"Jesus, *V*. Maybe have some chill," Dominic snapped.

He even has a nickname for her, Carrie thought.

"It's fine. A lot of people ask that. Yeah. . .I did. And I served in the Marines before that, so I've seen some stuff. But that's in the past now," he said with a forced smirk.

"Trent, I'm going to find your books right now," Sally said, scrolling through her phone. "What's your pen name?"

Carrie respected what Sally was doing, trying to shift away from the awkward conversation. Everyone knew that asking a cop or soldier if they killed anyone was a no-no. Everyone except Vanessa, apparently.

"Um, it's Steve McQueen."

Carrie burst out laughing, but nobody else seemed to get the joke.

"That's hilarious. I'm assuming it's a play on Stephen King?"

"You got it."

"What the hell? The internet isn't working on my phone. Sorry, Trent. I'll have to check when we get back to our—" Sally's words were cut short as the lights went out, sending the cafeteria into darkness.

"Everybody stay calm. It's probably just the storm causing a temporary power outage. Security will likely go check the generator to see why it didn't kick on and resolve it," Dominic said.

Carrie hoped he was right. But as she looked over at the windows to check the severity of the storm, it didn't look that bad yet, so how the hell could that have caused a power outage? After watching the storm for a minute, her eyes adjusted enough to see the janitor, Amelia, backing slowly away from the window. She stumbled, almost tripping over her chair.

And then she screamed.

CHAPTER 6

JEROME BROWN WAS in the middle of watching the Detroit Lions lose to the Packers on his phone when the internet went out. It was bad enough that he had to work the front desk on Thanksgiving when there were only eight people in the entire building working the holiday. Then his phone glitched out, further ruining his Thanksgiving tradition of watching his Lions lose. And finally, the power went out altogether, sending the entire call center into suffocating darkness. The generator should have kicked on within seconds, yet Jerome gave it a good five minutes before he decided he needed to do something.

Is the storm even that bad out there?

It sure looked dark as fuck, but he didn't recall hearing about anything more than a few inches of snow coming their way today. He was the only security on duty because of so few staff in the office, but out of instinct, he grabbed his radio. Realizing there would be nobody to answer on the other end, he set it back on the desk and grabbed his flashlight.

"Just fucking lovely. Work when everyone else is home, then miss the damn game."

He turned the flashlight on and stood from his chair. As he stepped around the desk, ready to head down to the generator, the walkie-talkie blasted static from its speaker.

"Fuck!"

His heart slammed in his chest, and he was thankful nobody else was around to see him spooked by a radio. The static intensified, then decreased in volume like it was riding an electrical wave.

"*Giiii. . . vvveee. . . us. . .*"

Jerome froze, waiting for the voice to return. Instead, the static picked back up, the volume rising to the point where he had no choice but to cover his ears. He ran to the radio and picked it up.

"Who's this? Hey! Who was that?"

When nobody responded, he fumbled for the dial, turning the volume all the way down until the power clicked off. The lobby returned to silence, but his ears were ringing. He forced a yawn to try and make his ears pop to no avail. Once the buzzing calmed a bit, he turned to head for the generator. The cone of illumination lit up the lobby, casting light across multiple chairs and plants. They were objects he'd seen countless times, yet in the dark they looked foreign. Jerome shook his head and marched forward when one of the plants moved. No, not the plant, but something *behind* it.

"Oh, hell no," he muttered.

He paused, watching the plant for a few seconds, but nothing happened. Here he was, a grown-ass man, acting like a child afraid of the boogeyman. Confident he was seeing things, he continued forward, his work boots echoing off the tile floor. The generator was at the far end of the building and, considering its size, would take a good five minutes to reach. Of all days, this had to happen when Mr. Sinclair was on-site. Every passing second without power restored felt like a death sentence to Jerome's job security.

He rounded a corner, now entering the empty office area where the tech team typically sat. The hallway traveled through the center of the floor with rows of cubicles on each side. Usually, even when he'd do his nightly rounds, there were at least a few people working in each department. The place was a ghost town today. The flashlight almost reached the end of the tech area, where Jerome would take another turn and head downstairs to the mechanical room, then out the back door to where the generator was located.

Something skittered to his left, moving behind one of the cubicle walls. He whipped the light in its direction, only to see an empty desk with a *Batman* calendar staring back at him. He aimed the light left to right, traveling across the office, but still didn't see anything.

"Is someone there?"

He loathed asking such a stupid question—clearly *something* was there. He just hoped it was one of the workers who was supposed to be upstairs putting in overtime. Jerome waited, trying to determine if he wanted to enter the labyrinth of cubicles or just keep moving toward the generator. The latter sounded far more appealing, but it was his job to make sure the place was safe. He stepped between the first set of cubicles, scanning each and finding nothing but standard office equipment. As he started toward the next row, he heard another sound close by. This wasn't the same skittering he'd heard before, which had sounded like a pack of rats fleeing into the shadows. Instead, it sounded more like something aggressively chomping down on air, clacking its teeth together over and over.

Jerome's free hand instinctively went to the firearm on his belt, ready to grab it if necessary. He took a deep, controlled breath to steady his nerves, then slowly stepped forward. As he leaned around the corner of the cubicle, a flash of movement disappeared around the other side as if it was playing a game of hide-and-seek with him. The movement was swift, but he could've sworn he saw a tail.

Fuck this.

He pulled the gun from his holster and charged forward. The tail was there for an instant, then gone again, this time toward the back of the tech floor. Jerome swallowed down the fear and picked up his pace, determined to see what the hell had found its way into the building. The sounds increased from the figure, the clicking noise picking up speed. It was followed by labored breathing. It had to be a fucking rabid animal—raccoon, cat, something. But that tail had no fur.

When Jerome was only a few feet from the corner, the noises stopped.

"What the hell. . ."

He aimed the light at the floor, holding the gun steady in his other hand, then slowly stepped around the corner of the last cubicle. The atrocity in front of him was far worse than anything he could have imagined. A trail of slime led to some type of creature that Jerome had never seen before. It wasn't a tail he'd been following, but a long, slender tube of flesh with jagged legs that resembled those of a scorpion. The creature's skin rippled as if there were much smaller wormlike monsters swimming beneath the surface. As if the thing needed to become any more nightmare-inducing, it turned when it sensed him, and the front of the creature had a face of spiraling teeth decorating the surface, with no apparent mouth beneath them. The sharp tips tore through loose skin, leaving trails of blue sludge.

"Oh Jesus! Oh fuck!" Jerome stumbled backward, dropping the flashlight to the floor. The light rolled around, making the beam circle around the office like a searchlight on a lighthouse. The light path stopped just short of the creature, casting it mostly in shadow.

Jerome aimed the gun, ready to fire. The snakelike beast launched, and as it did, the loose skin on the front of its face parted, revealing a mouth full of razor daggers with saliva dangling from each piercing tip. Before Jerome could pull the trigger, the thing was on him. He felt the pain before he realized what was happening. The teeth latched onto his stomach, sucking like a powerful vacuum. He screamed, dropping the gun as he tried to beat the thing off him. The pain gave way to a partial numbness, where all he could feel were the teeth catching like barbed wire around his belly button, digging in as the thing twisted like someone wringing wet hair.

He grabbed hold of the creature and tried to pull it off, but that was a mistake. Not only did the teeth latch on even more, but the skin on his hands burned. He let go and noticed his palms were blistering where they had touched the slimy skin. Something wasn't right with his stomach. Whatever this thing had done to numb him, it was almost as if it paralyzed him from the chest down. Even through the numbness, Jerome could sense something pumping into him, like he was connected to some fucked-up umbilical cord.

"Get the fuck off me!"

He knew he couldn't pry the thing off. He needed to get his gun. When it dropped to the floor, it couldn't have fallen too far from where he was. He looked around, spotting the weapon just out of arm's reach. With everything he had, Jerome attempted to shimmy his way over to it, all while his insides continued to be filled with some foreign substance.

It's. . . so. . . close. . .

And then he had it in his grasp. He immediately brought it up and took aim. It was the first time he got a real detailed look at the creature.

What the fuck is it, and where did it come from?

The body was pulsating as it pumped him full of its fluids, and he could sense whatever was swimming beneath its skin now inside of him. He fired the gun, exploding a hole in the creature's insides. Blue liquid sprayed onto his face, instantly burning his cheek and chin. The creature's grip loosened, but not entirely. So he fired once more and watched as the thing twitched, swinging sporadically from side to side. And then it stopped, falling off his body to the floor.

Jerome looked at his stomach and screamed. Little wormlike shapes pressed against his skin, looking as if they were trying to force their way back out of his body. Suddenly the numbness faded, and the pain came roaring back. White flashes spread across his vision, and then Jerome blacked out.

CHAPTER 7

CARRIE COULDN'T STOP thinking about Amelia's reaction to the lights going out. Thankfully, Fred went over to talk with her and calm her down, but now that she was sitting with the group, the fear in her eyes sent a chill down Carrie's spine. Fred had grabbed a flashlight from the cafeteria office, setting it in the center of the table to give them some light.

"What was it that you saw?" Fred asked Amelia.

"I. . .I saw something when I went out for a smoke break—I suppose I should start earlier, tell you about my past. My son died of an overdose a few years back. My life has been a living hell ever since. I won't bore you with my home life, but I tell you this because when I was out smoking, the sky turned dark all of a sudden, like the most intense storm was about to hit. But it was *darker* than that, like nightfall dark. I stared up at the sky, trying to figure out what was causing it. That's when I saw movement in the darkness. I can't explain it, but I swear whatever was creating the darkness was right there behind the clouds, suffocating the sky. And then, I heard voices. Not just any voices, but my dead son, telling me his death was my fault."

"Oh Lord. I'm sorry, hon. But that's just gotta be the guilt still buried inside. There's no way that could have anything to do with what's happening right now," Sally said.

"Yeah, except when I was just looking out the window, I saw him. I know it seems impossible. But I swear on everything that's holy, I saw my son staring back at me from below."

"Something strange is happening—I think we can all feel it— but we need to take a breath and try to figure this out," Fred said.

Just when they were starting to relax a bit, they heard a muffled scream, then what sounded like a few gunshots coming from the umbilicus of the call center.

"What the fuck was that?" Dominic yelled.

"Sounded like shots fired. Is it terrorists?" Vanessa asked, panic dripping from each word.

"Terrorists? Are you fucking serious? We're a damn pharmaceutical call center. This isn't *Die Hard*. What could they even want with us?" Dominic asked, holding on to the last bit of his composure.

"Okay. We have two options. We can either stay here and wait this out, or we can try to figure out a way to get the power back on and go see what caused that commotion," Fred said, the mild-mannered chef now gone.

"Commotion? It sounded like someone fucking dying, man. I don't want to go anywhere near that. And no offense, I could care less if the power comes back on at this point. I want to get out of here," Dominic said.

"Someone could need our help. I don't expect any of you to want to go, but I have to. Thank the old cop in me. If you don't want to come, I suggest trying to get in touch with security at the front desk and leaving the premises," Fred said.

"I say we just leave. Sorry, Dominic, but getting us to come in on Thanksgiving was bad enough. I'm not about to stay with the power out and something clearly wrong here," Trent said.

"Don't apologize to me. I'm right behind you," Dominic said.

"Either way, do what you'd like. But I need to go see if someone needs help," Fred repeated.

"I'll go with you, Fred," Sally said.

"Me, too," Carrie replied.

"Anyone else?" Fred asked, scanning the remaining uncommitted.

"I'll come with you guys. I'm not so sure going outside is the smartest thing after what I saw," Amelia said.

"Vanessa, I'd ask you, but I think we all know you'll do whatever Dominic does," Sally sniped.

Vanessa didn't respond, just stared at Sally like she wanted to slap her in the face.

"Well, that settles it then. Whoever's coming with me, let's go. The rest of you, I wish you the best. All I ask is that you send help if you can reach it," Fred said.

And with that, the chef grabbed the flashlight and took off in the direction of the commotion, followed by Carrie, Sally, and Amelia. Carrie knew it was the right thing to do, but she just hoped it wasn't going to be a huge mistake.

CHAPTER 8

ALBERT SINCLAIR DIDN'T like to admit when he was scared. It made him angry, weak. Vulnerability wasn't something his parents accepted growing up. The phrase "born with a silver spoon up your ass" often got tossed around for those born into wealth. But for him, it wasn't a silver spoon, it was a boot up his ass. His dad was a coldhearted man who wanted to teach Albert what was needed to survive in this world with the sort of power their family held. He couldn't afford to be weak, not when he'd have the world bowing at his feet, begging for a dollar every time he let his guard down. And his parents were right. When he was a child, he resented them, wanting to grow up like other kids and have fun. Enjoy normal hobbies.

When Albert was old enough, his dad forced him to come into the office and learn the ropes of the pharmaceutical company. At that point, the business wasn't worth half of what it was now, but their family was still one of the wealthiest in the United States. Albert had turned the fortune into a mega-fortune, now one of the wealthiest families in the *world*. So to say his parents rubbed off on him would be an understatement, which is why he despised himself right now for being scared.

They were in the elevator on the way down to the lobby when the power went out. It had only been a few minutes since they'd been stuck in the dark box, but it felt like an hour. Albert knew the main reason he was scared was because of how his parents punished him as a child. One of his mom's favorite forms of discipline was to lock Albert in the closet with the lights off for hours at a time whenever he talked back. The dark elevator immediately brought back those horrible memories. Shapes started to take form in the darkness, easing some of his fears, but not completely.

"Are you close to getting it open?" Albert asked Ed, trying to hide the tremble in his voice.

"It's not budging, Mr. Sinclair."

"Keep trying, damn it. The generator should have kicked on by now. Can you try to reach the front desk on your phone?"

Ed stopped his attempt at prying the elevator doors apart, wiped the sweat from his brow, then reached for his phone. He closed his eyes, hesitant to break the bad news that Albert knew was coming.

"No service in the elevator."

They couldn't use the emergency phone in the elevator without power. Which meant they were officially trapped. Albert walked up to the door and kicked it as hard as he could, not because he thought it would break through, but because rage consumed him. He kicked over and over, feeling the vibrations jolt through his leg with each impact.

"Fuck!" Albert yelled, panting. "Leave your phone light on so we can see in here, at least."

He slouched down and sat on the elevator floor, leaning his head back against the wall. Ed turned the phone light on and set the cell on the floor, then went back to work trying to pry the doors open. There was a crack of light peering through, but it was dull. Still, any light was better than the obsidian box they were in. It was progress. Ed stopped to take a breath, filling the tight space with an eerie silence. Albert closed his eyes, trying to think.

With a sudden jolt, the elevator shook, and at first, he assumed Ed was back to work, ramming his meaty shoulder into the doors. Then he opened his eyes and saw Ed frozen in place, staring up at the ceiling of the elevator.

"Sir. . .something landed up there," Ed whispered.

They remained quiet, listening for any movement. Was it possible someone had fallen into the elevator shaft and landed on top of the car? Just as Albert started to speak, the elevator shook again. Ed stumbled into the wall, then grabbed hold of the railing on the side.

"What the hell is that?" Albert snapped.

As if the culprit decided to answer them, something banged on the roof repeatedly. Dust particles fell in the darkness, landing on Albert's face. He spat the disgusting taste from his mouth, wiping it out of his eyes. Was that a hole starting to form in the ceiling?

Was something trying to break into the elevator? Maybe it was someone trying to help, the security guard at the front desk coming to break them free. Except he knew that couldn't be true. How would anyone know they were in the elevator when the power went out?

Albert could see enough to notice the small opening forming above, but not enough to see who or what was responsible for it. Then a flash of movement on the other side of the metal gash gave him a quick glimpse, and what he saw prickled his skin. Long leatherlike claws ripped at the metal. The claws were attached to matching black skin, on which the phone light cast an unpleasant sheen.

"Shit! Ed, do something!"

Ed grabbed his pistol and aimed above.

"I can't fucking see it in the dark! What if I shoot the cable holding us up?"

"Just shoot it! I don't give a shit about the cable," Albert snapped, pressing himself firmly against the wall like it somehow added more protection.

Ed fired the gun, momentarily robbing Albert of his hearing. An incessant ringing took over, which somehow weakened his other senses. For the next thirty seconds, Albert watched the scene unfold like it was a muted television. The flash bang of another shot simultaneously lit the fear in Ed's eyes. Ed, who Albert had never seen scared in all the years he'd known him. The clawed hand now pushing through the new opening, reaching in for them. And then, just as his hearing started to come back to him, Albert heard screams. It took him a second to realize it was a mix of Ed and the thing on top of the elevator, both bellowing in agony. A bluish liquid dripped through the hole, landing on Ed's hand. The brute's eyes opened wide, staring down at the sludge-like liquid covering his skin. He dropped the gun to the floor, no longer focused on the creature above.

"It fucking burns! Fuck, fuck, fuuuck!"

Albert no longer cared if his fear was visible. He was a kid again, locked in the closet. The creature was his mom and dad doing everything imaginable to make his stay in the confined space as uncomfortable as possible. He cowered in the corner with his eyes glued to the ceiling.

An insidious odor filled the tight space, and when Albert

realized it was the skin on Ed's hand melting, he leaned over and retched on the floor. The thing's arm extended like a black mamba seeking out its prey. It latched around the top of Ed's head, covering the entirety of his hairline. Ed's eyes bulged as he squealed an unnatural cry. Blood slowly slid down his face as the creature dug into his scalp. His legs flailed as they were lifted off the ground. Ed weighed close to three hundred pounds of muscle, and this thing lifted him like a toddler.

"Heeelp! Get it ooooff!"

Albert had no plans to get up and help. All he could hope for was that when this thing was done, it would move on and leave him alone.

The elevator shifted and the thing's claws tore into Ed's head, ripping the scalp clean off. Ed's body broke free and slammed into the wall, dropping to the floor in a heap. The phone light lit the exposed skull on the top of his head as blood poured out around the perimeter. Albert realized the reason the elevator shifted was because one of the cables had snapped, and the cart now leaned at a slight angle.

The creature growled like an idling lawn mower, then slammed its hands back into the ceiling, caving in the structure even more. Albert had only seen its arm and claws, and that was more than enough. He couldn't imagine what the rest of it looked like.

Ed's body shook, spazzing like it was being electrocuted by an invisible force. Albert knew he had to do something. He spotted the gun a few feet away and wondered if it had any bullets left. He'd never fired a gun in his life—he always had people to do it for him—but pulling a trigger seemed easy enough. Maybe he could get a good shot from the floor, out of the thing's reach.

"Ed. . . Can you hear me?" Albert whispered.

Ed didn't respond with words. Instead, he moaned incoherently. His back was to Albert, so Albert couldn't see his face. He was going to have to act on his own. He got to his hands and knees and crawled quickly over to the gun, careful to avoid the blue puddles burning through the carpet. He grabbed the pistol and crawled back to his corner, out of reach. His heart was a rollercoaster, blasting into his chest at full speed. He took a deep breath and aimed the gun at the hole, which was now much wider. The creature continued to work above them. Albert just needed a good shot and he'd take it.

And then the hole widened enough for the thing to fit both clawed hands into the opening, prying the metal apart. The black void above filled with the outline of the creature crouched over them, staring down. For the first time, Albert saw its hideous face. A black leathery canvas with tiny blue dots for eyes. The skin looked like it had been petrified for years and just got its first taste of fresh air. Around the eyes were little, jagged spikes, which traveled all the way up to the top of its head in a spiral pattern. The body was long and slender, yet all muscle. The worst part of all was the mouth: a significant overbite with a line of black fangs that hung down to its chin.

"Holy fuck."

Albert aimed and fired, and while it was too dark to see where he hit it, he knew the bullet connected. If the smack of the bullet entering skin wasn't enough, blue liquid poured out of the wound, landing on the floor below, splashing across Ed's unresponsive body. The creature opened its maw wide, revealing a black tongue beneath the razor teeth, and bellowed so loud Albert thought his eardrums had exploded. It lunged off the roof out of sight, and when it did, the elevator shifted back. Albert sat in place, still in shock from what he'd just witnessed.

He only had a second to relax before a snapping sound drew his attention above once more. He expected the creature to be back, but instead, the space was empty. Another *snap*. And then, as the elevator began its free fall, he understood it was the cables holding them in place. The elevator plummeted below and all Albert could do was close his eyes and pray.

CHAPTER 9

TRENT HATED THE idea of splitting up, but he also had no desire to go deeper into the building, where they heard those. . .*sounds*. It was sometimes funny how things unfolded. The night before, he had been standing on the roof of his parents' high-rise condo a few hundred feet above the city. He'd been ready to jump to his death, never to be missed by anyone. Then his phone rang, and he answered to hear Dominic on the other end, begging him to come in on Thanksgiving. As ridiculous as it sounded, he was wanted for a day. He was *needed*. It was enough to convince him to put off his plans, at least for a day.

Now, the thought of death terrified him. Would he have even jumped if the phone never rang? Or would he have been a giant coward like his entire family thought he was?

He was borderline genius in school, graduating at the top of his class and getting a full ride to Stanford, where he also finished above the pack. That should have been enough to make his parents happy. That *should* have been his start to adulthood, where he'd blossom into a real man. Except, that never happened. After he graduated, he struggled with severe anxiety. The thought of having to handle everything on his own after a life of being told he wasn't good enough was too much of a burden. So, he started an entry-level job at Sinclair Pharmaceuticals hoping he could slowly work his way up.

What he never realized was just how much he hated being a part of the real world. As a child, he didn't have to talk to anyone more than the bare minimum. He didn't have to worry about upsetting friends or breaking some girl's heart because he was never around long enough to form those types of relationships. His family moved around from city to city, and he was left to himself more often than not.

He snapped back to reality when another loud *bang* came from somewhere in the building. This sound was different, unlike the gunshots from earlier. It sounded more like a car crash, metal on metal.

"What the hell was that?" he asked.

Dominic stopped and Vanessa grabbed hold of his arm. Fred had taken the flashlight, so their phone lights were all they had, and in such a large building they were about as effective as a butter knife on a steak.

"I don't know. I think we should take another way down," Dominic said.

"We can't go back through the cafeteria, and we can't go toward that noise that sounded like it was coming from the main entrance area. So what's that leave us?" Trent asked.

"Just like during the fire drills. We go down the side stairwell and out the back," Dominic said.

"Dom, I don't know. Maybe we should just wait it out in an office somewhere? Until help comes?" Vanessa suggested.

"Yeah. . .maybe. I—"

"You can't be serious. We'd be sitting ducks if we stayed here. You heard those growls, or whatever the fuck that was," Trent snapped.

"It's just, the janitor, she sure seemed like going outside was a bad idea. Seeing her dead son and shit," Dominic said.

"She's fucking crazy. What would her dead son have to do with all this? Our best bet is to get out of here before whatever the hell that is finds us. We can get help for the rest."

"Please, Dom. We need to hide somewhere," Vanessa pleaded.

"Damn it! I don't know what the hell to do, guys. This is so fucked—"

Vanessa pulled on his arm, dragging him down a side hall toward a section of personal offices.

"We're safer waiting in here, Dom. I don't care if Trent wants to come or not, that's on him."

"No, I'm the supervisor to all of you. It's my job to look after you."

"Jesus, man, I'm not a toddler. If you want to go with her, that's up to you. But I'm going toward the exit. And if I need to be the one to go for help when I get out, I'll do it," Trent said.

Dominic shook his head, then said, "Just be safe, Trent."

And with that, he followed Vanessa down the dark hallway,

leaving Trent to himself. Trent watched them disappear into the darkness, then when they were gone, he turned back toward where they'd been heading. With trembling hands, he moved through the darkness, his small beam of light barely giving enough illumination to avoid tripping over his own feet. At least the sounds they heard before didn't repeat. But the silence that followed was almost worse. What the hell was out there? Why was it here? One minute they had all been quietly working before enjoying a nice meal, then everything went to hell.

Maybe it was meant to happen? Maybe the reason my phone rang was so I could be here to save everyone. Or maybe, maybe this was a punishment from God for trying to kill myself. Make me suffer a long, terrifying stretch before killing me slowly in front of the only people I know outside of my home.

Up ahead, a dim light penetrated the darkness from around a corner. He sped up, hoping it was one of the others, or better yet, a police officer coming to help. His quickening steps brought him to a sprint, and he reached the end of the hall, turning left. Trent stopped in his tracks.

It wasn't a flashlight or a person. Instead, he spotted a spiral design defacing the wall, as if it was rendered by fluorescent blue paint.

"What the hell. . ."

Trent observed the strange pattern, not only wondering what it meant but what the hell had painted it. And then a stench hit him, a mix of copper and overcooked meat. He approached the symbol, noticing the smell growing stronger the closer he got. He reached out to touch the glowing liquid, then stopped himself. He didn't know why, but his mind told him to get away. Instead, Trent reached into his pocket and pulled out a pen. He reached out again, this time allowing the pen to touch the foreign substance. The blue liquid continued to ooze down the wall, forming around the tip of the pen.

A sizzling sound emitted, then the tip of the pen turned to mush as it melted away.

"Son of a bitch."

Suddenly he began to think he made a mistake coming this way by himself. What if the thing that did this was still out there? And what did that symbol even mean? After a moment of considering his options, he decided to continue forward, praying that he would find a safe exit before things got worse.

CHAPTER 10

ARRIE FOLLOWED CLOSE behind Fred and Sally, keeping her eyes on Amelia as best she could in the dark. As much as she wanted to believe what the janitor insisted she saw—especially with all the strange occurrences taking place—the fact that she claimed to see her dead son seemed too far-fetched. They had made it all the way to the end of the second floor when the loud rumble occurred. It sounded like a freight train crashing into the building, even shaking the floor a bit. What they didn't find was the source of the gunshots. There was a trail of blood and some other strange substance, which they had been following through the stairwell and onto the third floor. The longer they went on, the more Carrie reconsidered her commitment to offer help. Maybe the others were right in leaving.

Either way, she was too far into it to back out now. They reached the dead end of the third floor, another empty dark space in a sea of dark spaces. Fred turned to face them.

"Listen, I understand if you all want to meet up with the others. Whatever this is leading to, I think we can all agree it's not good. But this blood tells me someone is hurt. I'd say now is the time you need to decide for sure what you want to do," Fred said.

Carrie would have never pictured this version of Fred, the nice cook who remembered everyone's order. Here he was, a true leader and fearless soul, willing to do whatever was needed to help others. Carrie thought about all of the horrible men in her life: from her dad, who walked out on her as a child, to Reed, who looked for any excuse to show his dominance. Then she looked back to Fred and realized, as sad as it was, he was the nicest man in her life. She wasn't about to let him down.

"We've come this far. I'm not going anywhere," Carrie said.

The others didn't say anything but gave a nod of approval. Fred turned and opened the door to the stairwell, ready to go up to the fourth floor, and gasped. Carrie looked over his shoulder into the weakly lit space and stifled a scream.

Sprawled out on the stairs was the security guard from the front desk. He was facing the opposite wall, displaying the back of his uniform which was covered in splotches of blood. From where they stood, it was impossible to tell if he was alive or not.

"Hold this door open and aim the light for me, please," Fred said without taking his eyes off the body. He handed the flashlight to Sally who aimed with trembling hands.

"Be careful," Sally whispered.

Fred approached the guard and kneeled. Carrie entered the stairwell behind Fred but kept her distance.

"Sir? Can you hear me?"

"Is he breathing?" Carrie asked.

"If he is, it's too weak to see in this light. I—"

"Kill me," the man uttered, then coughed.

Fred grabbed the man's shoulder and rolled him onto his back.

"Holy shit," Fred whispered, backing away.

The guard slowly turned toward them, his face caked in blood and vomit. A puddle of blue liquid covered the floor next to his head. His eyes flitted erratically as if they were watching an invisible bug flying around the stairwell. The front of his uniform was ripped in the center, his stomach covered by tattered cloth that clung to his skin like bloody papier-mâché.

"I said, fucking kill me! They're eating me alive, man. . . Please."

Fred slowly closed in on the man and Carrie noticed the confidence he had before had all but vanished.

"What happened? What's eating you alive?" Fred asked.

The guard started to respond, but instead, his cheeks expanded, then he vomited all over the front of his shirt. A concoction of blood, puke, and the blue substance dripped down to the floor. Carrie noticed something moving in the vomit and pulled back on Fred's shoulder.

"Fred, there's something moving."

"Look! Look what they did to me!" the guard shouted, echoing through the narrow space.

He tore his shirt back, revealing his full stomach for the first time. Something swam beneath his skin, traveling through his ribs.

But the worst part was the area surrounding his belly button. It looked infected, with blue and pink lines expanding out across the rest of his abdomen. The center of his navel looked as if something had stabbed him repeatedly with a small knife.

"Jesus Christ, man. What the fuck happened to you?" Fred asked.

"Something got in here. I think I killed it, but there may be more of them. It wasn't. . .it wasn't anything that could have come from here."

From here? What the hell does he mean?

As if knowing Carrie needed an answer, a loud screech blasted from somewhere deeper in the building. The guard quivered, attempting to force himself up to a sitting position.

"Please don't leave me here."

"We won't. And we're not going to kill you either. But I need you to try and relax. We'll help you get out. Is that sound from the thing that did this to you?" Fred asked.

The guard shook his head aggressively. "No way, man. The thing that did this to me was like some fucking worm-thing with spider legs. No way it could have made that sound."

Fred locked eyes with Carrie and they shared a second of silent concern.

"Is anything hurt besides your stomach? Can you walk?" Fred asked.

"I think I can. My legs are fine, but I'm weak. They're doing something to my body," the guard said in a pained tone.

Fred and Carrie helped him up. She couldn't avoid being disgusted by the vomit covering his clothing, but she did her best to hide it.

"What's your name?" Fred asked.

"Jerome."

"Okay, Jerome. Tell us everything you know. Anything that could help us. We need to get somewhere safe, and that thing didn't sound too far away. We might not have much time."

"Whatever they are, I think they tried to communicate through my radio. I heard a voice. It said to give it something, but I have no fucking clue what they were talking about. Next thing I know, that creature was trying to burrow into my damn stomach."

Amelia entered the stairwell leaving only Sally back holding the door. She pushed past Carrie and came face-to-face with Jerome.

"They said it to me too. When I was on the roof. Whatever this is, they want something. Did they. . .did they make you hear things? Or see things that weren't there?"

Jerome shook his head, and Amelia looked disappointed. Still, Carrie thought they were on the verge of figuring something out, even if it wasn't the answers they wanted.

"I think maybe it's something in the air outside that does it. I think that until they have what they came for, we're stuck here. We need to figure out what that is," Amelia said.

"If what you say is true about the sky, I think you're on to something. We don't know if they will leave us alone if they get what they want, but I think either way, if we find out what that is, we have some leverage," Fred said.

"That shit wasn't from this world, man. How in the fuck are we supposed to figure that out?" Jerome asked.

Before anyone could answer, the same bloodcurdling screech came again, this time much closer. It sounded like it was in the stairwell above them.

"We need to go. Now. Let's head back down to the second floor and we can hide out in the walk-in freezer until we come up with a plan," Fred said.

Carrie hated the idea of going back to where they started, but Fred was very convincing, and he was as confident as anyone could be given the circumstances. She looked at Sally in the doorway to gauge her thoughts about it all, and all Sally did was shake her head and shrug. Carrie smiled, feeling the bruise on her cheek as she did. A friendly reminder that even before she was dealing with monsters here, she had been living with one for years. Hell, maybe one of these things would take her out to dinner before killing her. It seemed a fitting way to go out.

A burst of movement a few levels up caught all their attention. They looked up to see an elongated black arm speeding by the open space above in a blur. It was only two floors above them now.

"Go! Get back out to the hall. We need to move quick," Fred snapped.

He helped Jerome out through the door, and the rest followed. Carrie slammed the door shut behind them. The group sped back down the hallway, making it to the end as they heard the door blast open behind them.

CHAPTER 11

DOMINIC SHUT AND LOCKED the office door, then turned to face a terrified Vanessa. While he liked the power of being a leader, this wasn't exactly what he signed up for. Still, he felt a sense of pride in keeping Vanessa safe. He knew the real reason she gave him any attention was to advance her career, but he put blinders on, allowing himself to pretend that a girl this attractive could be interested in him otherwise.

They made sure to pick an office with the shades already drawn, hoping if there was anything on the outside looking in, they would remain hidden. And that was one feeling he couldn't shake—the constant sense of eyes watching him from every dark corner. Dominic wasn't sure if this was the best decision or not, but he didn't want to admit how scared he was out in the open, not after what they'd heard. They hadn't even seen the culprit of the horrifying noises yet, which made it even worse. What the fuck could make those sounds?

"Dom, what's happening?"

"Hell if I know, Vanessa. I think for now, we'll wait it out in here. It wasn't just that wailing I heard. Did you hear the other sounds?"

"The gun? Of course," Vanessa said.

"No. Like something scratching in the ceiling or the vents. No matter where we went, I kept hearing it."

Vanessa furrowed her brow in concern. Was he hearing shit? He couldn't explain it, but it was a skittering sound like claws scraping along metal. As if something was following them through the ducts and watching their every move. That thought brought his attention to the ceiling, and he breathed a sigh of relief when he realized the exposed vents from the floor below weren't visible in the office. Although they were likely still there, hidden by the ceiling tiles.

"Dom, you're scaring me. We saw how that janitor was acting, and now you're acting weird too. Maybe that explosion was like a gas leak or something?"

He considered it. It was possible, but that didn't explain the blackout. All the uncertainty made him happy about his decision to lie low. Let the others try to be heroes, he wasn't paid for that. He went behind the desk and sat in the office chair, burying his face in his hands. How long would they need to wait here? He was starving, only getting a few bites of the amazing Thanksgiving meal that Fred had prepared. And he was supposed to meet his mom after work to take her Black Friday shopping. It was an annual tradition. With his face still buried, he didn't hear Vanessa approach the desk until her hand touched his leg, sliding up toward his crotch.

"You know. . .since we're in here, why not have some fun? I've always wanted to break one of these offices in with you."

"You can't be serious. How could you even concentrate on that right now?" Dominic asked. He found her sudden shift in mood a bit jarring.

"It could take our mind off it. . ."

She said it so seductively. Dominic immediately felt goosebumps spread across his flesh. That wasn't the only thing he felt spreading. His hand instinctively went to his pants, covering the growing erection from view. It was pointless, though; she knew exactly what she was doing.

"Oh man, *V*. I don't know if that's a good idea right now. What if the others find us? I could get fired."

"I think your little buddy disagrees with you, and that adds to the fun, doesn't it?" she asked, stroking the outside of his pants.

He couldn't deny it. The fabric on his thigh stretched as her hand rubbed the length of his shaft. Their relationship was obvious to anyone who paid attention, but that didn't mean he was comfortable being open about it. It was a big no-no to have sexual relations with one of your subordinates—not just at Sinclair, but pretty much anywhere. Still, his sexual urge was winning out against his morals.

He grabbed her arm and pulled her close, kissing along her neck, biting gently the way she liked. She moaned as she climbed on top, straddling his lap. Her hips thrust, teasing him. Dominic pulled back on her hair, then stuck his tongue in her mouth, which tasted like cranberry sauce—a fine dessert indeed. He couldn't handle it anymore, wrapping his arms around her and lifting her body onto the desk. She aggressively swiped everything off, ignoring the sounds of the items smashing onto the floor.

The way the phone light on the desk lit up her contours and accentuated her round breasts beneath her silk shirt, he couldn't wait to rip it off. He undid his belt, then started to unbutton his pants, when he heard that same skittering sound above. He tried to ignore it, assuming he was just hearing things. But then dust particles fell from the ceiling tiles, swimming weightlessly in the phone light.

He looked up at the ceiling, pausing his sexual pursuit. Vanessa groaned, irritated by his hesitation.

"What is it? You can't be worried about the others finding us. The door's locked, Dom. Don't tease me like this."

He shook his head, then pulled his pants down. Vanessa opened her legs, giving him easy access beneath her short skirt. Noting that she needed no aid getting wet, he licked the palm of his hand and stroked himself. Then he was inside her, thrusting against the desk. For a moment, all thoughts of the fears outside the room vanished.

But then he heard the scratching again.

He paused and Vanessa pulled him close, forcing him back inside her.

"Don't you dare stop," she snapped.

He complied, but his focus was on the noises above. He felt himself shrinking inside her, something that would normally never happen.

Then he saw a vibration in the acoustic tiles, traveling across the ceiling.

Something was moving right above their heads.

"*V. . .*something's up there," he whispered.

She let her head fall back in defeat, but in doing so, she saw the same thing he was seeing.

"What the fuck!"

"Be quiet," he snapped.

They watched the tiles moving as though giant cockroaches were traveling their hidden path down to the cafeteria. Except whatever was making the drop ceiling move that way had to be far bigger than small insects. Dominic backed away from the desk, blindly grabbing for his underwear, pants around his ankles. His eyes were glued to the ceiling. This time, Vanessa didn't pull him back. She shimmied off the desk and clung to his arm. But then the movements stopped, the room returning to complete silence. Dominic could hear himself still panting and made a point to try and control his breathing.

"Are they gone?" Vanessa asked.

"I think—"

His sentence was cut short as the ceiling in the far corner of the room caved in, sending tiles flying in every direction. Dominic instinctively guarded his eyes as Vanessa screamed. A hunched figure lurked in the darkness, too shadowed to make out any features, except for the eyes. Two beady, blue dots that were too close together. Dominic heard the same sound he'd heard earlier— a rhythmic clicking, like bones grinding together. Now that the thing was this close, he realized it was coming from the creature's mouth—its teeth clacking together as if chomping on an imaginary meal.

"Do something, Dom!"

He wasn't focused on Vanessa and her demands. Instead, he remained locked on the figure. The alien creature emerged from the darkness like a nightmare given form. Its sleek, black, leathery skin glistening with an oily sheen under the dim light filtering from Dominic's phone.

"Oh my fucking God. . ."

It lunged from the corner of the room over the desk in one impossible motion, landing on his chest. Vanessa screamed again, but Dominic couldn't see her as the hideous creature blocked the entirety of his view. The impact slammed him into the wall, and he fell onto the floor, but the thing clung to him. Behind the creature, Vanessa continued to scream, but they weren't the same cries of panic as before, instead now an agonizing scream filled with pain. The creature on top of her lover didn't come alone. Unsure of what was happening to Vanessa, Dominic heard a sick ripping sound, followed by what he could only describe as a suction cup popping. Vanessa squealed, but Dom had his own problems. The creature's elongated arms dangled so low the claws scuffed the rug beneath him. It lowered its head close to his, and for the first time, he found himself staring into its blue eyes. They were cold and calculating, filled with an otherworldly intelligence that sent shivers down his spine.

"What do you want?" he asked.

The creature stared at him, exhaling its rancid breath in his face. It scanned his body, and he felt his limbs turn to jelly. It lifted one of its hands, the long piercing claws only inches from his face. Its slimy fingers wrapped around his throat, squeezing slightly but not enough to choke him. If it wanted to, it could snap his neck with ease. He realized it was just trying to hold his head in place, and then he saw why. It took its other hand and with one of the fingers, pointed to his forehead, inching closer.

Does it want my fucking brain?!

If only that was true. If only the thing ended his life quickly. Instead, it pressed the end of the largest claw into his forehead, pushing until it broke through the skin. At first, he didn't feel anything. And then his skin started to burn. Like acid being poured beneath his skin. He screamed, but the creature didn't miss a beat, continuing to carve something into his forehead. His crotch warmed, and he realized he'd just pissed himself.

"Please. . .I. . ."

The words wouldn't form; his mouth went numb, paralyzed by either the pain or whatever had been inserted into his head. While he couldn't talk, his other senses kicked into overdrive. Vanessa stopped screaming, but the suction sounds continued. After what felt like minutes, the creature pulled back its hand as if to admire the art it created. Tears traveled down Dominic's face, but the rest of his body wouldn't move.

The alien creature stepped off him, and for the first time since the attack, Dominic saw Vanessa. If he could have screamed, he would have, but all that escaped his throat was a deflated moan.

Her body was convulsing on the floor, and something was on top of her, latching onto her stomach. Her legs were spread, and he saw the place he'd just been penetrating. He tried to blink, but his eyelids wouldn't work. Something crawled into her vagina, he was sure of it. The thing on top of her looked like a giant snake or worm, with pointy legs that clung to her abdomen while it pumped something into her stomach. The convulsing stopped. She wasn't moving. Was she dead?

Dominic looked to the edge of the desk, spotting his cell phone. He knew he couldn't call anyone, but he desperately wanted to see what it did to his head, as the burning sensation wouldn't go away. He pushed with everything he had, and his body lurched forward, falling against the desk leg. The impact knocked the phone to the floor next to him, the light almost blinding. He was able to move his hand enough to grab it, but his fingers tingled like they were asleep, completely numb outside of the pins and needles feeling coursing through them.

After a few moments, he managed to get the camera open and flip it to selfie mode. He couldn't believe what he was seeing. A blue spiral design had been carved into his forehead like some tribalistic tattoo. The skin around the design was bubbling and melting, sliding down his forehead in a wax-like pus. The alien creature turned to face him once more, its black skin blending with the shadows, its blue eyes burning into him. He thought maybe it was going to let him live, just sit paralyzed until someone found him and put him out of his misery. But then it stepped closer, again kneeling to his level. Its mouth opened wide, exposing even more black daggers inside its mouth, clacking aggressively.

Its tongue shot out of its mouth, impaling his throat, suffocating his already strained breathing. He felt it tear through the other side of his neck as everything started to fade. The last thing he saw before everything went black was Vanessa sitting up, watching him die with a smile on her face.

CHAPTER 12

THE GROUP MADE it to the walk-in freezer without any further incident. Carrie was relieved, but it felt like a ticking time bomb. That. . .*thing*, it was following them. They could hear it the entire time they trekked through the building back down to the cafeteria. But it was as if it was taking its time, hunting them, and enjoying every second of feeding off their fear.

Jerome's condition seemed to be worsening the longer they went on, making Carrie wonder if they made the right choice to take him in. What if he slowed them down to the point that they couldn't get away if needed? She couldn't live with herself if they'd left him, though. As long as he was alive, it felt cruel to leave him for dead. She just hoped it wasn't all for nothing.

Fred double-checked the lock, then stacked boxes in front of the door to add an extra layer of protection. In the small glimpse Carrie got of the creature, she wasn't sure a bunch of canned goods would stop it from getting to them if it really wanted to. After Fred was done stacking boxes, he walked over to Jerome who was now sitting in the corner against the wall, holding a bag of half-frozen peas against his forehead. The freezer was still cold enough to see their breath, but it was starting to warm up with the power out.

"Good thing Vanessa isn't here in her little miniskirt, huh?" Sally joked.

Carrie turned to face her and realized the smile was forced. Sally was always the one to try and lighten the mood in times of stress, whether it be falling behind on work or giving relationship advice to Carrie—which often went in one ear and out the other. Sally was a constant source of comfort for Carrie.

"Do you think this is the right call? Hiding in here?" Carrie whispered.

Sally looked at Fred, who was still helping Jerome get comfortable.

"Who knows? All I know is, I trust Fred. He knows what he's doing, as best he can in this situation, at least. I don't know about you, hon, but I'd like to live to see Christmas."

"Yeah, well, who knows where I'll be spending Christmas this year?"

"As long as you're not spending it with a new black eye, who cares? That's the best gift you could ask for. Anyway, this place seems as safe as any for now. Plus, we got food and drinks. We can wait this thing out until help comes."

After a moment of silence, Carrie shifted her attention to Amelia, who she'd almost forgotten was even there since she kept to herself. The janitor sat in the corner opposite Jerome, watching him like a hawk. It was hard to believe the story she'd told them after coming in from the roof, but she sure seemed believable. It wasn't as far-fetched now as it would have been first thing this morning. If they were truly trapped in the building, how would they get out? Carrie pulled out her cell phone again, hoping a miraculous few bars of service would pop up. Instead, she had the same empty space where the bars usually showed. A thought came to her, and she unlocked the phone screen.

"What are you doing, hon?" Sally asked.

"We don't have service—we know that already—but none of us have tried SOS mode, right? Even when you don't have service, can't we get a message to someone for help? Why haven't we tried nine-one-one yet?"

The sudden hope drove her heart into a frenzy as she quickly dialed 911. When she held the phone to her ear, she expected nothing in return, just a dead signal or even silence. Instead, an annoying buzzing sound blasted through the small speaker. Carrie pulled the phone back and cringed. She was about to hang up when it sounded like someone talking through the static.

"Put it on speaker!" Sally said.

Carrie almost dropped the phone but managed to turn speaker mode on. Fred turned and left Jerome to himself, and Amelia got up and surrounded Carrie with the others.

"*Giiive. . . Epochal. . . dieee. . .*"

More static—this time louder—blocked out whatever was being said.

"Who is this? We need help!" Carrie shouted into the phone.

Fred put his hand on her shoulder to quiet her, but it was no use. Static now occupied the other end completely. After a moment, the line went dead, and with it, any hope Carrie had of reaching someone outside. *What the hell was that, and what were they asking for?*

"That's. . .the same voice I heard before I got attacked," Jerome said with a grimace, still in a great deal of pain.

Something pounded on the outside of the freezer door, startling them all. Amelia yelped. The pounding continued, and all Carrie could think was that the creature had found them, and it was here to finish the job.

"Quiet," Fred whispered.

"Let me in! Please. It's coming," a muffled voice said from the other side of the door. It wasn't anyone Carrie recognized.

Fred looked at the others, then approached the door.

"You can't be serious! Don't let anyone in here. They said it was coming. You'll kill us all," Amelia said.

"If you all feel the same way, I'll wait. But I can't in good conscience leave someone out there to die," Fred said.

Carrie and Sally looked at each other and the mom in Sally took over her facial expression. "I agree with Fred. We can't leave someone out there."

Carrie sighed. She felt selfish for wanting to leave the door locked, but she knew they were right. Sally would help anyone and everyone she could. Hell, she was offering the sanctuary of her home to Carrie to avoid further harm from an abusive asshole. Why should the person on the outside of the door be any different?

"I say we let them in. Then we shut and lock the door as quickly as possible."

"No. . .no, no, *no*. I beg you, don't open that door," Amelia whispered.

"I'm sorry, we voted and made a decision," Fred said.

Amelia didn't respond. Instead, she backed away from the door as the person on the other side continued to pound. Fred moved some of the boxes he had just stacked moments before, then unlocked the freezer door and opened it. The person standing in the opening was the last person Carrie expected to see.

It was Albert Sinclair.

He looked battered and beaten, his five-thousand-dollar suit ripped and torn in places, scratches and cuts decorating his normally smooth-skinned face. The owner of Sinclair Pharmaceuticals stumbled into the freezer, dropping to the floor. Fred shut and locked the door again, then shifted his attention to Albert.

"Are you okay?"

Albert rolled over onto his back, inhaling deep breaths. While his body looked like it had been through a car wreck, his ice-cold stare was still there. He glared at Fred for an uncomfortable minute.

"Do I fucking look okay?"

"Listen, man, I'm just trying to help. What happened to you?"

Carrie wondered if Fred even knew who Albert was. He either didn't know or didn't care. Most people in the office wouldn't even dare make eye contact with Mr. Sinclair, let alone talk to him casually. Even in the situation they found themselves in, it was hard for her to let that guard down.

"We got trapped in the elevator when the power went out. Something tried to get in at us. And then it got Ed. The elevator broke free and crashed to the ground below. That's the only reason I made it out of there alive."

"Holy shit, that was the sound we heard?" Carrie asked, immediately regretting it. The thought of getting fired while they were running from some monster hell-bent on killing them seemed ridiculous, but it was a fear she couldn't shake.

"Thank God for the braking systems elevators have these days, even with the power out. It's likely what saved you from becoming a puddle of guts," Fred said.

"Did it follow you?" Amelia asked from the corner.

Albert looked at the janitor with disgust, as if even hearing her voice would infect him with some disease that only low-income, working-class people carried.

"How the hell should I know? I shot it with Ed's gun, it took off, then the elevator crashed. When I came to, it was gone. What is that thing?"

"We don't know. But Amelia here thinks we're trapped inside until they get whatever they came for," Fred said.

"*They*? There's more than one of those fucking things?"

"We've only seen one, but we've heard others. And Jerome said something different attacked him," Carrie said.

The mention of Jerome prompted them all to look at him, and what they saw wasn't pretty. Even with the cooler temperature, the security guard was glistening with sweat. Every single breath he forced out appeared labored. His eyes were closed, and Carrie couldn't tell if he was sleeping or fighting for his life.

"You say it— *they* want something. Do you know what?" Albert asked.

"Right before you came, we heard one of them say something on Carrie's phone. We couldn't make out what it was saying. Then the phone died. Epo. . .something," Fred said.

Albert's eyes lit up, and his mouth hung open. He stared straight ahead, through everyone, as he appeared to realize what they were talking about.

"It's real. . .the Epochal Tempora. If they want it, it must be real."

"What is that?" Sally asked.

Albert scoffed as if she should know exactly what this thing was that a pack of monsters wanted. He walked past the group and straight to Sally, standing only a few feet from her face.

"It's bigger than anything you could comprehend. I wouldn't expect any of you to grasp the importance of this device, not just to our world but to many worlds beyond. It controls time. It can travel dimensions. It's the most powerful object in existence."

Sally stared at Albert like he was crazy, and Carrie couldn't blame her. That sounded like something straight out of a low-budget sci-fi movie: a mad scientist about to solve his biggest mystery. Had they not been through what they had tonight, she was sure that she and Sally would have a good laugh over it with a glass of wine later. Fred had heard enough and charged toward Albert, grabbing him by the shirt.

"What the fuck, man. What are you talking about? If you know what's causing this, you better fucking tell us right now."

"I suggest you take your hands off me," Albert spat.

The tension could melt the remaining ice in the freezer. Fred and Albert stared at one another without saying a word while the others watched on in silence. Carrie was fuming inside. She had dealt with enough asshole men in her life, and she wasn't about to deal with more with her life on the line.

"Enough with the big dick competition, guys. It doesn't matter if you're a chef or the fucking owner of this company. If we don't get them what they want I think it's clear we'll all die tonight. So if you know what they want, Mr. Sinclair, please let us know so we don't spend our last moments in a damn freezer together," Carrie said.

Fred sighed. "She's right. If you really know what's going on, you need to help us. How do you know what they're here for?"

Albert fixed his suit jacket and looked around at everyone. "Because I have what they want."

CHAPTER 13

RENT MADE IT to the main lobby after taking a few detours to get there. Along the way, he encountered a few more of the symbols painted on the walls, adding to his confusion. Now, he had an escape right in front of him. All he had to do was push through the front door and get the hell out of there. But he was nervous to walk out the exit, as it was pitch-black out even though it was early afternoon. And as crazy as he thought the janitor was, he wasn't sure he wanted to take the risk and find out if what she said was true.

Before he left for help, he decided to look out the window for a moment and watch for any sign of trouble. That was when he heard a hissing sound and turned to see a blanket of smoke coming from the elevator in the corner of the lobby. The doors had been forced open and the thick cloud suffocating the inside of the elevator hid the interior. Hopefully, the others didn't try to come down the elevator only to have it crash at the bottom. That wouldn't make sense considering there was no power, but he had heard a crash earlier and now knew what had caused it.

He approached the door, chastising himself with each step, knowing it was a terrible decision. He needed to know if the others were hurt or not. Some of the smoke entered his lungs, triggering a coughing fit. He covered his nose and mouth with his shirt, then entered the tight space. His glasses began to fog immediately. The inside of the elevator was bent and warped, the metal walls almost folding in on one another. Trent kneeled to fit within the tight space and spotted a body on the floor. He jumped back with a start, smacking the back of his head on the edge of the wall.

"Hey, man. . .you okay?"

It was a stupid question. The man wasn't moving. He just remained curled up like a pretzel with his head hidden beneath his arms.

He's dead, Trent thought.

Instead of turning around and leaving, he decided to check for a pulse. He rolled the man onto his back, then jerked backward again, this time avoiding hitting his head. It was a security guard, one he hadn't seen working at the front desk before. The man's head was barely hanging on his neck. The top of the scalp had been ripped from the skull, which had been crushed, revealing part of the brain. He backed out of the elevator, scolding himself for going there in the first place. He needed to get the fuck out of here.

With one last glance out the window, Trent took a deep breath and exited the building. He wasn't sure what to expect, but when he walked out it was deathly silent. The janitor told them she heard a bunch of voices, so maybe she really was crazy. Still, that didn't explain the darkness that engulfed the call center. He looked up at the sky, mesmerized by the sight.

It was as if an obsidian ocean flowed above, swaying back and forth, a calm current. It was impossible to tell if he was looking at clouds or a bare sky. But then he saw more movement behind the initial curtain. As he continued to stare into the abyss, a small hole opened in the center of the sky. His eyes were locked, frozen on the new discovery.

"Why don't you do it? Kill yourself. Nobody would miss you. . . Right, Trent?"

"Give us the Epochal Tempora."

"Come closer. . . We will help you. . ."

It wasn't just one voice, but many, and they were all overlapping with one another, yet he could hear each one so clearly. And they were convincing. He wanted to do everything they asked of him. Whatever he could to help. Even if it meant killing himself. And though he had never before heard the words "Epochal Tempora," he knew exactly what they wanted at that moment.

The small hole in the sky vanished, again covered by a smoldering darkness. He snapped back to reality with his ears buzzing.

"What the fuck. . ."

Trent realized he still had his phone in his hand for the light and decided to check if being out of the building brought back service. Unsurprisingly, there wasn't a single bar. The sounds returned, but he gathered if he didn't look at the sky, they would have more trouble getting in his head.

Don't look up, whatever you do. Focus on the ground and run for help.

He took off in a sprint, heading toward the parking lot. The call center occupied a ten-acre piece of land surrounded by trees. Albert Sinclair had specifically selected the location away from the city because it would save on taxes. Right now, that made it impossible to go anywhere close for help. Trent stopped running when he came to a sudden realization: he'd left his keys in his desk drawer. Even if he got to his car, there was no way he could drive.

Then you run. Run until your fucking feet bleed if you have to.

He thought of the closest place to go for help, deciding the Shell station where he'd often stop to get gas on the way in and out of work was the best spot. Did they have power? Were they also trapped and being hunted? It was the best option either way. As he started in that direction, the buzzing sound came back. He tried to ignore it, force himself to keep going. All that did was cause the humming to crank up even louder until he couldn't handle it anymore, and then he looked up at the sky.

The hole was back, this time much bigger. It seemed eye contact triggered something, as Trent began to feel a pulling sensation inside of his body. He kept running, but it was getting more difficult with each step as if the building itself was a magnet pulling him back. He hadn't come this far to go back. The rest of them were depending on him to get help.

Who are you trying to kid? They probably think you tucked your tail and skipped town.

The pulling sensation intensified inside him, working its way through all his limbs. Suddenly, he couldn't move anymore. He looked down at his feet, which were now a few inches off the ground. His body was elevating, being pulled as if a powerful vacuum was sucking him upward.

"Ahhh! Fuck!"

The pain was unbearable, wrapping around his spine in a viselike grip, twisting up to his neck and head. His eyes throbbed, the force pushing them out of their sockets until they could no longer move without completely ripping from his head. The higher he floated, the more intense the pull.

His body shifted, now in a horizontal crucifix position ten feet off the ground. He had no choice but to stare up at the sky. At the widening hole that reminded him of a giant eye watching him.

"You should have listened to us. . ."

The voice in his head was met with a clawing pain behind his eyes. If he could've moved his hands, he'd consider ripping them out himself. Something exploded inside his stomach, sending a warm rush through the rest of his body. His fingers curled up, locked as if he was having a tonic-clonic seizure. His legs snapped back, bringing the heels of his shoes to the center of his spine. He didn't think his body could bend anymore, but then his head snapped back in the other direction, now touching his feet. Trent knew his spine was broken. He could hear it cracking inside of him, breaking into tiny fragments as the pull strengthened.

If there was a single silver lining, it was that he now couldn't see the space above him with his head facing the ground. But what he could see was that he was now fifty feet in the air, continuing to rise. His glasses shattered, which up until they cracked and fell from his face, he hadn't realized were still on his head. His eyeballs had pushed them off and were now completely out of their sockets, resting on his cheeks. It was a strange feeling—the bottom of his eyes touching his skin. An imaginary hand wrapped around his throat, choking away the remaining air he was able to inhale. The warm liquid inside of him forced its way up his throat and out of his mouth, splashing the sky in crimson. And then his eyeballs tore completely from their sockets, exploding into gore and white fluid.

As Trent took his last breath, he was thankful that he couldn't see what happened next to his body.

CHAPTER 14

T HE GROUP DECIDED it was best if only a few of them went to Albert's office to obtain the object. Jerome's health appeared to be deteriorating, and they feared if they left him alone that he'd die without help. Fred and Sally would go with Albert, while Carrie and Amelia would stay with Jerome.

"Please, be safe. We got a Christmas movie marathon waiting for us tonight," Carrie said as she hugged Sally.

"I will, hon. This is what needs to be done. If we can get it, this might all be over."

"Fred, you take care of my girl, you got that?"

"I'll do my best. You guys stay safe too. Don't leave unless you have no choice. When we get the object, we'll come back down here. Keep Jerome's gun on you at all times, just in case."

"*Object. . .* Stop talking about it like it's a damn pawn shop item," Albert snapped.

"I don't give a fuck what it is. You put us in this situation, and now we need you to help get us out of it. I'd really prefer it if you handed me your gun so I can protect us if necessary. I can't imagine you're any good with that thing," Fred said.

"I'll hold onto this, thank you very much. I got myself down here because of it," Albert said.

Fred shook his head in annoyance but didn't fight the issue. They said their goodbyes and Carrie watched them leave before sealing the freezer door shut. She looked at Sally like she was the mother she had always wanted, and she'd be crushed if anything happened to her. As much as she wanted to go with her and help, her background in nursing made her the default option to stay with Jerome and care for him. Amelia was too scared to go with the others, so she decided to stay put.

Carrie went to college to become a nurse and even worked at a hospital for a few years. It was how she'd met Reed. He was a patient who had been admitted to the hospital after a terrible car wreck. He worked his charm on her and ended up asking her out on a date. Fast-forward a few years, and he had forced her to quit the job, saying they never saw each other and that he didn't like the idea of her touching other men to care for them. When she argued it, he slapped her across the face—just another day in their relationship.

Carrie checked on Jerome, who had yet to wake from his pain-induced nap. When she was certain there was nothing that she could do for him at the moment, she walked over to Amelia.

"I'm sorry about your son. I can't even imagine going through that."

"Thank you. I hope nobody ever has to go through what I did. We think as parents we know our own kids. That we've taught them what they need to succeed in life. All I ever wanted was to provide a good life for him. . ."

Amelia wiped away a tear, and Carrie regretted bringing up her son.

"I'm sure you were a great mom. It's always easy to look back and blame yourself after the fact. But whatever that voice outside was telling you, it wasn't really him. You have to realize that."

"I don't care if it was really him or not. It's a feeling I've lived with for the past two years, regardless of what some imaginary voice tells me. *Regardless* of what my husband thinks. He's just as much to blame as I am, but you'll never hear me say that. It does no good. 'Reflect, not deflect.' That's what my therapist always says."

"Well, your therapist is wise. I like that saying. Except in this situation. We can blame Albert Sinclair all we want," Carrie said with a smirk. Amelia laughed.

"I'm scared. This all seems like make-believe, doesn't it? One minute, I'm going out for a smoke, the next, I'm hiding out in a freezer from some pack of monsters."

"Yeah, it's hard to comprehend, that's for sure. But as long as we stick together, I think we can make it out of this. I'm sorry if you feel you get the cold shoulder from us. I think it's just hard for people to open up to those they don't regularly converse with. You and I see each other every single day and we've talked, what, maybe three times?"

"That'd be two more times than with most people here. It's okay, I get it. Before this job, I probably would have been the same way. You'd think as adults we wouldn't judge others in society by what they do for a living, but it's human nature, I suppose."

Carrie pondered on that statement and had to agree. Humans could be a real bitch. She glanced back at Jerome who was stirring. His brown skin had faded to a greyish color, his face covered in severe burn marks. She had never seen anything quite like it. If he made it out of here alive, there would be a long road to recovery, and that's if he didn't die from an infection.

Both Carrie and Amelia walked over to Jerome as his movements increased.

"You think he'll be okay?" Amelia asked.

"I don't know. Let's just hope the others get help before it's too late," Carrie said, kneeling down. "Jerome, how are you feeling? Can I get you anything?"

He mumbled in his sleep, and she noticed his eyes bouncing around behind his closed eyelids. His breathing continued to come out forced.

"I guess we just let him sleep it off until we know what to do next?" Amelia asked.

"Yeah, I—"

Jerome's eyes shot open as a guttural sound forced its way out of his chest. Carrie and Amelia backed up as his body began to twitch. His eyes were glossed over, the pupils all but vanished. In their place were tiny wormlike insects crawling around the whites of his eyes. His bellowing didn't stop, instead it got louder. His mouth opened wider, cracking his jaw. Carrie had no idea what to do, but instinct told her to stay back. Jerome's hands curled, his fingers clawing at the tile floor. Fingernails snapped off his digits, cracking into jagged ridges as blood flowed from the wounds.

"Jerome! Snap out of it!" Carrie yelled.

He continued to writhe, his mouth locked open. The sound coming from him sounded like someone choking on air as they attempted a powerful yawn. After a moment of his body thrashing around, it stopped. His eyes remained open, staring at the ceiling. Carrie wasn't sure if he was breathing anymore. His mouth remained agape, his jaw clearly broken.

"Is he dead?" Amelia asked.

"I don't know," Carrie whispered.

They stood in silence, unsure of what to do. The thought of being locked in a freezer with a dead body sent gooseflesh across Carrie's already cold arms. She decided she had to check on him, see if he was still breathing. As she closed in, something moved in his mouth, hidden in the dark cavity of his throat. She had hoped it was his tongue moving, but she knew that wasn't the case.

There was something *inside* of Jerome.

Her breath caught in her chest. She didn't dare move, afraid that if she did, whatever was nesting inside Jerome would react. Amelia saw it as well and gripped Carrie's arm tight.

"What the hell is that?" Amelia whispered.

Carrie didn't answer.

They couldn't leave, but the last thing she wanted to do was sit here waiting for something to eat its way out of Jerome's body and come for them next. Carrie looked around the freezer, which suddenly felt much smaller than it did before. She gripped the gun tightly but had no intention of firing it if she could help it. There really was nowhere to go. No escape. She walked to the door, deciding that if they did plan to make a run for it, she wanted to make sure she knew how to get the door open quickly. She didn't like turning her back on Jerome, feeling his dead gaze burning into her. Amelia was still frozen in place, watching the movement inside Jerome's mouth. Was it fingers? A leg? A fucking small body?

After sticking the gun in her waistband, Carrie started moving some of the boxes for an easy escape. Then she heard a scratching sound. At first, she thought it was on the other side of the door, but then she realized it was coming from within the freezer. It wasn't until she turned around that she understood it was coming from Jerome's stomach. Whatever was inside him was now trying to dig its way out.

"Oh, to hell with this. Let's go!" Carrie yelled, throwing the stack of boxes to the floor.

"We can't. It's a death sentence out there, Carrie."

"It's about to be in here too. Come on. Help me move these boxes out of the way."

Amelia rushed over and they lifted a few of the heavy ones together, dropping them to the floor. The sudden *bang* of the heavy box startled Carrie, but she composed herself and moved to grab another. The *bang* came again, but this time neither of them had a box in hand. She whipped around to see Jerome cracking his head on the wall. He repeatedly pulled back and launched himself headfirst, each strike splitting his skull a little more.

Carrie snapped out of it, realizing that the thing controlling Jerome's dead body was trying to break free. They needed to leave. Now. She turned back to the door, fumbling with the lock mechanism. After getting the freezer door unlocked, she attempted to open it, but it jammed after a few inches.

"Shit!"

She looked down and realized a small tin can of tuna had fallen from one of the boxes, now wedged between the floor and bottom of the door. Behind her, she heard Jerome's bones continuing to crunch against the wall, the sound like cracking a dozen eggs at the same time. Amelia cried out as Carrie kicked the tin can from beneath the door, pulled it open, and turned back to call for Amelia. But she was too late.

Jerome's body was split down the center, a pile of viscera and gore splayed across the floor in front of his collapsed limbs. In the center of the organs and blood stood a small black creature like the one they'd seen in the stairwell. Its hands and feet contained daggerlike claws traveling up to each ankle. It crawled toward Amelia. The janitor froze in shock, and all Carrie wanted to do was run in and grab her, pull her to safety, and lock that thing in the freezer. But as she approached Amelia, the creature dropped low and sprinted on all fours, jumping up and latching onto Amelia's neck with its short but deathly fangs.

"No!" Carrie screamed.

Amelia pulled at the creature, but all that did was stretch her skin that its teeth had clamped down on, separating it from the flesh. Amelia cried out as blood pumped from the new wound. It bit down on her hand, a blue fluid leaking from its mouth onto her fingers.

Carrie cried in the doorway, knowing she had to leave Amelia if she was going to live. There was no saving her new friend. Amelia turned to face her with wide eyes. When she realized that Carrie was leaving her for dead, she reached out, begging for help. Carrie fought back more tears, pulling the door shut as Amelia's screams continued to bounce off the walls inside, muffled by the steel door. With one final look back, she turned and headed into the darkness.

CHAPTER 15

SALLY FOLLOWED CLOSELY behind Fred and Albert. She didn't trust Mr. Sinclair in the slightest, but he was their only hope. He was responsible for getting them into this situation, collecting dangerous artifacts like they were fucking Pokémon cards. The look in his eyes when he realized that he held something so powerful, so dangerous, was disturbing. They made it to the eighth floor without running into any of the creatures, but they *heard* them the entire way. Lingering in the darkness, traveling around the building in the shadows. Something seemed off. They were either waiting for the right time to strike, or they were concerned with other matters, only killing people who crossed their paths. Maybe they would leave in peace if they got what they wanted. Or maybe they were just toying with their prey.

When they got to Albert's office, the owner stopped outside his door.

"You need to understand one thing right now. There are only a few people who know about this room, and they know not to say a word. When this is all done, I expect you all to sign something in writing. If you ever say a word about this place, there will be colossal consequences. Do you understand?"

"Whatever, man. I don't give a fuck about your room. I just want the thing these assholes came for. So let's get on with it," Fred said.

Albert unlocked his office door and entered. Fred turned to Sally, but his eyes widened as he looked over her shoulder. Sally turned and, coming from the darkness, Vanessa leaned against the wall, clutching her stomach.

"Oh my God, Vanessa," Sally whispered, running to her coworker. "Are you okay? Where are Dominic and Trent?"

"Trent left to go find help. But they. . .they got Dom. He needs our help. Please, come."

Fred poked his head into the office to see what Albert was doing and then back out to Sally. "One of us should really stay here with him. I'm not sure I trust him alone with this device."

Sally knew he was right. As much as she didn't want to leave Fred's side, if they left Albert alone, who knew what he'd do? She would volunteer to help Vanessa.

"I'll go. I'll try to be as quick as I can. But please be careful with him," she said.

Fred nodded and forced a smile. With that, she turned and headed down the dark hall with Vanessa.

After heading down a few flights of stairs, they finally reached the office Vanessa said they had been hiding in. On the walk, Sally thought she noticed Vanessa staring at her, observing with a strange intent, unsure what was going through her coworker's head. Vanessa opened the door to the office, backing away so Sally could enter ahead of her.

"He's in here. I can't look. I'm afraid they hurt him bad, Sally. I think. . .I think he might be dead."

Sally walked in slowly, aiming her phone light in front of her. From where she stood, all she saw was the office desk, the floor covered in papers, and scattered office utensils. Behind the desk, a beam of light aimed above, and in the light, she saw a shadow on the ceiling—the outline of a head. She inched closer, afraid of what she'd see on the other side of the desk.

"Dominic?"

When he didn't answer, she continued. She rounded the edge of the desk and stared down at what was left of her supervisor. His body was a mangled mess. His eyes were frozen in a permanent mix of fear and agony, his mouth open in a silent scream. When she spotted the hole in his throat, she covered her mouth. Loose strands of torn skin hung down the outside of his neck, covered in congealed blood.

A snapping sound came from somewhere behind her in the darkness. Sally spun around, confused by what she was looking at. Vanessa stood rigid in the corner; her mouth opened wide. Her eyes had glossed over to a cloudy gray.

"Vanessa? Are you okay?"

Sally aimed her phone light at Vanessa, and that's when she noticed something rippling beneath her skin. Her eyes followed the movement, which started at the top of Vanessa's breasts, traveling through her cleavage and down beneath her silk shirt. Sally couldn't believe she missed it before, but now she noticed the multicolored veins branching out from Vanessa's belly button, identical to what they had seen on Jerome. She was infected by those things.

Vanessa's hands dropped to her side, her fingers curling into gnarled claws, digging into her palms. Her mouth opened further, her eyes rolling back in her head. Were these things smart enough to trick Sally into coming here? Was this a trap? She started for the door, but Vanessa was in her way. She had nothing to defend herself, so she turned to search through the mess of desk supplies on the floor behind her. She spotted a pair of scissors and picked them up.

When she turned back toward the door, Vanessa was crouched on all fours, her stomach stretching open in the center. Something was pushing through the skin of her belly like some deranged pregnancy. A clawed hand ripped through Vanessa's abdomen, tearing apart her body with a disgusting ripping sound. Sally attempted to run past her, making it to the door, when she felt a sudden pain shoot through her ankle. She turned back, ready to strike Vanessa with the scissors, but she noticed Vanessa's body splayed apart on the floor like an extra layer of skin. What had her ankle captive was the most horrifying thing she'd ever seen.

The small black creature was far more powerful than it had any right to be, digging its claws into her exposed skin with a firm grip. She attempted to kick it off, but all that did was force its claws in deeper. She gripped the scissors, prepared to strike, then remembered what their blood did to Jerome's skin. But the pain was excruciating; she needed to take a chance and get it off of her.

Its body was close to two feet long, saturated in slime. She couldn't see the face in the darkness, but the thing appeared to be trying to get close enough to bite her. Before she could react, it sank its long fangs into her calf, pumping her bloodstream full of its poison. She lifted the scissors and drove the metal tips into the creature's back. Its grip loosened as it let out an ear-piercing cry. Sally kicked it with her free foot, sending it tumbling across the floor and into the mess that used to be Vanessa. A trail of blue liquid covered the floor in its path, but that didn't stop it from getting up and coming back at her. It charged toward her, but she was too far from the door to get out in time.

"Get down!"

Carrie stood in the doorway. Sally fell to the side, then heard the thundering *crack* of a gunshot. She got to her feet and saw the creature writhing on the floor in a puddle of its own fluids. Carrie fired again, this time hitting the thing dead center in the head. The creature dropped to the floor and stopped moving. Still, Sally couldn't take her eyes off of it. The fear that it would jump up at any second and come back for her filled her thoughts. But it didn't move.

"Sal. Did it get you?"

Sally glanced down at her ankle in shock because as much as the initial bite hurt, the pain had vanished. She slowly shook her head and got to her feet, looking over the rest of her body.

"Carrie. . .that thing came out of Vanessa's body. I watched it rip right through her like it was nothing."

"The same thing happened to Jerome. It got Amelia. I couldn't save her. How. . . How the hell could something grow that quickly inside of them?"

Carrie walked over to Sally and hugged her tightly. The smell of fresh gunpowder wafted up from the pistol in Carrie's hand. They stood there in silence for a moment, embracing one another.

"Where's Fred?" Carrie asked.

"With Albert, in his office. We need to go back there now. Hopefully by the time we get there, they'll have the fucking object these things want so bad."

"I can't help but feel there's no way out of this—"

Sally interrupted her with another hug, unable to hold it in. "Hey, hon. We're going to be okay. There's light at the end of this horrible tunnel."

"Thank you. For everything. You're always there for me when I need you. I don't know what I'd do without you, Sal."

"You'd find a way. Us fighters always do. Plus, you saved *my* ass, not the other way around. Let's get back upstairs."

They headed toward the stairwell and the whole time, all Carrie could imagine were a bunch of tiny, blue eyes staring at them from the dark corners.

"What if this doesn't work? I mean, what if we get this thing, they take it, then kill us anyway? Who's to say they don't want us all dead? I don't see why they would try to trick us into following them into a dark room while we're trying to get them the thing they wanted," Carrie said.

"Well, they don't know we're trying to get it for them. To them, we're probably the ones trying to stop them from getting it. If it doesn't work . . . let's just hope Trent has help on the way. I don't know, hon. I can't figure out our own species, let alone another one."

Carrie couldn't help but let out a laugh. Even after everything they had been through, Sally still found a way to get a smile from her. As they walked into the stairwell, heading up to the top floor, she hoped their plan worked. She knew the creatures were following them; she could hear them in the shadows the entire way.

CHAPTER 16

FRED KNEW THAT Albert was stalling. He knew it from the moment they reached the top floor. The pace slowed, the conversation drawn out. All the telltale signs were there. He just wasn't sure *why* Albert was stalling. Why would this prick even remotely consider *not* giving the device to those things? Sure, there was a chance they would just kill them all once they got what they came for. But if that was the case, there was no hope anyway. It was the only shot they had at surviving. Currently, Albert was lumbering around his office, acting like he didn't know where he left the keys to the hidden room. Fred had waited long enough.

"Hey, man. Enough fucking off. What's your deal? Why are you trying to prevent us from getting this thing?"

Albert turned to him with a scowl spread across his face. Fred had seen his type many times before. A power-hungry asshole who refused to give up what little control he held.

"You don't understand. This is my life's work, not just some small obsession. Do you know what this object could do for mankind? There's a reason these things want it so badly. But I'm being honest when I say I can't find the damn key. Normally, the door opens with a scan of my finger, but with the power out, it can only be opened manually."

"I just find it hard to believe that a man as successful as yourself would simply misplace a key so important to you. And if you can't find it, we need to find another way in. Where do we get access to the door?"

Albert didn't answer, but he didn't need to. His eyes briefly looked over Fred's shoulder at the bookshelf. Fred assumed it had to be somewhere along the wall but wasn't sure exactly where. He turned and began throwing books to the floor, looking for access.

"What the hell are you doing? Careful with those!"

Fred ignored him, swiping across the shelf and knocking handfuls off at a time. Finally, he located the finger scan pad and with it, a keyhole. He turned back to Albert.

"Give me the damn key."

"I could have you arrested for this."

"Then fucking do it. If we make it out of here alive, be my guest. But for now, my only concern is getting into this room."

Albert closed his eyes and sighed.

"It's on the top shelf, up there to the left. If you feel around, you'll find it."

Fred shook his head and turned back to the bookshelf, standing on his toes to feel above his head.

As he was about to give up and tell Albert to come grab it himself, he heard movement behind him, turning just in time to see Albert bringing down a large paperweight across his temple. Everything went black.

CHAPTER 17

CARRIE AND SALLY walked quietly through the darkness, careful not to make too much noise while moving quickly to get back to Fred. Carrie was happy to see Sally had avoided any serious injuries. She also realized just how close they were to a far worse outcome. Had she arrived a few seconds later, Sally would have either been dead or joined those things in becoming some type of host to the creatures.

Sally put a hand on Carrie's shoulder to stop her.

"Do you hear that?" she whispered.

A clicking sound from above.

They were currently in the stairwell, working their way to the top floor, but something was up there, lurking.

"Let's cut through this floor and go up the stairs on the other side," Carrie whispered.

Sally nodded, then slowly opened the door to the main floor. This level consisted of mostly larger offices for presentations and team meetings. Each office contained glass walls, with long, rectangular tables and projectors built into the ceilings. There weren't many places to hide if needed, but at least if there was anything in one of the rooms, they would see it through the glass.

They moved quietly, passing the first few offices without issue. Carrie turned off the phone light, worried it would give them away if something was, in fact, lingering in the corner somewhere. Sally clutched her arm and stopped her.

"I can't see a damn thing without my glasses, hon. I need that light."

"It's okay, hold onto me, I'll just feel along the wall until we reach the next stairwell."

As they started to move again, something scurried above their heads in one of the ducts. Behind them, a scraping sound came from the door they had just exited. They were maybe halfway down the hall, with plenty of ground to cover before they reached the stairs.

"We need to move quickly," Sally whispered.

Carrie reached out and felt the wall to one of the offices, the glass cold to her touch. She picked up speed as her hand slid along the smooth surface, her other hand reaching out in front of her to make sure she didn't walk into anything. Sally stuck close by her side. The scratching from behind them intensified, and then the door began to thump as something banged against the other side of it. Up ahead, Carrie could faintly make out the end of the hall as they closed in. Whatever had been moving above them reached the end first. The ceiling above rattled, right over the exit door.

Claws suddenly sliced through the thin drop ceiling, tearing at it with ferocious intent. They had no choice but to go beneath the monstrous hand. Carrie pulled Sally, moving just short of a sprint, then barreled through the exit door to the stairs. Without looking back, she took the stairs two at a time, reaching the next level before she stopped to let Sally catch up.

"You okay?" she asked.

"Yeah, don't wait for me, hon. Just go. Get to Fred."

There was no chance she was going to leave one of the most important people in her life for dead. She noticed Sally was now moving with a limp, something she hadn't picked up on before when they were moving slower.

"Did you hurt yourself?"

Sally looked down at her feet, then back to Carrie.

"I rolled my ankle coming down the hall."

It wasn't ideal, but they were so close; they just needed to make a few more flights and get to Albert's office. The door beneath them burst open as something entered the tight space. That prompted Carrie and Sally to get moving, and they made their way up to the next level with only one more to go. The clicking sounds of the creatures were getting closer but Carrie didn't dare look back. Her lungs burned, her bruised cheek throbbed, and her quads were on fire. But she pushed through it all, determined to reach safety.

"There's more than one of them!" Sally warned.

The statement prompted Carrie to look back over her shoulder, and even in the darkness, she could make out two figures moving behind them. One was on the side of the wall, crawling on all fours.

She considered taking a shot at one of them, but she didn't want to stop and take time to aim. Plus, she had no idea how many bullets were left. Instead, she turned back and picked up the pace.

They reached the top floor, pushing through the door without slowing down. Albert's office was halfway down the hall. Carrie ran, pulling on Sally's sleeve and hoping her ankle would hold up enough to run. The monsters were hot on their trail, ripping through the door and entering the hall behind them. When Carrie made it to the office door, she prayed it was unlocked.

"Hurry, they're coming!" Sally yelled.

Carrie grabbed the door handle and turned it. Relief flooded her when the door opened, and she quickly entered and pulled Sally behind her. Then she slammed the door shut and locked it, not sure if the lock even mattered. Carrie leaned over, resting her hands on her knees, taking deep breaths to try and regain her composure. The adrenaline would wear off eventually, and she knew her body would feel like it had been hit by a freight train. She looked over to Sally, whose eyes were locked on something on the floor behind Carrie.

"What. . ."

She turned, but it was too dark to make anything out. How Sally spotted something without her glasses was a miracle, but the shape of something on the floor was definitely there. Carrie pulled out her phone and turned on the light. It landed on a leg. She moved it across the floor, realizing it was Fred. Her heart sank. He wasn't moving.

CHAPTER 18

"**F**RED!" SALLY SAID, limping over to the cook.

Carrie aimed her light at his face, and he didn't flinch. He was either out cold or dead. She kneeled to check for a pulse when she heard something move on the other side of the wall. She aimed the light toward the bookshelf and noticed many books scattered across the floor. *What the hell happened here?*

Fresh blood pooled beneath Fred's head, so whatever happened to him had to have just occurred. Carrie found a pulse and sighed in relief.

"He's alive, but something struck him on the head and he's bleeding pretty bad."

"Where the hell is Sinclair? That bastard has to be responsible."

Carrie scanned the room, lighting up as much as she could with the phone light. From what she could see, there was nobody else in the office with them. Fred began to stir at her feet.

"Whoa, easy does it, Fred. You got hit pretty hard by the looks of it," Carrie said.

Sally walked around him and crouched by his side, rubbing his cheek.

"Hey, hon. You scared us. Those things are out in the hallway; it's only a matter of time before they come for us. Can you move?"

Fred groaned, lifting his head from the puddle of blood. He squinted at the light, so Carrie aimed it away from him. He blinked away some of the grogginess and looked around.

"That son of a bitch hit me when I was trying to get in. Where is he?"

"You were the only one here when we arrived," Carrie said.

"What about the others?"

Carrie and Sally looked at each other, trying to determine who should break the news. Sally gave in.

"Well, Vanessa was trying to trick us. She was going to kill me, but Carrie got there in the nick of time and saved me."

"And Jerome. . . he changed," Carrie added. "One of those things came out of him and it got Amelia. I tried to help her, but it was too late. I ran and, on the way up to find you, I heard the commotion. I'm lucky I found her when I did."

"But those monsters followed us. We need to get this thing and try our plan," Sally said.

"He must be behind the wall. The room's in there, but if he locked it from the inside, I don't know how to get to him. I tried to tear that damn wall apart before he hit me. It's got metal between the Sheetrock."

They stood there for a moment in silence until an idea came to Carrie. She recalled hearing the things traveling above them in the ducts. She aimed her light above, locating the drop ceiling.

"What if I climb through the vent and crawl to the next room? Do you think that would work?"

Fred scratched the back of his head and winced again, accidentally hitting his wound.

"I think so. But that sounds pretty fucking dangerous. Not just because of Albert, but those things."

"Any other ideas? Because believe me, I don't want to do it. I'm claustrophobic as fuck, but I know I'm the only one who will fit in there. No offense, Sal."

Normally, Sally would have laughed, but she was too focused on the dangers that awaited them.

"Yeah, you're right. Are you sure about this?" Fred asked.

Carrie wasn't sure, not at all. But they were followed by multiple creatures in the hall. Too much time had passed for them not to try and break in, which made her wonder just what the hell they were out there doing. She didn't want to give them too much time to reconsider.

"Yes. Once I get in, I'll unlock it from the inside and let you in."

"And if he attacks you? He's unhinged. If you get in there, he'll do whatever he needs to do to stop you."

"I'll worry about that when I get in there. Let me try and talk to him."

"Well, okay then. Let's find a way to get you up there."

After a few moments of stacking whatever they could on top of Albert's desk, Carrie could finally reach the ceiling tiles. She pushed up on one, angling it so she could pull it out of its place, then tossed it to the floor. She lifted her head into the hole and aimed her phone light in the direction of the hidden room. The path was nothing like she expected. After watching too many movies, she'd assumed there would be an easy way to climb in and crawl right over to the next room. Instead, she was looking at a mess of wires and beams, along with the HVAC system she needed to get access to. She spotted a way in, then quickly realized she had no way to unscrew the access door. She crouched back through the hole, looking down at Fred and Sally.

"I need a screwdriver or something. There's a vent cover I need to open."

Fred ran to the desk, checking the drawers beneath Carrie. She heard him swearing to himself as he checked each drawer, finding nothing. Then he found a drawer with a bottle of wine and an opener.

"The bastard has expensive bottles in his desk for any occasion."

"Hand me that wine opener. Maybe that will be able to loosen the screws enough to pull the cover off," Carrie said.

"Be careful not to strip the screws. If you do that, we'll never get them off," he said, then handed her the corkscrew.

Carrie looked one last time at Sally, who nodded without a word. With that, Carrie hoisted herself up through the hole, grabbing onto one of the beams. She hoped it was only the darkness that brought out the worst in Sally, but she couldn't help thinking something was wrong. Sally was hurt more than she was letting on.

CHAPTER 19

THE MOMENT CARRIE'S feet were up through the hole, claustrophobia set in. She hated tight spaces, especially dark, tight spaces. The sad thing was she didn't feel much safer up in the ceiling than she did out in the open with those things. She held the phone in one hand and stuffed the wine opener into her pocket so she had more strength to crawl. Dust motes floated around in front of her. This space was last traveled likely when the building was built. She army crawled along the beam, careful not to fall off; if she did, she'd fall through the ceiling tiles.

One of the advantages of no power was that she didn't have to worry about a live wire electrocuting her while she crawled over them. She had no idea what any of them went to and assumed that when the power was on, at least some of the wires held sufficient voltage to give a helluva shock to her system. She made her way to the duct cover, navigating through a network of multicolored wires. When she reached the duct, she set the phone light on the beam ahead of her, then pulled out the corkscrew. After inspecting the tip, she angled the end into the first screw, hoping to catch the thread on the screw head. She pressed down hard, but her hand slipped, scraping her knuckles along the cover. It hurt like hell, but she held in the curse that wanted to force its way out.

She took a deep breath and tried again. This time, the tip caught in the screw, and she noticed it begin to turn. Carrie methodically repeated the process, eventually getting all of the screws out. She had no idea how long it took; it felt like it was too long, regardless. Once she got the cover off, she set it down and shimmied into the duct. This space was even tighter, and a battering of doubts struck her all at once. *What if I get stuck? What if there is no door on the other side and I have to try and crawl backward to escape? What if I get in there and Albert attacks me?*

There was a good chance all of those doubts would happen, yet she found herself moving forward. Just like Sally told her she had to do in life. Move forward. Leave Reed behind with these awful creatures trying to kill everything in their sight.

Every movement was met with an echoing *thump* as the thin metal layer of the ducts warped and bent with each movement. *So much for sneaking up on Albert*, she thought. She repeated the same process over and over. Slide the phone ahead with one hand, pushing the light forward, then wiggle her way a few inches at a time. After passing a few openings on each side that must have led to different rooms, she spotted the next duct cover ten feet ahead and was thankful to be almost at the end. Her chest tightened the moment she crept into this space, and she couldn't wait to be out of it.

She went to push forward when the metal beneath her left knee shifted like a cookie sheet in a hot oven, making a loud *thump* that echoed through the duct. Carrie froze, listening for any sort of reaction below. When she didn't hear anything, she prepared to start back up, but something scraped against the side of the duct behind her, producing a sharp, metallic sound that sent her teeth on edge. It was like nails on a chalkboard. She tried to look behind her but couldn't move enough to get a good look.

The entire duct began to vibrate as something rattled through the space behind her. She picked up the pace, no longer caring about the light. She wanted both hands free to move faster. Given how fast she was moving, she was making too much noise to know for sure if the thing behind her was closing in.

It must have come from one of the side ducts.

Unless it got Fred and Sally . . .

She couldn't allow herself to think that way. She needed to reach the other room. When she made it to the next cover, there was another duct that went left. She crawled into it, making enough room to turn around, then lined her feet up with the cover. She didn't have time to unscrew the thing, so she started kicking it with all the force she could muster. The sounds from the vent got louder, closer. Carrie risked a glance toward the path she'd just traveled and saw the hunched figure of one of the larger creatures crawling on all fours. Her phone light displayed all of its hideous features, especially its elongated teeth that hung down in front of its jaw. It started clicking its mouth, chomping at the air in front of it.

Carrie brought her focus back to the cover, kicking it repeatedly.

"Come on! Fucking break!"

Her feet throbbed with each kick but finally, the cover bent out, folding in on itself and falling through the ceiling tile into the room below. She wasted no time, squeezing through the hole feet first, then dropped to the floor. Her feet smacked off the hard surface and she lost her balance, falling into a glass display, which promptly tipped and shattered on the floor.

"No! What the fuck have you done?"

It was Albert, running over to the destruction. He wasn't there to check on Carrie; he walked right past her, picking up something she couldn't see.

"Albert, one of them is coming! You need to get the device. Now!"

He ignored her as more movement came from overhead. She got to her feet, forcing the pain to the back of her mind. Albert was distracted by one of his prized possessions getting damaged; she had her chance to try and let the others in. She limped to the door, noticing the key still sitting in the keyhole. All she had to do was turn it and open the door.

"Don't fucking do it."

Carrie turned to see Albert aiming a gun at her, and she kicked herself for forgetting that he had one from earlier. The background noise of creatures moving through the ducts continued to increase, vibrating the ceiling above them. It reminded Carrie of a mole traveling underground, watching the dirt trail inch closer. They were almost to the opening.

"Albert. . . If you don't listen, we are going to die. Can't you fucking hear them coming?"

"Stupid girl, I hold the power. They won't do anything to me. This thing next to me, this is what they want. Whoever possesses it is a god."

"And then what? What good does that do you?"

Albert laughed.

"You really don't get it. The possibilities are endless. If I want to go back and be responsible for ending a war, a hero to all, I could. If I decided to wake up one day and stop 9/11, I could. I could even go back and stop your parents from meeting if I wanted to be petty. Prevent you from ever being conceived."

He'd lost his damn mind. Carrie didn't know what to say. Albert reached into the glass display and grabbed the object. She immediately recognized the swirling symbol they had seen in the hall. He looked at it in awe, and she could have sworn she saw a glow in his eyes. She remembered she had the wine opener in her pocket and wondered if he was distracted enough so she could remove it to defend herself.

The creatures didn't give her a chance to act first. One of them exploded through the ceiling hole, landing on the floor next to Albert in a slithering crouch. It was one of the larger ones, its bright blue eyes narrowing to tiny slits as it spotted the Epochal Tempora. Albert, to Carrie's surprise, didn't flinch. He showed no fear in the face of the beast. He really was *that* delusional to think they wouldn't harm him with that thing in his hands.

"I see you've found me. I think you know who holds this, holds the power. If you don't do as I say, I'll wipe you from existence, just like that," he said.

The creature clacked its teeth together, drooling from its overbite. Above it, another of them peered from the hole, staring down at Albert. Carrie didn't know what to do. Albert was focused on the inhuman visitors. Carrie slowly backed up toward the door, keeping her eyes on the stare down as she did. She risked a glance at the key still in the lock, then quickly reached out and turned it before bringing her focus back to the room. The creature above clicked its mouth, communicating with the taller one on the floor.

"Albert, you need to give it to them. You're going to get us all killed."

He ignored her, but the creature turned toward her, opening its mouth wide and baring more teeth beneath its overbite. Albert pulled the trigger, shooting the beast. The thing roared, then charged at him. He fired again but missed, the bullet puncturing the wall behind Carrie's head. The second creature hopped down from the ceiling, leaping toward Albert.

He backed up away from them, bumping into Carrie. When he realized she was there, he grabbed her by the neck, aiming the gun at her head.

"These people want it for their own selfish reasons. I can get rid of your problem."

Carrie couldn't believe he was blaming her for the Epochal Tempora. He pressed the gun further into her temple. She didn't doubt for a second that he'd pull the trigger. The creatures inched closer to them. She reached into her pocket, and when she felt the wine opener, she squeezed it, pulling it free. Albert looked down just as she thrust it into his flesh. He let go of her, dropping the gun and clutching at his neck. Carrie watched as both creatures cornered Albert, pouncing on him. He dropped the Epochal Tempora.

The creatures were on him, tearing at his flesh, ripping him to shreds. He screamed in agony, and Carrie was thankful she couldn't see anything in great detail. She reached down and picked up the device, seizing it tight as tears traveled down her face. Albert's cries had stopped, but the sounds of his body being ravaged continued well past his last breath.

Eventually, when his corpse was unrecognizable, they climbed off, covered in crimson. They turned around, coming face-to-face with Carrie. She trembled as they inched closer to her, unsure of what to do.

"Please. . . Take it. We didn't want this."

They moved slowly, observing her with each step. She closed her eyes, afraid of making any sudden move.

"Kneel down, show them we mean no harm," Fred whispered from behind her.

She opened her eyes, looking over her shoulder to see the doors now open. She didn't see Sally with Fred. When she turned back to the creatures, they were now only a few feet away from her, giving Carrie a detailed look at their bodies. The smell coming from them was revolting, a mix of coppery blood and raw meat. They were close enough that she could feel them breathing on her. Carrie lowered to one knee, holding the cube out toward them.

"Please. We mean no harm."

The taller one snatched it from her hand; the brief touch of its gnarled claw grazing her skin sent a shiver down her spine. She stood up and backed away slowly, bumping into Fred. They both remained silent, waiting for the creatures to do something. The smaller one crouched low and crawled toward her on all fours, snapping its teeth aggressively. Carrie had a brief thought that she had made a huge mistake, that they were going to kill them after all. But then the larger creature wrapped its free hand around the jagged shoulder of the other, stopping its advance. The crawler growled, but the other clicked its mouth, communicating in their native tongue.

It focused on the Epochal Tempora, raising it high enough to be at eye level with Carrie. Then, it twisted the cube, and a bright glow emitted from within the device, lighting up the room in a blue hue. The brightness intensified, burning Carrie's eyes. She shielded her face but could still hear the clicking of the alien creature as it manipulated the cube. Carrie realized it wasn't just a random blue light coming from it, but as the creature aimed it toward the wall, the spiraling symbol they had seen numerous times tonight appeared. The design was burning the wall. The Sheetrock started to dissolve, creating a hole in the center of the symbol. It wasn't just a hole, but a portal. The space shimmered like the surface of the ocean.

The creatures moved toward the wall, side by side. Carrie and Fred didn't dare move. And then they both walked through the portal, the wall pulling them into an infinite void. The spiral simmered, dulling to a barely visible light. The humming sound that warped through the room also diminished to nothing. After a moment, the only sounds were Fred and Carrie's heavy breathing. Neither talked for a few minutes, until Fred put his hand on Carrie's shoulder.

"I think it's over. Look."

He pointed to the windows in the office, which still had the shades drawn, but in the tiny slits visible, daylight was back in full force, the snow once again falling from the sky. Carrie leaned her head on Fred's shoulder and wept. She buried her face in his chest after catching a glimpse of Albert Sinclair's mangled remains. Fred rubbed her back until she pulled away, a thought occurring to her.

"Wait. . .where's Sally? Why isn't she with you?"

She immediately saw the hurt in his eyes, the thin wrinkles in both corners now lined with tears.

"She didn't want to tell you. One of those things hurt her. She's. . .not doing too well."

As Carrie pushed past Fred to head into Albert's main office, the power came back on, bathing them in light. It was something they took for granted most days, but right now, it was the best thing Carrie could ever hope for. That was until she spotted Sally slouched against the wall in the corner of the office.

CHAPTER 20

S**ALLY'S SKIN HAD** turned deathly pale, sweat glistening on her face. She looked at Carrie coming to her and forced a smile. Carrie knew the moment she saw her friend that she was close to dying. She couldn't lose Sally, the only person to look out for Carrie her entire life. She was the mom Carrie never had. The best friend she always dreamed of growing up.

"Hey. . .hon. I see you did it. I knew you would."

"How? You. . .you seemed fine on the way up here," Carrie said, unable to say more as she began to cry. She thought back to the events leading up to this moment and understood that she was too preoccupied to notice that Sally had been walking slowly, moving with a limp. Carrie assumed it was something minor, but obviously Sally had been lying to her.

"Don't be mad at me, please. I didn't tell you because we needed to get up here. Whether I said anything or not, that was always the goal. Had I told. . . Had I told you, we would have wasted even more time."

"No. . .no, please. I can't lose you, Sal. Where did it get you? We can get you help."

Sally provided a half-hearted smile but shook her head. She reached out and rubbed her hand along Carrie's cheek.

"See? Nobody can tell. It's between you and me. Do me a favor? Don't. . .don't you dare go back to that monster, you hear me?"

Carrie's lips trembled as she nodded. She looked up and down Sally's body, trying to locate the wound, gasping when she located it. Starting at the back of her thigh and traveling all the way up to Sally's midsection, her clothes were stained a dark maroon, torn to shreds to reveal part of Sally's insides as she bled out. Carrie leaned her forehead against Sally's, careful to avoid the wound.

"What am I going to do without you? I can't—"

"You can. You've proven tonight you are stronger than you give yourself credit for, hon. The first thing I want you to do is drink that glass of wine for me. Then maybe watch a Christmas movie. Just not *The Family Stone*. You know I hate that movie," Sally said with a chuckle. Carrie couldn't help laughing herself. Even on her deathbed, Sally had to remind her about her poor taste in movies.

"I love you. I'm so sorry I was too late."

"Don't say that. You saved more than just me tonight by getting up here. Stay strong. Stay. . . I—I can see their light. I think they're coming back. . ."

Sally's eyes faded, freezing just over Carrie's shoulders, never to move again. Carrie lost it, crying uncontrollably and refusing to let go of her dead friend's hand. Fred put his hand on her shoulder.

"She was a great woman. And she'd want you to remember her for that, not this. Let's go call in help, okay?"

Carrie stood from her crouch, numbly reaching for her cell, then remembered she had left it up in the duct. Fred realized she didn't have hers and pulled out his own. While he was on the line with the dispatcher, Carrie took in the huge mess they'd made, the floor covered in glass and artifacts. She didn't dare touch any of them, afraid of what they might be capable of doing. It was the rich trying to get richer, the powerful trying to gain even more power. It made her sick.

Once Fred disconnected the call, they made their way down to the lobby to wait for help. Carrie's entire body hurt, the bruised cheek now an afterthought. She had no idea where her life would take her after this or who she'd tell this story to. What she did know, was that as soon as she got out of there, she was going to have that glass of wine.

WE WERE WHO WE WERE

GAGE GREENWOOD

CHAPTER 1

LAST WEEK'S SNOW had melted and refroze again, creating a slippery, chopped-up walk to Walter's front door. Tess took careful steps, bringing her anxiety to new heights. What was she doing here? Why was she doing this? The answers sat heavy in her throat.

Ice broke apart under the weight of her boot, and the slush hidden underneath gushed up, penetrating her skin. Her toes curled from the pain. The cold burst was nearly enough to turn her around, but she'd come too far. When a person decides to act on stupid thoughts, they can only travel so far before they have to see it through, the idiocy of it all, consuming them from within. Who are we if not the product of our dumb decisions?

When she finally reached the door, she knocked once, too gently. But it was enough because she heard movement in response. After a moment, the rustling deep within the house stopped. She considered knocking again. Maybe Walter hadn't heard the knock after all, and the shuffling inside was a coincidence or part of Tess's imagination.

But then she heard Walter's voice, that rugged scratchy voice like a braking train Tess heard echoing in her brain for as long as she'd known it. She hadn't heard it in years, and even then, only in small bursts. "Yes, Your Honor." "Thank you, Your Honor." But it never left her, always dancing on the periphery of her subconscious.

Now, he just said, "Be right there."

Be right there. And then what?

While she waited, she scanned the yard. The evening's darkness masked the faraway portions, but a floodlight revealed a back deck, a well house, and the border of deep woods lining the other side of Walter's place.

Footsteps grew in volume and Tess's throat dried. She coughed. Would Walter remember her? He probably had no idea who she was, or why she was there, but she knew he'd seen her in the courtroom, sitting next to her mother.

The door opened, and Tess felt her heart rip from her chest as if it were tied to the door as it pulled inward. Walter had changed a little. His hair pulled further back from his forehead, and grey stubble peppered his face. Deep pools of black swam under his red glossy eyes. Amazing what only a few years can do.

Recognition crossed his face, and his eyes widened. "What are you doing here? You shouldn't be here." He looked around as if someone might be hiding behind a tree, ready to arrest him anew for being in breathing range of Tess.

"I'm not here to. . ." She sighed, already flying off script despite having recited it repeatedly since early this morning. "I just wanted to talk to you."

His mouth stayed closed, but Tess could see the bump from where his tongue glided across his lower teeth. His eyebrows wrinkled, and finally, he said, "I don't think that's a good idea."

"I just. . . I need to talk to you. I need to do this. Please."

She expected more resistance, but he wiped his forehead and said, "I guess I owe you more than I'll ever be able to repay." He stepped out of the way and waved her in.

She hesitated, regretting every decision that led her here, but she gave a slight nod and followed him inside.

She'd imagined his house many times, or his mother's house rather. Walter lived with her before prison and returned there when he was released. One of the benefits of living in a small town was Tess heard all of this information whether she wanted to or not.

She'd pictured a cozy little place with cheesy beach designs. Airy and light blue. The kind of decorations older women in Tanner's Switch, Rhode Island doused themselves in. But she also imagined a little mess made by the homecoming of her wayward son.

What she found stopped her feet in their tracks. The front hall led to a kitchen in front and a living room to the left side. The furniture in the living room was all flipped over. Not thrown over, but perfectly placed upside down. The couch and chairs were angled thanks to their headrests, but the coffee table, end tables, and television stand were all standing leg up. The television itself sat in front of the stand, on, and playing the aquarium screensaver from Roku.

Walter guided her into this room, so she only got a quick glance at the kitchen, but from what she could tell, the table was upright. However, the chairs were all placed on top of it like at a closed restaurant.

Walter bent down and grabbed the coffee table, flipping it upright in a single swoop. He did the same to two chairs, and grabbed an ashtray off the windowsill, sliding it on the coffee table. He did all of this with such grace, Tess would have guessed he'd been practicing it.

"Doing some moving?"

He furrowed his brow. "What do you mean?"

She pointed to the tv stand, which remained upside down. "Just, everything was turned over."

"Oh," he said, reaching into his pockets and pulling out a pack of Marlboro Reds. "No."

He offered no other explanation, and Tess didn't push it, but her nerves fired, and a tiny voice screamed for her to turn back, to run away from this.

Walter sat, pulled out a cigarette, and lit it. He didn't offer her one. "You're Jay's sister, right?"

She nodded and took the only other chair on its legs. "Yes."

"And I just got out of jail for killing him."

She nodded again, wanting to let him know she wasn't angry, at least not at the moment, but she also knew it wouldn't ease either of their growing anxieties.

Smoke poured from his nostrils. "If it makes you feel any better, I thought I deserved a longer sentence too."

Tess sighed. She hated this. It's true, her mother ranted and raved about the injustice of Walter only getting two years when Jay's punishment was eternal, and Tess herself had deep hatred for Walter. Her emotions were so tangled and knotted, though, so unable to parse that furious rage with the feeling of guilt at wishing a young guy a ruined life in a tit-for-tat game. Walter was to blame. She refused to call it a mistake. He was drunk. He drove. That puts the fault squarely in his lap. But she knew things everyone else didn't, and those pieces of information led to a city of questions. If she could get answers, close some of the doors, she might be able to unknot some of those emotions, come out the other side with some semblance of resolve. Because maybe Walter wasn't to blame as much as everyone thought.

Walter sat staring at her, waiting for her to say something. She crossed her legs and wrapped her arms around her stomach, suddenly feeling cold and exposed. "I just wanted to ask you something."

He flicked his cigarette ash into the tray. "Okay."

The smoke filling the air irritated her eyes, making them watery. It didn't help her dry throat either. "Do you know Tim Burns?"

"Everyone knows Tim Burns. One of the loudest people in every room, even though he never has anything good to say."

A slight smile cracked through Tess's façade. In another life, she and Walter may have gotten along, may have even made good friends. "Yeah, he's an idiot. A walking, talking meme, just ranting about the dumbest political shit every night at—"

"—Cuddy's." Walter finished for her.

She shook her head. "Always at Cuddy's. I love that place. It would be perfect without Tim."

Walter took another long drag, pulling hard as if the cigarette were a joint. As the smoke slid out of his nose in a stream, he said, "You're dodging the point."

She rubbed her face, taking in as deep of an inhale as Walter had, praying the oxygen freed her from the self-made muzzle keeping her quiet. "As much as I hate Tim, the asshole knows things. He hears things."

Tess noticed something, then. The walls were bare. Plain white, only marked by sporadic nails protruding through the drywall with nothing hanging from them. She counted six lone nails. What did they used to hold? Where did Walter put the artwork or family photos that gave the room its identity? Coupled with the flipped furniture, the whole feeling of the night squirmed in Tess's stomach.

Pulling herself away from the observation, she said, "I overheard him talking about a conversation he had with Colin."

Walter's head shot back against the headrest at the mention of his friend's name. Trying to recover from his obvious reaction, he shifted and rested one leg over the other. "And what did Colin have to say?"

Tess wished she had a smoke now. She'd quit but saw the cigarette like a single picket, the start of a fence she could hide behind while she spewed the craziness she planned to unload on Walter. She'd known insanity long before she'd overheard Tim Burns telling Colin's tale at the bar, known it before Walter went to prison, even. But to admit it out loud to someone else was entirely different.

"Colin admitted he went out drinking with you, that you both spent a couple hours at the bar, complaining about your workday, and drinking Guinness. He said you left, and that you'd both had way too much alcohol to be driving. But he said that happened on Tuesday, October 5th."

Walter's eyes darted from one side of the room to the other, much like when he first opened the door for Tess. She couldn't help but feel he worried someone could hear all of this. And that gave her hope.

He sucked another drag and then jabbed the butt into the ashtray with a hint of aggression. "So, he got the day wrong. What's the big deal?"

Tess read his face, seeing the lie. He knew why it was a big deal. "He said that you drove home on Tuesday night, and you both saw a crazy blue flash, then boom, you were like ten miles down the road from where you'd been, and you hit my brother, who was walking on the shoulder after his car broke down a few miles back."

"Sounds like a wild story."

She couldn't read his face any longer. Was it anger? Fear? But she knew what wasn't there. He showed no signs of disbelief, nothing to match his words. She decided to meet his coyness with her own. "It sure does. Yet, here I am, asking you about it."

He sat back down and raised an eyebrow. "You gonna tell me you believe it?"

She leaned forward, wanting him to see her eyes. "I do."

CHAPTER 2

Years ago.

TESS SAT ON her bed, staring out the window. Rain poured down heavily. She watched as the water spilled over the sides of the family's 5-foot aboveground pool. A blast of lightning flashed in the woods behind the yard's picket fence. Following it, the loudest boom Tess had ever heard. She yelped and recovered just before falling off the bed and onto the hardwood.

A giggle escaped her, embarrassed by her reaction. She checked the hallway through her bedroom's open door, hoping no one caught it, especially not Jay. He'd never let her live it down.

Her father was downstairs in the living room, watching a ball game. Tess could hear the announcers ranting about something. The only light outside her bedroom came from across the hall, where a thin, blue flickering danced from Jay's room into the hallway like a malfunctioning disco ball. Her mother must have already passed out because no light or peep escaped from the other bedroom.

Another crash of thunder rocked the house and Tess clenched her bedsheets. Her father swore so loudly, Tess clearly made out the F word. His feet stomped across the floor, and while it hadn't rattled the house with nearly the ferociousness of the thunder, it still had its way of crawling into Tess's bones. It took Tess a moment to catch on to what happened. They'd lost power.

She turned away from the window, and suddenly the darkness scared her. Before, light was only a click away, but now, the thunder had stolen the power, and she couldn't get it back. The absence of it suffocated her. Not seeing her chest rise and fall as the breath came in and out made her feel like she wasn't taking in any at all.

She gasped, moaned. Was she literally drowning?

The flickering still came from Jay's room. He must have something on battery power. But he hadn't made any recognition of the loud thunder or the power going out, so Tess worried he might be sleeping. Still, she needed something, a familiar presence, a little light.

She ran across the hall to his room, relying on instinct and her astute knowledge of the house to guide her, to keep her from crashing into the walls made invisible by the pitch black of the power outage. Whatever light came from Jay's room did nothing to give her sight. It was as if it existed on another plane, showing itself but wholly avoiding its primary function.

When she groped the threshold, she scanned the room, first noticing the source of the light. The blue power button on Jay's CD player. She knew the player well, had stolen it from him on multiple occasions to listen to her 10,000 Maniacs CD. So, she knew the power light stayed continuously lit. It didn't flicker the way it was now. Maybe this new pulsing was the result of the batteries running low, but she didn't think so. It certainly was malfunctioning, but it looked like it was talking as if it were sending messages in its own form of morse code.

Crazy, she knew. Thoughts that were the product of her fears piling on top of each other.

Then something moved by the window, and she yelped like an idiot before realizing it was just Jay staring out the window.

He turned to her and put his finger to his lip. "Shhh." Then he waved her over.

Because of the darkness, she couldn't make out much of his features, but the storm of red growing in his eyes was impossible not to see. It nearly glowed like a neon OPEN sign.

She crept to him, unsure why she wanted to keep quiet, but knowing it was important. Jay pointed into the distance, somewhere out there in the darkness. There was nothing to see but an ocean of black. She knew what existed from their viewpoint, the neighbor's houses across the street, another line of houses going down the intersecting road, and far in the distance, Park Ave, a main road completely absent of traffic. No headlights. Just darkness.

Park Ave always had cars driving down it, even at two in the morning.

But now, all she saw was nothing. The sound of rain made Tess feel like they sat at the bottom of a waterfall.

"What?" She asked Jay.

He leaned into her, whispering in her ear, "I keep seeing a blue light."

She turned to the CD player. "It's that." She pointed to it. "I think it's busted."

He slowly turned to it. She shivered at how slowly.

"Not that. Bigger than that. Just watch."

Behind them, their father stomped by toward his bedroom, oblivious to their late-night adventures, and probably extremely pissed to miss the end of the Red Sox game.

She stayed with Jay for what seemed like hours, but it was probably only fifteen minutes, staring out the window at the dense darkness of a neighborhood suffering from power failure. No blue light came. In fact, no light came of any kind. Not a single car headlight. Not another bolt of lightning. Nothing. Finally, she relented, stood up, and put her hand on Jay's shoulder. "I have to go to bed."

His ability to stay still, to stare so intently without blinking or shifting or twitching, impressed her, but it also worried her. What could stop Jay so dead in his tracks? He was always moving, always exerting more energy than anyone around him could handle.

He never offered a response, so she sighed and walked toward the door. As she reached it, he said, "There it is!"

She whipped around but saw nothing. Choosing not to upset him, she said, "I must have missed it," instead of, "Are you seeing things that aren't there?" Or "It's probably just lightning, dude."

Jay made a weird croaking sound so haunting it nearly knocked Tess to her knees. Then his head fell back. With his upper body straight, the back of his head hit his spine, so he looked directly at his sister without turning his torso from the window. Tess screeched at the sight, the unnatural angle. It was humanly impossible.

Jay's croaking grew louder, rumbling like a generator. His bloodshot eyes rolled back into his head. Tess went to scream again but her lungs wouldn't work, as if the night had struck her in the gut and sucked the wind out of her.

Then Jay said something in a voice that didn't belong to him. Couldn't. No trick or vocal manipulation could make Jay's sweet quiet voice turn into something so high-pitched and vulgar. "I am who I am," he screeched.

I am who I am.

His head shot back up, and his body collapsed to the floor where his limbs went wild, flailing, kicking, punching. It looked like someone electrocuted him.

Tess found her voice. "Mom! Dad!" With all the power her throat could handle, she called for them until they barged into the room, ran past her, and flanked Jay.

Tess's mother put her hands under Jay's head and propped it on her lap. "You're okay. You're okay," she said over and over. Then, to Tess's father, "Call 911."

He shook his head. "I tried the phone when the power went out to report it. It's just giving static."

As they argued about what to do, Tess sat at the threshold of Jay's room, watching her brother shake uncontrollably. His words, and that voice, echoing in her brain. I am who I am. I am who I am. I am who I am.

CHAPTER 3

AFTER A FEW MOMENTS, Jay's seizure stopped. His parents helped him downstairs and gave him some water before piling everyone into the Subaru Legacy. On the ride to the hospital, Jay kept insisting he was fine. The seizure had passed, and for the most part, he did look fine albeit a little confused.

When they reached Park Ave, Tess learned why the view from her brother's room never had any headlights in the distance. Not one, but three trees had collapsed onto the road, and traffic detoured down Warwick Ave on one side, and toward Pawtuxet Village on the other.

While all of this explained the lack of light, the fact that three different trees in three different spots all fell down in a perfect way to block off her entire neighborhood from incoming traffic, just added to the eeriness. It also meant Tess's family couldn't get to the damned hospital.

Her father circled the block twice, as if going around again would somehow make one of the trees disappear.

Raindrops pelted the windshield and pinged off the top of the car. Jay stared out the window, occasionally taking a sip from his water.

As Tess's father turned left to make yet another trip around, Tess tapped Jay's shoulder. "How are you feeling?"

Before he could answer, Tess's mother scoffed and said, "Elliot, what are you doing? Just drive off the road and around the damned tree."

"What am I going to do? Tear up the Crouse's yard?"

"Yes! Your son needs to get to the hospital."

Their bickering grew louder while Tess continued to stare at Jay, who kept his eyes glued out the side window. He mumbled something, and Tess leaned forward trying to hear it over her parents shouting.

She couldn't stand it, their loud debating, and the frustration of not hearing her brother, who grew increasingly weird by the second. His feet were tapping ferociously on the backseat floor, and his fingers matched the rhythm against his knees. Tess's parents were so focused on the damn trees, they missed the forest, which in this case happened to be their son. Each rapid-fire tap of his fingers and feet came more and more forcefully, like an increasing windstorm battering against the windows. Only a matter of time before everything fucking shattered.

"FINE," Her father yelled. The tires screeched and the car shook hard as it went up the curb, onto Tucker Crouse's yard. It didn't fully clear the tree, snapping small branches under its weight as it sped through the grass.

Another big bump and the car was back on the street, past the roadblock and zooming away from the scene of the crime.

With that out of the way, Tess's mother caught on to Jay's strange behavior. "Jay, what's wrong?"

He ignored her, continuing to mumble unintelligibly. Tess glanced at her mother, hoping the woman could break into the mental blockade, clear this all up. Something was wrong. All of this, so unlike Jay.

On his best days, he was a wild spirit, so full of pep and vigor, he couldn't be contained. The adults went mad at his frantic nature, claiming he was too old for the behavior. Tess didn't think twelve was too old for anything, but she was only eight, so what did she know? She loved that side of Jay.

Now, slamming his feet into the floor, smashing his fingertips into his knees, and mumbling nonsensically, Tess wondered if something inside him broke. He was the CD player, flashing blue in weird rhythms, and just like the dying radio, she couldn't help but want to make sense of it, to find some pattern, a secret language hidden within the chaos.

Her father turned the car into the hospital parking lot. Tess hadn't realized how far they'd traveled. As soon as her father twisted the key from the ignition, Jay stopped. The tapping ceased, his rambling mumbles died in his throat, and he turned to Tess and their mother with a confused look on his face.

"What?" He asked. Then he furrowed his brow and scanned

the parking lot until his eyes reached the hospital building. "Why are we here?"

They rushed him inside, explaining everything to him on the way. He had no recollection of any of it, not even the seizure, which they'd already told him about before the second episode.

The rest of the night disappeared in a blur. Jay was carted all over the hospital for a variety of tests, meanwhile never exhibiting any of the symptoms again. After all the tests, and questions from doctors and nurses, Tess and her parents sat around Jay's bed while he fell asleep. As they waited for brain scans to come back, Tess's mother whispered, "He had a fever, right? When I touched his head in the bedroom, he felt like he was burning up."

Her father nodded. "Kid was so hot, it hurt me putting my hand on him."

Tess's eyes darted from Mom to Dad, trying to make sense of it all, and hoping the two people who always put things into context could do the same again.

"And what was his temperature here?"

Her father laughed. "98.2 they said."

Tess's mother crossed her arms. "Can something like that happen? A quick episode of a fever. I know high temps can cause seizures. Is that all it was? And it just. . .. What? Cleared up on its own?"

Her brother's chest moved up and down at a sweet, calm pace. The idea that a human could just malfunction so easily terrified Tess. Even if they left the hospital, cleared by medical experts, could Jay experience the same thing tomorrow? Could SHE? Could anyone? Was it possible to crack so easily? Were we all just eggs teetering on the edge of a table, one small breath away from splattering our insides all over the kitchen floor?

Tess was eight. She never really thought about death or health. She just lived. But picturing her brother writhing on the floor, she couldn't help but fear this new concept of weakness within us, this bomb in our bodies. Fear filled her. She could lose anyone at any time. No one was safe.

Ever. Not even her.

The doctor came in, rubbing his bald head and scanning Jay's file. He explained stuff to Tess's parents that went above her head, but she got the message. Nothing was wrong with Jay, and they should bring him right back if anything happens again.

At first, she was happy. Jay would come home with them, and the nightmare had ended, but then it sank in. Even the experts had no idea what caused it. A sense of dread washed over her. A monster crawled through their lives, and it could unravel them at any moment. Pull them apart. Rip them from their spools.

CHAPTER 4

WHEN THEY ARRIVED home at 4:30 AM, Tess's father called both her and Jay out of school, and everyone went to bed. The rain hadn't stopped, but the lightning and thunder had seemingly passed. Someone had cleared the trees from the road as well.

Tess didn't expect much sleep, her mind too busy racing around all she'd learned about the delicate nature of her existence. But to her surprise, the next thing she knew her eyes peeled open to a slice of sun beaming through her window. She glanced at her alarm clock. 12:32 PM.

She sat up. Clattering came from the kitchen. Plates or cups clinking together, probably as her mom unloaded the dishwasher. She heard her brother and mom talking and then a sound that filled her heart. Giggling.

Up on her feet in seconds, Tess ran downstairs and into the kitchen. Jay brought a spoonful of something to his mouth, but before it could land, Tess crashed into him with a hug. Despite his hot soup spilling from his spoon to the table, Jay laughed at the excited embrace from his sister.

She stayed in the hug for a long time, and he never asked her to stop.

"Alright, give your brother some breathing room," Tess's mother said.

As Tess had predicted, her mother was unloading the dishwasher. Jay went back to his soup as Tess hopped on the chair next to him. He pointed at the spilled puddle next to his bowl. "You owe me a spoonful," he said with a snort.

Tess's mother passed by her with a handful of silverware. "I'd offer you a bowl of soup too, but since you're just waking up, would you like some breakfast instead?"

"I'll just have soup too," Tess said. She always ate whatever Jay ate. "Sorry I slept so late."

Her mother smiled. "Oh please. We all would have slept in if we could have. Your father had to take Jay to Dr. Manzana before he went to work."

A bag of stones landed in Tess's belly. Her mother must have noticed the panic in her daughter's face, because she said, "Don't worry. The hospital always asks for a follow-up with the family doctors. It was just more of the same. Nothing else happened."

She stared at her brother for a moment. After a few slurps from his spoon, he noticed. "What?"

"What?" She shrugged.

"Why are you staring at me?"

"I don't know. How are you?"

He laughed again. He always laughed. "I'm good. How are you?"

She sunk down in her seat as she cracked up, just finding his normal demeanor worth the giggle fit. "I'm good."

Jay looked up to their mother, who had moved away from organizing the silverware and began pouring soup into a bowl for Tess. "See, Mom, Tess and I are both good. And we both didn't have school today. I think you should keep us home every day and we'll keep being good."

Tess's laughing fit grew into screeches. She spoke through the hysterics. "No more school."

Their mother placed a bowl in front of Tess. "You both got one day. Don't push it."

Jay looked at Tess and winked. "I'll just have another seizure tonight."

The giddiness and humor exited Tess's body. Her mother forced a smile, but her words came out stern. "Don't even joke. You have no idea how scared we were last night."

Jay put his hands up. "I know. I know. I was just kidding."

After Jay finished his soup, Tess slurped the rest of hers down, so she could tag along with whatever he planned to do for the day. She found him upstairs in his room, messing with his radio, his ear to the speaker as if trying to glean some muted sound.

"Wanna do something?" She asked him.

He turned to her and smiled. "Let's get into trouble."

"Yes!"

He stood up and jumped onto his bed. "Okay, here's the game. Are all the contestants ready?"

Tess climbed onto the bed and stood beside him, both of them bobbing on the mattress. "What are we doing?"

Jay pointed to the wall adjacent to them. "We are going to jump as high as we can on the bed, and then we are going to take turns slamming ourselves into the wall. Whoever makes the loudest smack, wins!"

Tess laughed. "Okay."

They both jumped and jumped until Jay had to crane his neck to avoid hitting his head on the ceiling. And then he launched himself into the wall. Tess was shocked by the sound it made. The whole room rumbled with more force than when the thunder crashed the night before.

Jay fell to the floor, laughing and yelling, "Ow."

"What was that?" Their mother yelled from downstairs.

This just made Tess and Jay laugh harder. Tess, knowing the games could end any second if her mom followed up with her question, flew off the mattress. Her shoulder and leg hit the wall first and made a big bang before she dropped to the floor and landed right next to her brother. They both exaggerated their pain, holding their arms, and cracking up between "OWWWWWWWs."

Their mother stormed up the stairs. "What the hell is going on up here?"

When she entered the room, she saw them laughing themselves to tears on the floor and smiled. "What are you goofs up to?"

"We were playing splat," Jay said, and a new round of hysterics broke out, their mother even adding to it, despite not fully understanding the joke. "Just keep it down, alright. And don't hurt yourselves. We don't need another trip to the hospital."

She shook her head and walked away.

Eventually, the laughing ended, and Jay and Tess stared at the ceiling from their positions on the floor, catching their breath.

Jay turned to her. "I like that we're friends."

Tess smiled. "Me too."

"I think siblings are supposed to fight, but we never do. Like ever."

"I know, right." She didn't know. Were siblings supposed to fight? She and Jay never did. Maybe the occasional bicker, but mostly they got along great.

"Especially since you're four years younger than me. I'm supposed to hate you."

She'd never considered it before, but they did have a big age difference, and all of her friends from school were in her class. She couldn't think of any kids her age that hung out with their siblings, and especially not any that hung out with twelve-year-olds.

Jay put his hands on his chest and laid straight, staring off as if looking beyond the ceiling to the late afternoon sky. "You're supposed to be a pain in the ass. I think that's why we're friends because you're not."

"Thanks." She didn't feel like it was a compliment, but she didn't know what else to say.

He rolled over, facing her. "I have to tell you something, but you can't tell mom and dad. You're my best friend, so I trust you. Can I trust you?"

She nodded, but the fun left the room, and she didn't like promising before she knew the secret. It scared her like Jay was dropping a weight on her back and telling her to swim.

"I know what happened to me last night."

Her pulse sped up, fear washing over into excitement. She wanted to know, wanted to loosen the worry she'd had the night before. A reason. All she needed was a reason, something that could make her feel protected. If Jay knew what caused it, she could avoid whatever it was. "What?"

"Remember I told you about the blue lights?"

She nodded.

"It was aliens."

First fear, then excitement, and now sadness. He was picking on her. Making jokes. "Stop it."

He sighed and squished his face. "I'm not joking. I think I saw something I wasn't supposed to see last night, and one of the aliens didn't like that, and he like, got into my head."

A light whine came into the room, almost too soft to hear, but Tess picked it up. Jay's face remained stone serious, and Tess wasn't sure how to react. Was she meant to laugh, or to pretend to believe him? Was he joking or not? It didn't matter, but Tess *did* believe it, at least a little. If he told her right now it was a joke, she'd still toss and turn all night now, worried about aliens getting into her brain. You can't tell something like that to a kid, even facetiously, and expect them not to be haunted by it.

Jay closed his eyes and shook his head. "It's okay if you don't believe me. Just don't tell mom and dad. If they think I'm crazy, they'll make me go to the doctors and I don't know if they'll like, put me in a crazy hospital or something."

Tess just nodded again.

"Promise?"

"Okay." Tess realized then that he wasn't joking with her, and she wished she could go back in time a few minutes and tell him she didn't want to hear his secrets. Not knowing what happened to him wasn't the scariest thing after all. Tess was eight. She didn't believe in monsters anymore, but she still had trouble sleeping in the full dark, worried about what existed outside her sight. She didn't believe in ghosts, but she still ran to the bathroom at night thinking one might touch her if she didn't quickly get the light clicked into the on position. And she didn't believe in aliens, but she believed her brother, and now she had a new nightmare licking her brain: entities that could get inside your head. What would they do once in there? Could they make her hurt someone? Or herself? Could they make her forget things?

"What did he do to you?" She asked, allowing herself to step further into the haunted house of her nightmares. Once you're enveloped in the darkness of your fears, it doesn't really matter where you move. It's all charcoal.

He opened his eyes wide, surprised by her question. He really assumed Tess wouldn't believe it. She'd believe her brother if he told her she was a giraffe.

"It's hard to explain. I guess I don't know. But I felt him in there. He was yelling at me." Tears formed in Jay's eyes, and he bit his bottom lip. "It really hurt." His voice broke.

Tess slid closer to him, hypnotized by his story. But she still heard that whining sound. In fact, she thought it might be getting louder.

"And then it was like I had no control over myself. And I was gone. I was just floating somewhere, and it felt awful, like a million darts thrown at me."

Yes, the whining was definitely getting louder. There was a static sound attached to it.

"And he screamed and screamed at me, but it was inside my head, so it was like someone reaching inside my skull and pressing on my brain and pulling and tugging and tearing it."

Tess caught herself not breathing. That noise. What was it?

"I'd never been so scared in my whole life. And, he was talking to me, but I couldn't understand him because his words weren't real words. But he said his name. I'll never forget that name."

Tess went to speak, but her voice squeaked. She cleared her throat and asked, "What was it?"

"Mahazael," Jay said, and as he said the name, the whining went to full blast and a voice yelled. At first, Tess thought the alien was in her head, hollering at her brain like Jay explained, but Jay shot up and ran to the radio. He kicked it, and as it smashed into the wall, it went silent. The whining gone. The static and the screaming vanished.

Tess stared, frozen in fear.

"He can hear me," Jay said. "He knows I'm telling you. Come on," he reached out a hand.

CHAPTER 5

TESS GRABBED HIS hand and Jay yanked her hard. They ran out of the room and down the stairs where their mother had just come to the landing.

"What the heck is going on with you two today?"

"No time," Jay said, leading his sister toward the back door.

"Will you both settle down a little."

"Sorry Mom, but fun is a must," Jay said as he threw the backdoor open. He crashed through the screen door, slamming it against the house and he and Tess ran into the middle of the yard.

Jay's face drove through a manic display of emotions, fear, anger, and Tess couldn't tell what the other one was, but it might have been the most prominent.

"Laugh," Jay said and followed his own instructions, letting out an exaggerated and poorly acted guffaw. His head raised to the sky, jaw wide open, and he laughed loudly, ridiculously. Tess caught her mother at the door, closing the screen Jay had left open. She stared at them with suspicious eyes.

Jay stopped his phony display dead and said, "Laugh. Do it."

Tess whispered a little *ha ha*.

He gave her a gentle shove, and while he didn't put any force into it, Tess hadn't expected it and almost fell into the grass at the center of their backyard. "You have to have fun. Don't just pretend."

She didn't understand. Jay clearly faked his laughter, so why couldn't she? He put both his palms to his lips, wrists together, and blew a raspberry. It caught Tess off guard, and she laughed for real. Just a small one before the reality of all the nonsense seeped back in.

Jay noticed and made his fart noises even louder. His eyes widened comically, and his cheeks turned red as he continued to blow out into his palms. Damn him. She hated how even when he scared the shit out of her, he could also make her laugh.

Within a few minutes, they were both cracking up again. What about the aliens? What about the radio going wacky? It didn't matter. Jay led and Tess followed. He could guide her to the depths of hell, and then to Denny's for burgers, and she'd take the whole ride and all the emotions that came with it. Jay wanted them to pivot, so she pivoted.

When they stopped their fit, Jay said through big breaths, "Okay, see. Fun is a must. Just have fun and everything is fine." He tapped the top of her head. "Tag."

She chased him as he darted around the picket fence lining their yard. Aliens. Screaming. Panic. Laughter. Tag. It didn't matter. She chased her brother. As always.

They played in the yard for hours. After tag, it was cornhole, then races, then kickball. Eventually, their father's car pulled into the driveway, and they all came in for dinner.

Tess never stopped thinking about what happened earlier, but the idea of it being real dissolved into the minutes of their day, a story unraveling with time. She still worried, of course, but now it was more for Jay's wellbeing than anything sinister.

At the dinner table, Jay acted perfectly normal. Everyone chatted while swallowing their chicken and potatoes.

"Glad to hear everything was okay today," their father said.

Their mother responded, "Huh. I'll say. Couldn't get these two to settle down for a minute."

Jay smiled with a mouth full of potatoes. "Fun is a must, that's what I always say." He spoke in a silly talk show host kind of way.

Things settled back into place as if the confession from Jay and the weird radio static were all part of some dream. Maybe Jay had played a prank on Tess, some elaborate scheme to freak her out.

After dinner, their father went to the living room for the nightly news, and Jay escaped to his bedroom. Tess helped her mother with the dishes.

"How was Jay today when you were with him?" Her mom placed a plate into the dishwasher.

Tess shrugged. "Fine."

A sigh escaped her mother's mouth. "Good. Let me know if anything weird happens."

"What kind of weird?" Tess ran a bowl under the water and handed it to her mom to place in the dishwasher.

"You saw him last night. If he seems sick or, I don't know. The doctors didn't know what caused it, so I don't really know what to look for. Just anything out of the normal. Okay?"

Tess nodded and ran some silverware under the blasting water. She debated on telling her mom about her brother's confession, but she'd just gotten accustomed to the idea the whole thing was an elaborate trick, and she worried spilling the beans on Jay would only bring the craziness to life again, somehow forging it into reality.

After they finished loading the washer, Tess ran upstairs to her room and turned on the television, waiting until *Boy Meets World* came on. She flipped through one of her *I Spy* books while she waited, and then two minutes before go time, she had to pee.

She went for it, running across the dark hallway. Her parents were still up, downstairs in the living room, and Tess could hear the *Jeopardy* final question music playing from all the way up here. When she crossed Jay's room she slowed to peek in and stopped dead in her tracks at the sight.

Jay sat on his bed, legs crossed, hands at his knees, staring wide-eyed into his closet. His mouth was opened wide. From the angle, Tess couldn't see what he was looking at, but a blue light flashed from within. She noted the broken CD player on the floor where Jay had smashed it earlier, so it couldn't be the cause.

"Jay?" Her words came out softer than she meant them to.

He didn't move.

"Jay?" A little louder.

Still nothing.

"Jay?"

Finally, he slowly turned his head to her in a mechanical fashion. His eyes and mouth remained wide open. When he looked directly at her, he stopped moving his head but said nothing, did nothing, just remained in that same frozen position with his eyes bugging out of his skull and his mouth draped open like heavy stones pulled his jaw down.

"Jay? What's wrong?"

In a blink, he snapped out of it, shot back, hitting his head hard against the wall, curling up in a ball, and he screamed. The sheer volume in it sent waves of shivers up Tess's body and she fell backward.

He didn't stop, just one long scream expelling from his body. He kicked his legs and swung his arms as if some invisible creature were trying to get close.

"Mom! Dad!" Tess yelled.

She heard their footsteps running to the stairs, and then flying up them.

"What is it?" Her father asked.

"What's going on?"

They ran past her. "Jay, what's wrong honey?" Their mother asked as she came to Jay's side.

The screaming stopped as Jay sucked in a breath, and as soon as he'd refilled his lungs, he went right back to it.

"Jay. Jay. Stop. It's okay. You're safe. What's wrong?" Their father said.

Meanwhile, their mom rubbed his back and said, "Shhh, shhh, shhh."

Tess stood in the hallway, watching, too afraid to approach. Her hands covered her mouth. The screaming was too much. She couldn't take the sound, so high-pitched and violent.

Jay didn't look like he did last night, the way his entire body tightened up and shook, but his legs and arms were flailing wildly.

She forced herself to move forward, taking slow steps into Jay's room. As soon as she crossed the threshold, he snapped out of it. The abrupt nature of the silence was almost as jarring as the initial scream. Jay gasped hard as if just emerging from an underwater swim. His eyes darted wildly, confused by his family surrounding him.

"What?" He asked.

His mother shot up out of the bed. "Okay, back to the hospital."

Their father rubbed his eyes. He almost looked like he might object but shook his head in argument with himself. "Yeah, let's go."

"What? Did I have another seizure?"

"No. Come on. We'll explain on the way."

Jay didn't argue, just stood up and followed everyone out of the room.

CHAPTER 6

T**HE TRIP TO** the hospital proved uneventful compared to the night before. No trees blocked the road, and Jay never delved into a weird catatonic mumble session. In fact, he went right back to his goofy self, cracking jokes, making weird faces, and being an all-around sport about going to the hospital once again.

It was a slow night, so they sent Jay right in upon arrival. The doctors opted to do a few more tests and to retest some of the stuff from the night before, but they also wanted to bring in some pediatric specialists and do some psychological evaluations. Tess's parents seemed concerned about that, but Tess didn't know why or what it all really meant.

After they put Jay in a wheelchair and carted him out of the room for some kind of test, a doctor came in, a pretty Hispanic woman, and sat down to ask Tess's parents some questions.

"Did your son ever say what he was screaming at? Did he explain how he felt to you while it was happening?"

Tess's father shrugged. "Same thing he said to you. He doesn't remember it happening or why he screamed."

Tess squirmed in her seat. A promise is a promise.

The doctor flashed her shiny white teeth. "Understood. He just seemed a little closed off when we talked to him, and sometimes children are just afraid to speak up to strangers. Which is good, right?" She laughed. "That's what we teach them. Don't talk to strangers. But in this case, we need to know anything we can about what he experienced. So, if he does start to remember and tells you, it would be very helpful for us to know that information."

Tess's mother leaned forward and whispered, "Do you think this is all mental?"

Her smile straightened. It was still a smile, but more matter-of-fact. A thin stream running across her cheeks. "I don't want to presume it's anything yet. But clearly something very scary happened to him and your family, and my job is to cover all the bases and make sure we get to the bottom of it for Jay and for all of you."

Tess liked the doctor. Hospitals were scary places, and so many people came in and out of their rooms and just got right to the facts. But this doctor worked hard to calm everyone. Her very presence eased the tension.

Her parents chatted with the doctor for a few more minutes, and then she left.

"Mom, what did you mean when you asked if it was mental?"

Her mother put her hand on Tess's head and scruffed her hair. "Well, whatever is happening to Jay is either physical, which means something is happening to his body, like an infection or a virus. Or it's mental, which means it's happening in his mind. It still means he's sick, but it's more of something his own brain is doing."

"Like his brain made him have a seizure?"

She laughed. Her father cleared his throat and chimed in. "No, honey. His seizure was something else. And what he has is definitely physical. The doctors just want to know if Jay was seeing something that wasn't there when he was screaming. Sometimes a physical sickness, like what Jay had last night, can cause problems in the brain."

Tess tucked her hands under her knees. Her heart raced. "I think he really saw something because I saw a blue light coming from his closet."

Her mother sighed. "The blue light was probably from one of his electronics. I saw in the closet, Tess, nothing was there. But I don't know if Jay was seeing anything at all. He may just have been screaming for no reason at all."

Tears formed in Tess's eyes, not for Jay but for herself. She had to betray her own brother. "He told me something earlier today."

They both turned to her.

"He told me not to tell you guys."

Her father gripped the arm of his chair. "Tess, you know not to keep secrets from us."

Her mother rubbed Tess's back. "I know you want to keep your brother's secret, but if you think it's something that will help him, you need to tell us. You want to help your brother, right?"

Tess nodded.

"So, tell us, Tess," her father said.

The words spilled from her mouth like water in a fountain. "He said during the storm last night, he saw aliens, and they were mad that he saw them, and they got into his brain and were trying to hurt him. But I don't think he imagined it, because his radio was doing weird stuff right after he told me."

Her father's face stayed the same stoic stony it always was, but her mother couldn't hide her concern behind her wrinkled forehead and curled mouth while she chewed on the inside of her cheek.

"I think your brother may have been messing with you, Tess," her father said.

"You saw him at lunch. He was perfectly fine. And then he was having a wild time with you all day. Don't you think if your brother really believed an alien got into his head, he would have been a little more upset all day?" Her mother added, sounding like she wanted to convince herself more than Tess.

Tess shrugged. No, she didn't think that, but if her parents weren't concerned by her confession, she wouldn't worry about it either.

Her mother looked to her father, "We should probably still mention it to the doctor though."

He agreed and left the room.

"I don't want Jay to hate me," Tess said.

"I'm sure your brother won't hate you. He'll understand why you told us. Besides, would you rather have your brother mad at you for a little bit, or for him to feel better?"

Tess found the question unfair. Why did she have to choose?

CHAPTER 7

HER MOTHER'S ASSUMPTIONS proved wrong. Jay was extremely angry at Tess for telling them. For weeks, he refused to talk to her, and whenever anyone asked him about the alien story, he confessed it was all a joke to mess with Tess. She didn't know which hurt more.

CHAPTER 8

WHILE THEY NEVER found anything physically wrong with Jay, they sent him to meeting after meeting, uprooting the entire family schedule. Since most of those meetings happened after Jay finished school for the day, but before their father returned home from work, their mother had to drive him, which meant Tess had to tag along.

With her brother not speaking to her, it made for rather uncomfortable trips. Jay became more erratic and destructive for a while. If his behavior prior to his seizure was wild and free, his new attitude was chaos unleashed. He yelled when he talked as if he were carrying a conversation in a convertible on a windy day. He jogged instead of walked. He slammed into things intentionally, ping-ponging his body off walls as he moved around the house.

He never wanted to sleep, staying up way past his normal bedtime.

This new cartoon version of Jay wanted fun all the time, never willing to relax, and even for Tess, it was exhausting.

She didn't know why they had to have so many appointments. The doctors never found anything wrong with him, and by Jay's own admission, he never had anything to say to the therapists.

For weeks, everything sucked.

And then Jay had another screaming fit.

Back to the hospital, back to testing, and all of it resulting in the same things. Nothing was wrong. See more doctors.

But one thing did change: Jay. He dropped the overexcited act and showed his true self. A scared boy.

On their way to a doctor's appointment, Jay stared out the window, temple against the glass, and said one single thing that broke him wide open.

"I'm tired."

It was like one of those trees from the storm had crashed down on their car the way those words hit. Not the words themselves, but the delivery, the meek and haunted tone in Jay's voice, the sadness.

Their mother glanced in the rearview. "Why don't you take a nap, Honey. You've been firing on all cylinders lately."

Jay balled his hands into fists and punched his temples. "I'm not tired like that. I'm tired of trying to keep it out of my head."

She sat up straight. "Keeping what out? What's going on, Jay. Talk to us."

For a second, he looked like he might shut down again, slinking into himself, and turning his head toward the window again, but then he said, "I think there's something wrong with me."

They turned into the parking lot of his psychiatrist's office, which was in a building within a series of buildings all lined around each other. Each place housed a different kind of medical specialist. On their first trip there, her mother joked, "You can get every part of you fixed up in this place, from your feet to your teeth."

"What do you mean something is wrong with you?"

He shook his head. "I'll talk to Dr. Renard about it," he said. "I'll tell you guys later."

The car pulled into an empty spot in front of the building, and Jay quickly exited the car, head down, defeated.

Sitting in the waiting room while he went into his appointment went by excruciatingly slow. It always did, but this time it felt worse. Tess just wanted it all to end, to see some results, something that would change their lives back to how they were. Before the first seizure, Tess understood doctors as people who fixed things and made the bad stuff go away. She needed that to happen again.

When the hour ticked over, Dr. Renard propped the door open and said, "Would you mind coming in for a minute?"

Tess's mother nodded and took her daughter's hand. "She okay to come in too?"

Dr. Renard glanced at Jay, who nodded, and she passed the nod along to their mother.

Tess marveled at the room, having never seen inside it. Shelves of books lined the walls, and the comfiest-looking couch sat dead center, where Jay currently rested. He scooted over, making room for their mother and Tess, who took seats next to him.

Dr. Renard sat in her chair and had a sip of her tea. After she swallowed, she said, "Jay gave me permission to discuss with you some of what we talked about today. Well, I urged him to, because we agreed the best course for him right now would be some medication."

Tess perked up. Medicine. That always helped, but her mother had the opposite reaction, sitting up, her eyebrows drooping. "Medicine for what?"

Dr. Renard showed no concern for the question. "I won't go into the details, but if Jay wants to later, he can. What you need to know is Jay confessed to hearing and seeing things that he understands aren't really there."

Their mother's jaw dropped, and she looked at Jay, and then back to Dr. Renard. "Hallucinations?"

"It's quite common, believe it or not, and from what I can glean from our conversations, I believe it's being brought on by stress, which could also explain the seizure he experienced."

"Seizures and hallucinations from stress?"

Dr. Renard nodded.

"He doesn't seem very stressed. We have a very good home life."

Dr. Renard put her hand up. "Of course. This isn't something you did wrong. Jay is suffering from acute anxiety. Nothing in particular is triggering his stress, it's just his brain's fight or flight going into overdrive."

"So, anyone can just fall over and have a seizure from anxiety?"

Tess didn't understand why her mother turned so defensive. She talked like the doctor was lying, but what Dr. Renard told them was good news. They had answers and solutions. Who wouldn't want that?

"No. Not anyone. But folks with other conditions, such as severe anxiety disorders, can."

"What will you be giving him? Antipsychotics or anti-seizure medicines? What's this going to do to him?"

Tess was impressed with Dr. Renard's ability to take her mother's jabs.

"We are going to start with some anti-anxiety medications because I believe that is the root of all of his problems. We will start him with buspirone and go from there."

Her mother reduced herself to a stuttering mess for a moment while she gathered all of the information, before seemingly relenting. She said, "What kind of hallucinations was he having?" She turned to Jay, to Dr. Renard, and back again, waiting for someone to answer her.

But Tess ended up being the first to speak and provide her mother with an answer. "Mahazael."

As the word left her mouth, Jay reached around his mom and gripped her arm. His jaw muscles protruded out, and he shook his head. No. A lump landed on top of Tess's heart and the strength of it dragged it into her gut. She didn't know why, but she knew she shouldn't have said that name out loud. She shouldn't even have thought of it.

CHAPTER 9

THAT NIGHT, Tess woke every few hours from dreams where a monster ripped its claw into her skull, pulled her brain out, and wrung it out like a soaked dish rag.

CHAPTER 10

IT TOOK A week or so for the medication to change Jay. Slowly, his excitability settled into his normal happy-go-lucky personality. He stayed hyper, but not off-the-charts hyper. His smile returned. His humor, too.

And after a few weeks, he even talked to Tess again. They played together, talked about music, walked to the convenience store down the road to buy candy.

And over time, Mahazael disappeared from Tess's mind. The seizure, the screaming, the bad dreams, they all eroded and disappeared like universes sucked into the black hole of her mind.

Just memories. But unimportant ones that never needed revisiting.

CHAPTER 11

ON TESS'S 14TH BIRTHDAY, Jay drove her to the skating rink so she could meet with some of her friends. While she skated around the rink, giggling with her girlfriends, a few of Jay's pals stopped by to hang with him and eat some pizza. Tess was old enough now to understand the sacrifice her brother made on a Friday night by not only driving her but sticking around to bring her home afterwards.

Soon, he'd graduate, and she'd mourn for the quality time he so often granted without complaint. He'd never grown too cool for her, never failed to be her friend.

She skated up to the rink wall by his table and said hello to Christian, Mark, and Jenna, Jay's three best friends. Tess didn't feel left out when any of them were around. They all treated her well, like a cool younger kid. She wasn't ushered in with praise and cheers, but they were all nice to her and didn't pick on her the way older kids can sometimes do.

"Happy birthday," Jenna said and held up a bag.

Tess couldn't believe one of Jay's friends actually bought her a present. Sure, they were nice to her, but they'd never done something like this.

"Thanks!" She took the bag and looked at it. A silver background with an array of colorful balloons. Her fingers touched the top of the bag but hesitated. Was she supposed to open it now, or was that considered rude?

She looked to Jay for answers but found something else entirely. His eyes were bloodshot, and he looked off. It probably went unnoticed by his friends, the changes too subtle, but Tess saw the floundering in his smile, and the twitching on the left side of his lip.

Jenna said, "You can open it now."

Tess peeled her eyes off Jay and dipped her hand into the bag.

The tissue paper crinkled as she moved around it until her fingers touched the hard edge of her gift. She pulled it out and gasped. Her eyes filled with tears.

"I painted it one night after leaving your house. Do you remember the night we sat in your backyard cooking hot dogs on the grill?"

Tess nodded, too awed by the painting to look away from it.

"I saw you two sitting on the picnic table talking to each other, and I thought it was so cool to see a brother and sister like that, so—"

"—friendly?" Tess guessed.

Jenna shook her head. "No. Not friendly. Like, you need each other. I wondered who you'd be without each other, so that's what's happening in the sky. Your faces in the front are you two as I saw you that night, and the faces in the stars are who you'd be without each other."

Tess wiped her eyes. It was a beautiful painting. She and Jay sitting next to each other on a bench, laughing. Happiness so apparent on their faces. Behind them, a celestial backdrop. Stars dotting the blackness. A streak from a comet. But the stars were designed to make two more faces, almost in a connect-the-dots fashion. Both unlike the ones on Tess and Jay in the forefront. These faces looked cold, distant, sad, and alien.

Tess peeled her eyes away and turned to Jenna. The girl held an awkward smile, waiting to hear what Tess thought of it.

"This is the best present I've ever gotten." And it was! Jay would leave soon for college, and this present came at just the right time, a token Tess could hang in her room to remind herself of her brother when she missed him most.

She skated around the wall and hugged Jenna. "Thank you so much."

One of Tess's friends called for her. Tess gave the girl a wait-a-minute finger and placed the painting on the seat next to Jay. "Keep this safe," she said and went back to her friends.

Her friends grabbed her hands as she reentered the rink, and they skated in a line, laughing and singing to Hit Me Baby One More Time as it blared through the speakers. But every time Tess passed her brother, she glanced at his face. He hid it well, joking with his friends and showing no signs of struggle, but he couldn't hide it from her.

He wasn't the kid on the picnic table in the painting, nor was he the lost boy in the stars, but he was lingering somewhere in between them, a lost fragment of space rock floating through the atmosphere.

Eventually, parents came and picked up Tess's friends, leaving her to herself. She returned her skates and put her sneakers back on while Jay said goodbye to his friends. He waited at the door for her with her painting in hand.

"What's wrong," he asked her as they walked to his car.

"With me? I was going to ask you the same thing."

He put his arm around her shoulders. "I'm good."

"You can't fool me," Tess said and stuck out her tongue, not wanting to sound too serious. She worried it might shut him down if she showed concern.

He chuckled. "I suppose I can't. I am okay, though. I just forgot to take my medicine today."

"Which one?" She asked. He'd been on so many different medications throughout the years and took about three a day now.

"All of them."

She slapped him. "Jay. You can't do that."

They reached his car, and he placed her painting in the backseat. Tess hopped in the passenger seat, and they drove off in silence for a bit before Tess broke it. "So, like, does not being on the medicine make you feel different?"

He gave a thoughtful frown. "Mostly not, but I feel a little anxious. I don't know if that's the lack of medicine, or just thinking about finals and stuff."

"Is it like a panic attack feeling or just stressed?"

He shook his head and pulled out of the parking lot, and that alone showed how different the lack of drugs made Jay. He always had an answer for everything, and a nod or head shake would never suffice.

Halfway home, he turned the car into a gas station and parked by the front door. "I need snacks and soda. You want snacks?"

"You buying?"

He nodded and she nearly jumped out of the car. They ran inside, and while Jay went to the coolers, Tess headed for the chocolate bars. She snatched up a pack of peanut butter cups, a bag of peanut butter M&Ms, and a Peppermint Patty. Jay met up with her holding two bottles of Cherry Coke and a bag of Doritos.

"You wanna know what it feels like?" He said.

Tess furrowed her brow. "Huh?"

"The not taking the medicine thing."

"Oh, yes!"

"It feels like someone is scratching my brain, trying to get in, but not quite able to. But it sort of feels louder and louder the longer I go without it."

Tess's stomach turned. It sounded awful. "Well, let's get you home so you can take them. It's not too late, is it?"

"Just for one of them."

Jay paid for their stuff, and they walked out. As soon as they hit the outside, Tess noticed the sparkling shards of glass on Jay's side of the car.

"What the fuck?" he said, running to it.

Someone had smashed out the back window. Tess jumped in front of Jay and went right to the door. "No!"

"You've got to be kidding me," Jay said.

Tess broke down, tears poured down her face. Anger, confusion, loss. She didn't know how she felt as she stared at her painting, now destroyed by a large slice trailing from top to bottom.

"Did they steal anything?" Jay asked.

Tess turned to him and yelled. "No, they just ruined my birthday present." She didn't mean to yell at him, or for it to come across as mocking as it did, but she couldn't help it. Why would someone do this? Why would someone smash Jay's window just to ruin something special for Tess? It made no sense.

CHAPTER 12

WHEN THEY ARRIVED HOME, Jay took his pills and Tess cried herself to sleep.

CHAPTER 13

SUMMER CAME AND WENT, passing by too quickly for Tess's liking. She hung out with her friends, and Jay hung out with his, and in between, they eked out whatever time together they could spare. Mostly, it came in the evenings, when both settled in for the night, and they'd watch scary movies in the living room.

July melted into August, and the days escaped her grasp, and the next thing she knew, Jay was packing his bags for his move to New York.

She cried in his arms before he got to the front door. And again, on the ride to the train station. And again, just before he boarded.

CHAPTER 14

THE FOUR YEARS Jay spent in New York, and the next four when he went for his master's at Plymouth State in New Hampshire, Tess spent missing him. She wasn't alone, and lord knew her own life went through its share of growth.

She had friends, plenty of them. She got her driver's license, graduated high school, and went on to the community college in Warwick. She kept busy, she kept happy. Fun was a must.

But at night, when she sat on her bed, studying, or reading, or watching television, she'd glance into the hallway hollowed by her brother's absence.

He came home often enough, but the visits were never like the times they'd shared together prior. Too busy. Too many people to reconnect with. Distance wasn't just measured in miles, but in the changing of their characters as they grew up. They remained brother and sister, and in that category, they still ranked high on the list of siblings who always got along, but they stopped being friends.

Years stretched into new lives. Jay found a job out of graduate school as a history teacher at Tanner's Switch High School. He married an English teacher. Tess came over twice a month for dinner.

She never married but had a steady girlfriend for a while. And another after that one.

Their father passed away suddenly, and they both consoled each other and their mother at the funeral, and in the few weeks before they all returned to their normal routines.

Jay and his wife divorced just after reaching the eight-year mark in their marriage. He told Tess it was amicable, but he seemed sadder than he claimed.

One night, about two months after his wife left their home, he called Tess, slurring an invitation to come by. He'd clearly been drinking, and the call came across more like an SOS than a friendly invite to chill.

CHAPTER 15

WHEN TESS ARRIVED, all the lights were off in Jay's house outside of a bright pulsing from the living room television. The front door was nearly closed, but not clicked into place.

"Jay?" Tess walked in slowly.

No response.

"Jay?"

The television had Jay's Spotify account up, where "Rookie" from BoySetsFire played loudly. The guitar riff echoed through the house.

She expected to see a half-gone bottle of Jack sitting on the end table but only found a Coors Light can. He must have drunk a shit ton of those to bring out the slurring he exhibited on the phone.

"Jay, where the fuck are you?"

She worried she'd open a door and find her brother hanging from the ceiling. She didn't think he was *that* depressed, but how often do folks make that kind of claim after they were proven very, very wrong.

They weren't siblings who lived across the hall from one another anymore, so she didn't feel comfortable opening doors in his house, but when does worry warrant such an invasion of privacy?

She gave a peek around the corners, checking the kitchen and dining room. With a deep breath, she climbed the stairs to the second floor.

"Jay? I'm here. You're being creepy."

When she reached the top of the steps, she clicked the hallway lights on, uncloaking the four doors housed up there, all closed. Jay's bedroom to the right, and a bathroom to the left. A computer room, and as far as Tess knew, an empty room across from where she stood at the top of the stairwell.

From the time she stepped in the house until the very second she reached the top step, she'd acted under the pretense that Jay was somewhere around her, and therefore she called his name loudly in an effort to find him, but as she viewed the many options at the top of the steps, two questions entered her head. The first: What if she was alone in here? And the second: What if she wasn't?

She said her brother's name again, but it slipped out of her mouth thin and whispery.

"Jay?"

She screamed as his door flew open, slamming against the wall. Jay stormed out, grabbed her hard, wrapping his arm around her and covering her mouth with his hand. She screamed again, but his grip muffled it well as he dragged her into his room.

When they entered, he let her go and slammed the door shut.

"What the fuck?" she said.

He put his finger over his mouth. His eyes were bloodshot, and his pupils danced wildly.

She whispered, "How fucking drunk are you? You look like shit."

"SHHHHHHH!" He waved her over to the window where he pointed into his neighbor's yard.

"What?"

"SHHHHHHH!" He yelled again, and then whispered, "Something is out there. It's hiding behind the fence."

"Jay, what are you talking about? Like someone is looking through your windows?"

He shook his head. "No. No. No. No. No. No."

His fingers were trembling, and Tess wondered if he'd been drinking like this a lot longer than she knew. He looked like an alcoholic, not someone having a bad night.

He ducked away from the window, and leaned against the wall under it, like a child freshly caught spying on his friends. Tess sat down next to him. "I need you to catch me up, here."

He sighed. "The last few nights, I've been hearing things outside the window." He tapped his middle finger against his forehead. "Sometimes it sounds like its coming from in here."

It had been years since Tess thought about Jay's pills. Even when he still lived at home, it was just a part of his routine that she barely noticed. And she had no idea if he still took any, if he took the same kinds, or if he needed them for entirely different reasons now, but something about this encounter reminded her of when they were young. "Did you stop taking your medicine?"

He looked at her as if she'd just slapped him in the face. "My medicine? What the fuck do you know about my medicine?"

She shook her head. "Jay. You used to take medicine all the time. I don't know what the hell you do anymore, but you're acting crazy and talking about noises in your head. What do you expect me to say?"

Something slammed outside the bedroom. Tess jolted so hard, she smacked the back of her head into the wall.

Jay smiled. "See. Something is here."

The slamming just sounded like a door closing, and it only happened once. No sound followed it. Outside of the faint sounds of BoySetsFire, nothing else could be heard anywhere around them. Maybe he had a window open in one of the other rooms and it caused the door to open and shut. But she couldn't lie, the force of the sound scared the shit out of her. "Nothing is here. It was just a noise."

He leaned toward her. "I know I sound crazy, Tess, but something is here."

She put her hand on his upper arm. Memories flooded back. Not completely, but they were filling in slowly. "Do you remember when you thought you saw something out the window when we were kids?"

He shook his head. "I don't know. Kind of, but that's not what this is."

"I'm not saying it is." She just wanted to distract him, to give him a few minutes away from his paranoia to calm down. "But what was it that you thought you saw? Do you remember?"

He tapped his fingers against his knees. "No. I can't remember."

"Did you see anything this time, or only hear it?"

He pointed up. "I saw a shadow moving behind the neighbor's fence, and it looked like someone was watching me through the spaces between the pickets. Last night, I thought I saw a blue light coming through the shade. But that's it. I think someone is fucking with me."

Tess snapped her finger. "A blue light. That's what you said you saw that night when we were kids. I remember now. There was a huge storm and you said you saw a blue light and you made me sit with you waiting for it."

He twisted his head and peeked out the window again. Two seconds, and he was back to sitting under it. "I don't really remember that."

She gave him a playful shove. "Come on. And you had a seizure that night, remember? How fucked was that? Why the hell did that happen? So random."

He turned his head to hear, his eyelids running away in each direction. "Oh my god. I thought something was inside my brain. Holy shit. I forgot all about that." He rubbed his eyes. "Am I crazy?" His eyes filled with water. "Am I fucking seeing and hearing things? Holy shit."

Tess put her arm around him. "Shhh. You're not crazy. I mean, you are, but we all are. I don't think you hang with stress very well. Isn't that what you were on? Anti-anxiety meds? Are you still taking those?"

"I've taken a million medications for a million reasons. Depression. Anxiety. Blah blah blah."

"Well, are you taking them now? Maybe the stress makes you paranoid or something."

"But that's what I'm saying. I've taken so many different things, and not always all the time. I went years without anxiety meds. But I was probably on sleep meds or depression meds or something. I am always taking something, but if one of them was stopping me from seeing and hearing shit, it doesn't make sense, because I wasn't always on anything. I switched and switched and switched, and suddenly I'm seeing a blue light out the window again like I did when I was twelve, and I had forgotten all about it until you reminded me. And I'm also feeling something scratching in my head, and I had that happen when I was a kid too, so either this is real, or I have something really wrong with me and it's coming back."

His words shot out like bullets, and he still had the slur.

"But did you take any medicine today? Any?" She made sure to keep her words even and calm.

He shook his head. "I just drank a lot."

"And when is the last time you didn't take any pills?"

His voice cracked. "I don't know."

She sighed. "What do you say we go downstairs and put on a movie. Distract our minds. You tell me if you feel or see or hear anything else, okay?"

He didn't answer for a second, but then he stood up, shut the window shade, and nodded toward the door. "Okay."

As Tess stood, a shiver crawled up her spine. "When you told me all that shit about the alien in your head, I was so fucking scared."

"You were scared? I thought it was in my head."

They both laughed as they made their way into the hallway and down the stairs. Making sure Jay didn't notice, she glanced around looking for the source of the slamming noise they'd heard a moment ago. All the doors were closed, and she realized it was highly unlikely the wind opened them and shut them again. But she saw no other potential source.

"What was his name? I remember you gave the alien a name and it freaked me out." She didn't know if bringing up the memories would help him or make it worse, but she had to try something. She'd never seen Jay look so broken. Well, not since he was twelve anyway.

"I don't remember. You're the one who keeps all this shit in her mind."

As they walked into the living room she put her hands in the air. "I didn't remember it either until you dragged me into your room."

They sat down on the couch, and Jay turned off BoySetsFire. "What should we watch?"

"Pleasantville," Tess said.

Jay laughed. "Weird choice. A great choice, but I have no idea if it's streaming anywhere."

Tess snatched the remote from him. "I'll look for it while you get us some snacks."

She wasn't really hungry but wanted Jay to feel comfortable in his own house again.

"Alright. What do you want?"

She shrugged. "Surprise me."

As he walked into the kitchen, he said, "Alright, pickles and Pop tarts."

She flipped him off.

As he fished around in the kitchen, Tess searched for Pleasantville. It wasn't streaming on anything Jay subscribed to, so she quickly signed into her Amazon account and rented it from the Prime app under her name before Jay insisted he'd get it.

She paused it and waited, and while she did the fragments of memory continued to crystallize in her mind. Jay entered the room holding a plate of freshly toasted iced cinnamon buns.

Tess jumped off her seat. "I remember. Mahazael. The alien's name was Mahazael!"

Jay gasped so hard he choked. The plate crashed onto the floor, shattering. His gasping turned to hyperventilation as he ran to the ornamental key hanger by the front door. "Tess, get the fuck out of here."

She jerked back. "Jay, what are you doing?"

"Tess, go home. Have fun. Forget all about this." He walked fast, going out the front door.

She ran after him, and when she reached him in the driveway, she grabbed his shoulder and yanked him around. "Jay, calm down. You can't leave. Don't get in your car." She tried to snatch the keys from his hand, but he moved them above his head, out of her reach.

"Listen to me. I'm not fucking with you. Go home."

She tried to pull him back as he opened the Volvo S60's door, and she grabbed at him a second time when he sat in the driver's seat. He showed no concern for whether he might hurt her as he forcefully closed the door. She pulled away just in time to avoid losing her hand.

The engine roared to life, and she pounded on the window. "Jay, you've been drinking. Don't be stupid."

The wheels skidded out on his cement driveway, and he zipped into the road. Before peeling out, he unrolled the window and yelled to his sister, "Don't forget when we were kids. Fun is a must." He sped off, leaving her dumbfounded in the middle of his driveway.

Neighbors peered out their windows at the scene, or what was left of it. She wanted to hop in her car and chase after him but also didn't want to entice him to speed up when he was already clearly not in the right mind to drive.

She went inside and turned his television off before sitting on his couch for a while, debating on whether she should wait for him to return or not.

It had been so long since she last worried about her brother, that she'd forgotten all about it, but now all the pain and fear flooded back. Jay was sick. He needed serious help. Tess wondered if this kind of behavior played into his divorce. She should call his ex-wife.

But a teeny tiny thought buzzed around in her brain, too. Something stupid and laughable. What if he wasn't crazy? What if Mahazael was really in his brain?

She had to go look for him. As she closed his front door, the speakers in front of the television released a small whine, even though she had turned the television off minutes ago.

CHAPTER 16

SHE DROVE AROUND for a stupid amount of time without any clue where to begin looking for him. Eventually, she folded and went home.

She crashed hard onto her bed, feeling terrible for how the night went. In the morning, she'd tell her mother and see what they could do to help Jay.

Mahazael.

She closed her eyes and tried to clear her mind enough to ease her into sleep, but the thoughts ran fast and violently in her skull.

Mahazael.

Someone knocked hard at the front door, and Tess jolted upright. It was way too late for visitors.

"What the hell?" Tess's mother stormed by her room, pulling a cardigan taut around her. "Whose knocking at the door at this hour?"

Tess's heart beat hard. Nothing good could come from opening that front door. It was either a crazy hallucination come to life, stranger danger, or Jay. Two were threats, and the last would destroy her mother in a completely different way if she saw her son in the state Tess had a few hours ago.

Tess ran down the stairs. "Mom, I'll get it."

"Who the hell is it?" Her mother said from the bottom step.

"I don't know. That's why I want to get it. Don't open the door."

Her mother stepped out of the way. "Well, you don't open it either."

Tess closed an eye and looked through the peephole. She couldn't see anything through it. "Who is it?"

"Tess? Ah, it's Christian."

Christian?

She unlocked the door and opened it. When she saw her

brother's old friend in his police uniform, she knew immediately why he was there. Her knees buckled. "Oh no," she managed.

Christian put his head down and sighed.

"What's happening?" Tess's mother said, not understanding.

"How?" Tess asked.

Christian shook his head as if shaking cobwebs out of his ears. "Looks like his car broke down on Route 1. He was walking on the side of the road, presumably toward the Cumby's in Charlestown."

At this point, Tess's mother figured it out, and she screamed a bloodcurdling wail that shook Tess's soul right out of her body.

"I'm so sorry," Christian said.

"No," Tess's mother yelled and pushed past her daughter. "You're lying." She slapped Christian, once, twice, over and over until Tess grabbed her and pulled her away.

She pulled her mom back inside, where the woman dropped to the floor and wailed some more. Tess wanted to console her mother but needed more answers.

"So did someone hit him?"

Christian nodded.

"Did you catch them? Did they hit and run?" She couldn't keep up with herself. It was hard to breathe.

"They called it in themselves. Stayed there until we arrived." He looked away for a moment. "I shouldn't tell you this, but because I know you, they were pretty obviously hammered, and they admitted as much."

Tess's mother stood up, a firestorm in her eyes. "You'll arrest them, no? They'll spend their lives rotting in a jail cell?"

Christian nodded. "The driver, yes. We already have him in a cell. He confessed to drinking and hitting Jay. Your son was on the side of the road. I would guess the driver is in big trouble."

But Tess thought he wasn't the only one guilty. She had attempted to play therapist to her clearly sick brother, and it caused him to flee in a panic. If she hadn't come over, Jay would probably still be hovering around his bedroom window staring at imaginary enemies. Hell, it was hard to blame the driver when Jay himself was driving drunk. It could have easily gone another way where Christian showed up at someone else's house to tell them their child died at the hands of a drunken Jay.

Maybe this person who ran Jay over would spend years in jail, but Jay was just a rock, Tess launched him from a slingshot, and this other guy hit him. The fact the man was drunk, and that Jay was on the side of the road would be a set of tools Tess would hold dear in the coming months and years, something she could cling to when the self-pity weighed too heavily. But she'd always know she played a part. At least, she would until that one night in Cuddy's.

CHAPTER 17

TESS MET UP with her friend Julia at Cuddy's after a long day of work driving elderly folks to and from their doctor's appointments, and to pick up their medications at the pharmacy. She loved the folks she interacted with but hated driving a van all day. It messed with her sciatica.

While Julia sat at the bar, Tess scooted her stool back and stood up, not wanting to sit any longer than she already had. The two girls chatted for a while, mostly about work stuff, funny things that happened during their day, what have you.

Julia was dating someone new. A guy named Jersey, which Tess automatically pictured as a douchey Jersey Shore type, but she recognized that was probably her jealousy talking. She and Julia had dated for a little while, and while Tess was the one to break it off, she struggled to see her ex with someone new.

When the daylight slipped away from the windows, and the bar lights stole the show, Julia asked for the bill and called an Uber. Since Jay died, Julia never drove herself to the bar. Tess hadn't mentioned it, but she noticed it, and she was thankful.

Without looking up as she signed her check, Julia said, "You should let me pay for your ride home, too. There's some sketchy dudes here tonight and you shouldn't walk home alone."

She put the cap back on her pen and looked up at Tess with a beaming smile.

Tess returned the smile. "I'm just not ready to leave yet. I need a few more."

Julia gave her a kiss on the cheek and said, "I won't stop you, but will you call me while you're walking home?"

Tess agreed and the two hugged before Julia ran out the door to her awaiting chariot in the form of a Ford Focus.

Tess's friend was probably unaware, but Walter had just gotten out of jail for killing her brother, and tonight she wanted to drink her confusion away. She didn't know how she felt about anything anymore.

She drank a few more Long Island Iced Teas, when she noticed a group of guys heading outside. One of them was Tim Burns, who she knew from high school, holding a cigarette between his teeth. She'd been at enough bars where Tim frequented to know he'd be in and out all night, smoking cigs in the lot. The only difference this time is she wanted one.

"Sup, Tess," he said as he walked by her.

"Hey Tim, do you have an extra cigarette I could have?"

"Nah, the pack only came with 20. No extras. But you can have one."

She faked a laugh at his corny joke and followed him and his friends outside.

It was a cold night. Freezing actually. Tess had to hold her head down to keep the wind from making her cry. The guys all stood in a circle, lighting their cigarettes. Tim handed one to Tess along with a red Bic lighter.

She hadn't had a cigarette in five years, and wondered if she'd cough on the first drag, but she didn't. Instead, she got a little lightheaded and felt the need to sit down.

"Sorry about Jay," Tim said.

Tess smiled and thanked him as she moved to a low wooden wall that ran along the perimeter of the bar, separating the now-frozen mulch from the cement lot.

As if she had disappeared completely, Tim said to his group, "That's Jay Creed's sister." He either didn't realize how loud he was, or he thought Tess couldn't hear him from the short distance between them.

The group all responded in recognition, from "Oh," to "Oh shit."

Continuing as if Tess weren't there, Tim said, "Colin's all sorts of fucked about it."

"He should be," one of the guys said.

Damn straight, thought Tess, but again, those flashes of doubt landed in her bloodstream. She caused Jay to go out. He drove drunk, too. Tess and her friends had driven home from plenty of bars after too many drinks. The only difference between her and Walter was luck. Tess only made sure not to drive after drinking once her brother died. If anything, she was just a hypocrite.

Tim said, "Can't blame Colin, though. He didn't drive. He was just sitting in the passenger seat for all of it."

"But he could have stopped Walter if the fucker wasn't good to go."

Tim punched his friend in the arm. "Oh yeah, how many have you had tonight and who is driving you home?"

The guy laughed. "Well shit. Point taken."

Another dude chimed in. "I know when I can handle my shit and when I can't."

Famous last words, Tess thought.

"Colin though, his mind is fried now." Tim said. "Doesn't remember shit about that night. He completely blacked it out."

"Or he was completely blacked out."

They all laughed.

"Nah. He told me that he remembers going out with Walter on Tuesday, which was like three days earlier. Said he remembers driving home with Walter and was like, 'Yeah, we had too much to drink,' but then he said he remembers this weird blue light coming over their car, and the boom, next thing he knows, Walter is skidding off the road, hits something, bump bump."

Tess cringed at the cavalier descriptions of her brother getting run over, but she couldn't move away, couldn't stop listening. She sucked in a long pull.

"They hit something else?" Tim's friend said like an idiot.

"No, you dipshit. He left the bar on a Tuesday and can't remember anything else until he hit Jay on Friday."

Tess snuffed her cigarette in the hard mulch and walked past them to go back inside. At first, she didn't think much of their conversation. Tim was notoriously wrong when relaying conversations. Plus, the idea of a degenerate alcoholic like Colin Read misplacing days didn't feel surprising, anyway.

After she killed one last Iced Tea, she ventured out down the same Route 1 that claimed Jay a few years earlier, and as promised, she called Julia. She didn't say much, the *bump, bump* from Tim's conversation still playing hard in her chest, especially when Walter just left his prison cell.

Julia ranted about a new show she watched on Netflix, but Tess hardly listened, too focused on her self-hatred, the icy walk, and her fear of passing vehicles.

At home, she hung up with her friend, dropped her phone on

the kitchen table and went right up to her room, where she collapsed on her blanket.

When she woke up six or so hours later, it was still dark outside, and a gusty rainstorm blew down on her window. She sat up and looked outside where the family pool used to be. She remembered always watching it during a rainstorm to see the plinks fill the walls too high.

Her heart sank as she fell back into the night of Jay's seizure. Colin mentioned a blue light. He saw a blue fucking light and suddenly it was three days later. Jay saw a blue light and had a seizure.

A blue light.

Her head swam with possibilities on what this could mean, and she spent the rest of the night and morning considering every fantastical idea she could fathom until she knew she'd have to go to Walter's house for answers.

CHAPTER 18

W**ALTER CLASPED HIS** hands together and leaned back, working to bring calm back into his demeanor after Tess claimed she believed Colin's crazy story. "Why would it matter? We still drove drunk. We still killed your brother."

His words felt like a bullet to the chest because he wasn't entirely wrong, but then, it clicked why it mattered so much. He was wrong. "No. That's not right. If the story is true, yes, you drove drunk, and you suck for that, but you didn't kill my brother. If something happened to you, and you were placed in that spot at that time, something else killed my brother, and used you to do it."

He reached into his pocket and pulled out the pack of cigarettes. As he tapped one from the pack, he said, "Do you hear yourself? We were drunk. At the time. When the police came, they gave us a breathalyzer. We were smashed. If we hadn't had a drink in three days, how could we still be drunk?"

She hadn't considered that, but when did logic fall into the equation? There was nothing rational about this, and thus, it should remain outside the dialogue. As she pondered this, Walter examined her closely, lighting his cigarette and staring her down.

"Why is this so important to you? I killed your brother. I'm a shit person. Why are you working so hard to give me a pass?"

She brushed her hand through her hair and stood up, the nervous energy blasting through her toes to her fingers. She wasn't looking to give Walter a pass. She needed one for herself. She'd told no one she went to Jay's house that night, that she played counselor for his severe mental illnesses, and the only way she'd ever relieve herself of the guilt was if Jay wasn't mentally ill at all, if instead, there really was something out to get him. Of course, she couldn't tell all that to Walter, especially since there were way too many gaps in her wild theories. "Because I know what Colin said was the truth. And I know you're lying." It was a stupid thing to say, but was there much difference between knowing and needing? Don't they often result in the same self-created delusions?

Walter's eyes turned to slits, stopping Tess's heart in its tracks. She suddenly realized her situation, sitting alone with her brother's killer inside his house without a neighbor nearby. The empty nails on the wall and the upturned television stand acted as a reminder of the uncanny world she sat in. Walter stood up and put the lit cigarette into his palm. It disappeared into his fist as he crushed it. Bits of shaved tobacco flurried to the floor.

His chest heaved, and his head shot back. Tess stepped away, eyeing the door. What had she done?

With his face aimed at the ceiling he screamed, "I am who I am."

And as she turned to run away, she stopped herself. No more running. She walked to him and slapped him hard across the face. "Stop. Snap the fuck out of it. No more of this 'I am who I am' bullshit."

She gripped his shoulders and shook him. "What the fuck is happening? Tell me."

He blinked and stared at her slack jawed. "You fucking idiot."

"Yes. I'm an idiot. Now tell me what you know."

He pushed away from her and glanced out the window. "You have no idea what you're doing. He'll hear you."

"Who? Tell me who?"

"Colin didn't see him. He just went from point A to point B, Tuesday to Friday. And to him it was a blip in time that he can't fathom. Did you know Colin killed himself a few days ago?"

She slumped. "No." She had nothing else to say to it, because it hurt to hear it, but she couldn't let her sadness derail her intent.

"He did. Because he thought he was, I don't know, fated to be a fuck up. But I don't. I fucking saw the thing that did it to us. It reached its hand back in time and ripped us three days forward. What kind of thing do you think can do that?" He looked out the window again.

"The kind of thing that killed my brother on purpose."

"Yeah, by literally bending fucking time you crazy bitch. And you believe me? You believe me and you still came here to poke that bear? Fuck you. Get out. It goes away if you don't think about it."

Fun is a must.

"So, you spend your entire life refocusing your thinking to avoid it? What kind of life is that?"

Walter slammed his palm into the wall. "A good one. I survived two years in jail when I had nothing to do but think, and I did it by forcing myself to forget that face. And every time I slip, it lets me know it's close by breathing in my fucking brain or bending a wall." He kicked the tv stand. "Or flipping my furniture over, smashing my mother's picture frames. Now get the fuck out so I can forget you both."

"I'll leave when you tell me his name."

Walter put his arms out wide. "I don't know his name. I know his face. I don't want to see it ever again. Eventually it'll stop toying with me, and it'll kill me like it did Jay, unless I just don't think about it, Then, it'll go away."

Walter grabbed Tess by the arm and dragged her toward the front door. "Now get out and don't ever come back."

As she pulled toward the door, she said, "His name is Mahazael, and I hope he hears me. I won't forget his name ever again. Come get me."

Before Walter could twist the knob, he dropped to the floor in a fit. He shook and twitched all over the floor with his mouth opened unnaturally wide. His throat gurgled, but through the phlegm, he said, "I am what I am. I am what I am."

Tess bent down and tried to lift him, but he was much bigger than her and stronger. She did the only thing she could think of and kicked him. Not hard, just a gentle kick to snap him out of it. It was all so crazy. She'd had this nonsensical idea she could come here and find out that Walter saw the same boogeyman Jay did and she'd be able to sleep at night, but in truth, when she came into Walter's house, she fully expected to hear a rational explanation. She'd walk out of his house knowing how the real world worked, but clinging to this asinine and otherworldly fantasy so she could convince herself moving on was possible. If there was a hope of a boogeyman it meant she didn't have to be one herself.

But now, she was in the thick of the madness, and she wanted nothing more than to blame herself, to accept her brother's insanity.

Walter jumped up, completely free from his seizure, and screamed. It sent Tess reeling backward into a wall. Walter punched his cheeks with both hands and then fell back again, slamming hard onto his back. And with an athletic jump, he was back on his feet, moving further from Tess. He stumbled over the furniture.

The television flickered to static and released a high whine. Then it flashed blue.

Tess stood frozen, watching the chaos of it all, an exploding star bursting in Walter's living room. He stood up straight, unnaturally so, as if Mahazael replaced Walter's spine with a steel rod.

"I am who I am. I am who I am. IamwhoIam. IamwhoIam." He said it over in rapid fire in weird whispered and exasperated bursts until the words all melded together into one non-word. "eyeamwooyam."

"Walter. Walter, stop!" She'd wanted to call out to Mahazael but hadn't intended to hurt Walter in the process. She could have just stayed home and thought about the fucker, and it would have come, according to Walter, but she didn't truly believe it until all of this.

Walter stopped. Breathed deep. Then slowly turned away from Tess, walked to the living room wall, and slammed his head into one of the nails.

She screamed as blood splashed on the white drywall on both sides of Walter. As he turned, revealing the mutilated eye socket, she covered her mouth in shock. Moving faster now, he moved to an adjacent wall, toward another nail.

"No!" Tess yelled and reached out a hand as if she could stop it on will alone.

Boom. His face slammed into the second nail.

His eyes were bloody sockets, oozing yellow and red down his cheeks when he turned back to her again. Why was she still here? Why was she watching this? Because she needed to see Mahazael. At any cost. But would she? Would he operate through Walter, run across the living room, and rip her to shreds?

She planted her feet firmly. No. He wouldn't do that. He toyed with his victims, and he could read their thoughts. He knew Tess wanted to see him, so he'd show himself.

But not before tearing her courage from her soul.

Walter placed both hands at his mouth and used four fingers on each side to pull his lips left and right. From where Tess stood, she could hear the tearing sound as Walter ripped his face in half.

She looked down and prepared to leave. Mahazael would come for her now. She didn't have to stay and witness his horror show. Of course, Mahazael could bend time itself, so she supposed he could return her right to where she stood and make her watch it over and over again if he wanted to. But she wouldn't just let it happen.

As she headed to the door, something knocked on the window to the left of it. A white face with large hockey puck-sized eyes stared back at her. Its face was oval and smooth.

"Mahazael," she said. Behind her, Walter screamed and gurgled, continuing to rip himself apart.

Tess opened the door, facing the boogeyman.

She expected instant violence. But nothing happened. He didn't break into her mind. He didn't rush to her. He just waited for her.

CHAPTER 19

SHE COULD HEAR her heartbeat in her ears and feel the pulse throbbing in her temples, but she stood firm. "You're the boogeyman."

If he weren't so inhuman, the creature would be unassuming. His limbs were as thin as book spines, and outside of his large black eyes, his face showed no ferocity. No teeth. Literally no teeth because Mahazael had no mouth. Only those black holes for eyes.

The alien lifted his arm, causing Tess to flinch, but she didn't move otherwise. Mahazael moved slowly, which Tess took to mean he meant no harm. Not yet anyway.

A finger extended from his bony pale-white hand and touched her forehead. She felt him inside her then, wriggling in her brain. It didn't hurt the way Jay described it. He entered gently.

And then he spoke, but it was a communication through her brain, and that hurt. It rattled and vibrated in her skull.

"What do you want?" It asked.

She tilted her head and cried. "I should be asking you that."

"I want nothing."

"Are you going to kill me like you killed Jay?"

It didn't speak in her head this time. Instead, it nodded.

"Why?" she pulled away from his finger and turned toward the bloodied body slumped on the living room floor. "Why all of this?"

Mahazael's eyes spun. Because they were deep black, she might not have noticed it, but they weren't perfect circles, so she noticed the warped nature of the spin.

"Why anything?" He asked in her brain. Apparently, he didn't need the finger to enter.

"That's a non-answer."

"I am who I am."

"What the fuck does that mean? We all are who we are."

He shook his head. "No. You were who you were. You are no longer you."

She spit in his face. It dripped down from his left saucer-shaped eye. If it bothered him, he didn't show it. Not even a flinch.

"You blame me."

"Yes. I blame you for everything."

"I do not understand."

She screamed in frustration. Again, he showed no concern. "You drove my brother insane. You killed him. You ripped through time and let two other people kill my brother. His whole life he suffered because of you."

The alien stepped backward. "You mistake your words."

She tossed her hands up, exhausted by the riddles.

"Because of me. For me. Different things."

She squinted. "Are you serious? You think he had a seizure and cried and suffered. . . For you?"

The alien pulled his hand up again, this time quicker, and he tapped on her forehead. "For you, too."

"HE DIED!"

"And you will too."

"Why? Why why why?"

"Because it is how things happen." The creature's face scrunched and he swooshed his hand. Tess felt the force of a wrecking ball against her ribs. She lost her wind and flew through the air, slamming hard into the cold, icy yard.

Fruitlessly, she ran around Walter's wellhouse and into the woods. At this point, the most she could do was save seconds, but she'd take them all. She had pushed this all to happen, but she hoped she'd find answers before she did, and all she received was more questions.

She ran into the woods, ignoring the pain in her side. The hard frost crunched under her feet. Sometimes she heard steps near her, and sometimes she didn't, but she ran on either way.

She did that for as long as her stamina allowed, which probably wasn't very long, but seemed like an eternity. Hands to her knees, she gasped for breath and waited for Mahazael. She couldn't have outrun him. The fucker could bend time. He could infiltrate her brain and force her to walk back to him. He could probably make her head explode or send her flying into outer space.

But nothing happened. Nothing fucking happened. Another

frustrated scream left her lungs, echoing through the vast universe
of bare trees surrounding her.

CHAPTER 20

AFTER MAHAZAEL SPOKE to her, she realized she couldn't assign reason to his actions, because he thought differently than humans. His rationale existed on a horrid plane beyond her comprehension. She hated to use the term, but his thoughts felt a lot like victim blaming. Like their pain was their duty and they were at fault for questioning that. But she wasn't even sure that was true. His words were too choppy, too cryptic.

Like the human brain's need to create faces in inanimate objects in an effort to establish familiarity, her mind tried to piece together a "why." Why had Mahazael abandoned his hunt? Why did he let her leave those woods and drive home to her bedroom?

Because he knew she'd wait for him. She'd spend every day thinking of him and fearing his return. By disappearing, he became the draft up her spine for all eternity.

She wouldn't let him win that way.

CHAPTER 21

IN A WAY, the planning gave her life more purpose. She knew she couldn't do anything until her mother died, unwilling to make that poor woman suffer more than she already had. And that meant living each day as normal, biding her time, planning how she would take the fight to Mahazael.

Her mother lived for another ten years, and that meant Tess did too. She kept her friendships to a minimum and refused to date again, not wanting anyone to get too attached. She did stay close with Julia, which she regretted, but she couldn't let her oldest friend slip away. It was selfish but aren't all binds?

After her mother's funeral, Tess had a small reception at her house, which mainly consisted of her mother's coworkers, because after Tess's father passed, her mom didn't really keep close to any of her old friends. Maybe in that way, she'd been just playing out the days like her daughter.

When the house cleared out, Tess cleaned. It felt like an insult to her mom to leave the place a mess at the end of the world.

And then time was up.

She went to her mother's cabinet, where she'd stored all of Jay's medication after he passed away. Wanting to see what she had to work with, she poured them all out onto the kitchen table and stared at the little hill in front of her.

Terror coursed through her. She knew what would happen if she swallowed them all. Her organs could fail. She could have a seizure. Struggle to breathe. A lot of folks think it won't be hard, that the pills will mask the pain, but that's not what happens. From everything she'd read, it could be excruciating. She hoped she wouldn't have to bear it, but her threat meant nothing if she weren't willing to go through with it.

She placed one on her tongue, no idea what it was, a little blue thing that looked easy to take down. With years to wait for this, and the pills filling up her cabinets all that time, one would think she'd have taken the time to learn about them, to know them.

Oh well.

She filled her mouth with water and swallowed. One down.

No signs of Mahazael.

She grabbed a second pill, this one white. Down the hatch.

She closed her eyes for a second, thinking through the repercussions of her actions. Julia, for one. But not just that. Ending it on her own felt like such a slap in the face to her family after the good life they'd provided her, even if that end was part of a greater plan with a bigger purpose.

When she opened her eyes, she nearly jumped out of her skin. Jay sat next to her. Not the Jay from the end, but the one from when they were kids. He had that silly grimace he made all the time.

"You owe me a spoonful."

She giggled which quickly turned into weeping. The prank was incredibly cruel, even for Mahazael.

The person she stared at was not her brother, but she couldn't help acting as if he were. "I miss you."

He placed his elbow on the table and rested his chin in his palm. "That never really goes away."

She pinched another pill in her fingers. "Might as well swallow this, then."

He shook his head. "No. You should just forget me."

She tilted her head, holding in a deluge. "I can't."

Jay sighed and slapped his palm on the table. "Then we have a problem."

Abandoning pretense, she spoke to Mahazael now. "Why didn't you kill me that night?"

He rolled his neck, causing his head to sway in concentric motions. "Killing. Humans are the ones who make that a first resort. For the rest of us, the fun is in the ruining."

"Why are you talking so normal now?"

"I talk how I want when I want."

"Will you finally tell me what this is all about?"

Jay shrugged. "As the person who formerly wore this skin would say, 'Fun is a must.'"

Tess's chair screeched across the linoleum kitchen floor, and she jolted out of her seat and put her face right in front of Jay's. "Never quote him. You're not worthy of his words."

Jay laughed. "I'll do what I want." He waved a hand and Tess fell to the floor screaming, holding up her arm with all of her fingers bent, bones snapped, fingernails touching the back of her hand. She clutched her wrist with the other hand. Sharp bursts of throbbing pain drove through her body.

"See?" Jay said. "You think you have some upper hand here. Hand. Haha. I didn't mean that pun. No. I could infest your brain and make you toss up those pills right now. I could rip your arms off so you couldn't even pick up the pills. I could turn you into a skin suit with no bodily functions. There is nothing I couldn't do, which should tell you that whatever I *have* done was by design."

She stopped her screaming to say, "You couldn't get into my brother's head. All those years, you couldn't get in. I know you weren't just fucking with him because he forgot all about you and he lived."

Jay stood up, hovering over Tess as she squirmed in pain. "I guess you got me on that front. Which means what happened to him was all your fault. You brought me back into his mind. Sure, he stopped taking his pills after the divorce, and he had itches in his brain, but my name would never come back, and the floodgates would have stayed closed."

He put his foot on her leg to stop her from flailing so much. "Forget me now, and I will go away again." He laughed a hardy and obnoxious laugh. "I mean, you know my weakness. Use it."

She rolled onto her back and rested her head on the floor. "No. Mahazael. Mahazael. Mahazael. I know you can torture me until I do whatever you say, and I know I'll eventually fold to that, but I'm going to make you do the work. So do it."

Jay rubbed his eyes, and she thought for a second, she'd actually gotten under his skin. But then he said, "You know what? You win."

She knew he lied, that he'd never let her win, and she still didn't know what winning or losing was to Mahazael. His wants and plans were still riddles. But he piqued her interest. Something cracked and then the pain disappeared. She looked down to see her hand back to normal. "What happens now?"

He licked his upper lip and scratched behind his ear. "We make a deal. You come with me while I show you something, and then I let you go. And not just you, but all of Earth." Before she could respond he raised a finger. "Wait. I'll do you one better. I'll bring Jay back to life."

Her guts twisted, knowing he absolutely could make that miracle happen, but also that he wouldn't, that the promises he made were more of his mind games. "Why would I ever trust you?"

He put out a hand for her to grab. "You wouldn't. But you have no other choice."

He had her there. She reached up and put her hand in his.

CHAPTER 22

THE FLOORS, WALLS, and ceiling melted away, and Tess found herself floating in a well of blackness. Thin strips of light flittered by. It took adjusting before she realized the light was actually stationary dots, and instead, she was the one moving. Flying. Speeding through nothingness.

And then she landed on her feet. A cold, metal floor kept her upright. Smooth, rounded metallic walls surrounded her, but they turned into a large window or screen in front. Mahazael appeared next to her, in his real form, no longer wearing Jay's face.

"The people I have hurt in my lifetime have had one of two reactions. If they learn the power of forgetting me, they spend their lives trying to do that. Eventually, they fail, but they try. The rest of them never learn how to stop me, and they cower in fear."

He put his long, thin fingers out for Tess to grab, and she did.

"But you challenged me. The first to ever do so. Even when you knew you stood no chance against my power, you refused to just give me your life." He laughed a horrific high-pitched screech. "I haunt so many minds. And I never tried to haunt yours. You were never one of my targets. Yet, you always called to me. In your own way, you never let yourself forget me."

"What are you getting at?"

"Now it is my turn to ask you why. Why, when everyone tried to forget me, did you do everything in your power to remember?"

She removed her hand from his. "I didn't. You were irrelevant to me. I just wanted to save my brother."

Mahazael whipped his face toward her and snarled. "Do not pretend to be so noble."

"Did my brother become one of your targets because he accidentally saw you that night in the storm?"

"Your brother accidentally saw me because I wanted him to."

"Why? And please just answer straight this time."

Mahazael stepped toward the large screen and waved his hand. An image appeared, frozen in a still shot. Jay stood in the middle of a cheatgrass field, holding a girl's hand. He looked around the same age as when he had the seizure. Tess didn't recognize the girl, and it stung that Jay may have had a friend or a girlfriend that she knew nothing about.

"What's this?"

"It is your brother, two weeks before the storm."

"Who is the girl?"

"Her name is Callie. She grew to take a lot of boys through that field. But that's unimportant."

"Then why are you showing me this? I asked you to tell me straight. You're just creating more riddles. Was that his girlfriend?"

"He liked her. She liked him too, well enough, but had no interest in relationships. Nothing happened between them outside of a kiss at an abandoned amusement park. She'd stopped talking to him by the time I came around just a few weeks later."

"He never told me about her."

"And that is my point in showing you this. What you knew of your brother is equally matched by what you didn't know. In fact, there's a lot about your brother he didn't even know."

"Like what?"

Mahazael waved his hand again, and a video took over the screen. It showed Jay sleeping, younger now than in the previous video. Maybe ten years old? He tossed and turned under his blue bedsheets. Sweat stained his pillows. He moaned and groaned.

"Would you like to see what's in his head?"

Tess nodded.

Mahazael did his fancy wave, and the screen turned black. She thought maybe the screen had turned off, but then something pulsed in the center. A blue light. At first, it was so faint, she could hardly see it until it grew larger and more intense. Within a minute, it swallowed the screen in brightness. Within the brightness, voices screamed.

"What's happening? I can't see anything."

Mahazael's oblong eyes spun. "You can't see anything?"

She shook her head but kept her eyes on the bright screen. "Just brightness."

"Why are humans so incapable of witnessing their superiority?"

"Says the guy who can bend and break my bones with a simple thought."

He moved in front of her, blocking her view of the screen. "You don't understand yet? I am not more powerful than you. Humanity chooses my path. I am your weapon."

She stepped back. "I don't understand."

"Everything I do to one is because another wanted it done."

She shook her head. "Bullshit."

He wrapped his fingers around her throat. "But it's true." He lifted her in the air. She kicked her feet but couldn't reach his body. She felt the pressure growing in her head and she thought it might explode.

"Who wanted Jay hurt?" She asked without saying the words out loud.

"Himself."

"Bullshit."

"He wanted you to suffer."

"Why?"

"So he could feel loved."

"Bullshit."

"Human love is bullshit."

"Fuck you."

"Don't point your anger at me."

"Did he know?"

"No. I read what he wanted, and I provided it. Humans often want something, but they aren't willing to go through what's necessary to achieve it."

"You read him wrong. He didn't want what you did."

"You must go now."

He dropped her and she fell through the floor, floating, floating. A small pain built in her stomach and then it stretched through her body, building into unbearable agony. Every muscle pulled and ripped. Her head throbbed so forcefully, she felt it in her throat. Her skull snapped as her brain expanded beyond its cage.

She howled as she exploded into a million shining pieces.

But even as little bright speckles, she could feel, could hear and taste and be. And recognize. And want.

It took a while, maybe a century, maybe a few hours later before she gleaned enough of her environment to make sense of it all. She was there, separated into parts, and floating, but she was not alone. Within the darkness of space, she noticed a giant slash mark that traveled from the top of everything to the very bottom, and across from it was a million more speckles just like her.

And one day, as she suffered in her own thirst and hunger, she stared through the slash mark at those speckles and recognized them.

"Jay?" She asked. "Is that you?"

And she wept into the silence. She knew then that Jay floated on the other side of the slash, and he too could see her, but could not hear her over the valley. He too called for her, knowing what he always needed existed just on the other side, but could never reach it, couldn't even call to it.

This was their eternity.

And she yearned for time reversed so she could have accepted that fun was a must when fun was an option.

"Jay?" She called again. And the yawning vastness responded with silence.

DARK MATTER DREAMS

ANDREW VAN WEY

CHAPTER 1

WANT TO tell you about the sleepover we had—Jake and Tyler and me, Lucas—and how we'd been planning it all summer, all year really. Jake's mom and dad had a fight and then she took him to live with her brother down south. It sucks now, 'cause Jake only comes to visit once a month. Sometimes, it's more like every other month. We haven't seen him since Christmas when his dad got drunk and tried to drive us to check out the eclipse but rear-ended some cop on the crosstown expressway.

Idiot.

It's been too long since we've kicked it and even Emma said Jake seemed different.

Maybe it was the haircut that kinda popped off his head like broccoli. Maybe it was the cigarettes he brought, saying he'd lifted them from his dad like that game we used to play. Maybe we'd just started growing apart.

Mr. Knowles once taught us how planets can fall out of orbit if their gravity isn't strong. Or if something like an asteroid smashes into it and sends it spinning off into space. I guess friendships are like that. Sometimes a rogue object shakes up our world and the next time we're in alignment, things are different.

I noticed Jake had an edge to him now; like he was trying to find the bad in things or pointing out how something else was better. The pizza my parents ordered, it wasn't as good as they made it in his new town. The girls in the bay were way hotter. Even the TV in our basement wasn't OLED with frame sync to smooth out our video games.

I guess I never noticed these things. But Jake did.

When my parents went to sleep, he logged on to his dad's TV Pass which had all the subscriptions, even porn. Like the kind where you could see every freckle and fold.

Mostly, it was the horror movies he was after.

He wanted to show us a cowboy movie where these cannibals cut someone in half. Tyler gagged and nearly puked up his pizza. Then, Jake found something else where a woman ripped her head open and a fetus came out and they killed all these cops. After that, it was this weird one where a witch made these naked women dance until they all exploded. But I wasn't really watching by then. Tyler had started building a couch cushion fort and I wanted to help out, even if Jake said it was sort of gay.

I didn't care.

I didn't care about his cigarettes. "Dude, these are menthols."

Or the girl he said he'd felt up. "They were like water balloons, for real."

I didn't care about the weird triangle stone he stole from the museum his mom worked for. "C'mon, let's just play with it and see."

I was kind of over him now.

See, I want to tell you we had a great night together. That we played games and laughed like we used to. That the divorce hadn't chipped away at Jake, like a thousand asteroids knocking him off orbit and into the cold darkness of space.

I want to tell you my best friend was okay. That what returned wasn't something bitter; a dying world off-axis and spinning all weird.

I want to tell you everything would be fine after that night; the last time we slept in the basement together.

But first, I want to tell you about the aliens and how they took us up into their ship.

How they ripped my whole family apart.

CHAPTER 2

FOR A CLASS 31 Apex Hominid, it amazes me how little humans dream. As I wave my fingers over the bedroom door and its mechanism turns—a knob, I remember—I can't help but to pity these hairless primates. They search the skies for answers or turn to superstitions. If only they knew what incredible energy they held in their minds.

Swaddled in darkness and dappled by a nightlight, this teenage girl's bedroom is a testament to the blindness of the human mind. Posters formed of inks and pulped plant matter decorate her walls, trophies to mediocre achievements adorn the bookshelves.

Some skinny musician, his body a frame of starvation. Posing, I believe they call it.

Tickets to a concert this girl attended are pinned to a corkboard.

Below it, a photographic representation of three grinning friends is fastened with. . .what is this translucent material?

"Tape," Ciron-64 informs me via the Overmind. *"Adhesive strips used to attach lightweight objects to vertical surfaces."*

"Tape," my thoughts echo back. I let my three fingers probe the material, learning all I need to. Tape. Tickets. Posters. A clipping from a magazine catches my attention: *We wear black because the world hasn't earned our colors.*

What a peculiar expression. I make a mental note to save it for Brellin, who collects human phrases.

As I glide to the girl's bed, a flicker pierces the darkness. Here it is, the apex of their obsessions, a smartphone.

"Tag it for study," Ciron instructs.

I conjure a mental spray, imbuing the device with enough kelons for extraction. Curious how the girl laid it bedside, close enough she could grab it upon awakening, eager to send simple messages to simple friends with such simple tools.

If only humans knew the network they shared when they dreamed.

"Jin'qua-33, please terminate ruminations and proceed with extraction."

A blue warmth blooms in my skull whenever Brellin-88 communicates through the Overmind. I know she feels it too, this mental backsplash as our thoughts entwine.

"I've got a gift for you," I inform her. *"But first, let me prepare the subject."*

The specimen, I note, is seventeen in Earth years; a female named Emma. Although their forms are repulsive, she is one of lesser offense to my senses. I wave my left hand over her; my proboscis sensing her status.

Name: Greenburg, Emma.

Hormones: elevated.

Mood: restless.

Sleep stage: NREM2.

Good. It's easier when they're not dreaming. Less mental interference means a faster study. A faster study means fewer subconscious scars when we put them back together. We've gotten fairly good at dissection over the eons.

I open a mind channel with Jorun-43, letting a wave of pleasant green co-mingle in our thoughts.

"Third subject requires gravity lift at. . ." My proboscis quivers between my first and third fingers, sampling the girl's mass. *". . .seventy-three point three kelons."*

"Her mass has expanded," Jorun thinks with amusement.

"Grown," Brellin corrects.

With a wave of my hand and a few well-trained thoughts, the girl's blanket curls and falls away. Her clothes follow.

Human curiosity #7,181: they have an aversion to their naked form.

Like many vestigial things, we Grays evolved beyond a fear of our flesh. When one is a part of trillions—when the nodes of the Overmind bind us across space/time—few secrets can hide beneath clothes. When one is always dreaming, there is no need for a bed.

"Have you seen their males when it's cold?" Soru-22 inquires, his amusement spiking violet in my brain. *"It's like tunnel slug trying to hide. Now, meet the beam, Jin'qua, we've still got. . .how many more?"*

"Four," I inform them. *"Three kids and the elder matriarch."*

"Five," Tenzin-44 tells us, his thoughts arriving in curt, silver waves.

My toes quiver as I sense numerical disagreement and the immediate misalignment it causes. I offer a soothing aura to my teammate. Tenzin is the junior extractionist and he's been practicing his low number counting. For our pluralistic species, single digits are tricky.

"Odd, our sensors can't agree either," Brellin conveys.

Back chatter builds in the Overmind, our crew's thoughts overlapping.

"We'll run a cross-check," I inform the team.

Peering inward, I open a visual feed directly to Tenzin's ocular systems. He's in a bedroom beneath me. I reference his prior memories: the operations briefing, the landing in the dewy meadow, the entrance through the kitchen which was so easily unlocked with our thoughts.

Tenzin is moving into the basement while I subdue and extract the parents. His mind registers three young life forms: boys. They have dismantled the furniture and laid blankets over cushions. They've fallen asleep watching TV.

My mind strains as I count the low number.

"Verified; three children," I inform the team. Confirming my suspicion, I close the connection as a discomforting wave of ochre bristles my nerves. Tenzin is displeased to be wrong.

"Are we certain?" he privately inquires.

"I know you've been working on your single digits," I think. *"And I know you put in a request for my role. Just remember, Tenzin, two is one too many for this job."*

I sense a frustrated backlash as his mind goes into a loop.

"Enough number games," Soru says. *"Council requests you locate the elder matriarch."*

"Greatfather," I think.

"Grandfather," Brellin corrects, her indigo thoughts conjuring a soothing infusion in my tired muscles. *"After so many studies I'm surprised Jin'qua forgot the word. That gravity must be distracting."*

"It's not the gravity," Soru responds. *"His mind is on your ovum, not the research. Tell me, are we certain we wish to incubate with such a human-touched brain?"*

"That's your mistake," I tell them. *"You assumed my brain even functions."*

A warm blanket suffuses our mental humor: Soru and Brellin high above in the cloud-hidden ship, and myself, here among these sleeping humans.

"Keep the Overmind quiet." Tenzin's thoughts cut in, bright and golden. *"We're still waiting on your subject, team leader."*

I don't like the way his thoughts echo. *"Affirmative. Encysting her now."*

I focus on the sleeping teen girl, letting my brain quiver and stretch. I conjure memories of the rock spiders that draped webs across the thermal caves from my youth. Sealed holes, sticky with glistening strands. How they netted my skin and clung to my feet. I see them so clearly it takes a simple *push* to bring my childhood dreams into the bedroom.

The teen does not flinch as the membrane seals her, toes to temple. She does not stir as I wave my hand and the transparent box—window, I recall—slides open, and cool air enters the room. The gravity lift's icy glow fills the room and she rises off the bed. I guide her into the conveyor belt of light. A few words burble from that gross vocal hole below her nasal passage.

"Mouth," Brellin softly informs me.

Yes. Emma murmurs something from her mouth. "Will you idiots shut up? Stop playing with that stupid toy and go to sleep."

Then she glides out the window, the gravity lift pulling her up, up into a dark and moonless sky, fattened with a single cloud that holds more than rain.

CHAPTER 3

ORU'S ASSESSMENT IS CORRECT; I've been distracted lately. Thoughts of propagating my genetics have grown more frequent as we revisit the Greenburg family. Few things make a Gray feel the pull of space and time more than how little time other species are given. And how far from home this research takes us.

While Tenzin prepares the three boys in the basement, encysting them together for easier transport, I seek a familiar face.

Harold Greenburg was nineteen Earth years when our research team selected him for a multigenerational study. He fit the profile: male, fertile, has a mate already impregnated and showing positive signs of gestation. Their genetics were excellent, free of most diseases that could pollute our data.

Best of all, they were rural people at the time.

Human curiosity #7,186: most have an aversion to open space and cluster together.

A dilapidated building in the middle of a city draws no attention. An old barn in a fallow field and their primal minds fill it with. . .what was that word?

"*Fear*," Brellin answers.

"*Right*," I think, gliding down the stairs. "*Tracking grandfather Harold.*"

A pleasing memory arises; young Harold stepping out of his truck to gaze up at a single cloud in the starless night sky; alone for miles all around.

Or so he thought.

My body comes to a halt near the old man's bed. I detect no life form in the room, not anymore. A quick scan with my proboscis reveals traces of warmth: the bedsheets, the pillow, the carpet. My hearts beat faster, flooding my senses with. . .

Fear, right.

The door to outside is open. The wind carries scents of juniper and pine and a hint of something beneath it; rotting gray matter.

"*Don't tell me you've lost him,*" Tenzin admonishes, pushing his way into my ocular systems. He's watching from within.

"*Not lost; merely misplaced,*" I try to quietly think. Another curious human feature: this one tends to walk in his sleep.

The chirping amusement of Gray thoughts rings through the Overmind, orange and jolly. A sleepwalker is an odd concept, I admit, since Grays never sleep.

"*Fascinating! The subject is neither conscious nor at rest.*" That's Elex-94, the lead xenobiologist. "*I propose we run a full biopsy this cycle.*"

"*Yes, yes,*" his twin brother Nivex agrees. "*We could run parallel studies.*"

"*I propose we harvest more memories for our crystals,*" Ciron chimes.

Soon, the science and data analytics teams are all thinking on top of each other. I dampen their discussion. My senses need to focus.

Stepping outside, I scan the yard filled with vegetation. Dozens of plants chosen for appearance and nutrition.

"*Garden,*" Brellin sends me the word. "*Maybe we could build such a thing?*"

My feet skitter on the soft life underfoot, green and frequently trimmed. Grass. Despite my ability to glide, I find humans are best tracked when I engage with their world.

Another whiff of aged brain and a body on the downslope towards dysfunction. There he is, Harold Greenburg, standing at the edge of a pond. My proboscis sways, reading the scent notes in the breeze.

Sweat.

Dementia.

Synthetic medications and some alcohol, too.

Beneath it, a ping of something metallic and tart.

"I know it was you, Mister Jay," the old man says. "Late summer. No moon. When I saw the weather report I remembered. It's been about, what? Fifteen years?"

Even though their language is rudimentary, I cannot reply. Human communication requires the precise modulation of sound within narrow frequencies, a limitation my kind transcended long ago.

Still, I give Harold a slight nod to assure him I understand.

"Fifteen years," he repeats. "Jesus, Emma was in diapers, wasn't she? Lucas wasn't even a damn twinkle in my son-in-law's eyes. Where'd the time go?"

I want to convey my gratitude. We have learned many things from his planet and from the locked halls of his mind. I want to tell him he's widely known to researchers across Shy'ran. I want him to know his suffering isn't in vain. But hominid minds lack an Oneirogenic Hub, so their thoughts can never be connected, only erased.

Yes, there is a broken dignity to this human that stirs my emotions. Empathetic hormones flood my bloodstream. I sense I'm looking upon something like the last sunset of a season.

"I suppose you'll be taking me up now, Mister Jay," Harold speaks. "You and your little Gray men. Funny, how no one ever believed me."

He raises his head skyward and I can see the loose skin on his neck. He wears the decades like the trees wear moss.

Another ping. There it is again; a tart, metallic sensation. I scan the surface of his mind. My fingers probe between the old folds and layers.

I pause at his prefrontal cortex, where a decision is forming. The word *PLAN* in black shadows.

Then the parietal lobe; his seat of spatial awareness and navigation. Two words in leathery brown: *POSITION* and *HAND*.

His flaring amygdala and limbic systems causing his emotions to spike white hot. *END*.

That twitching motor cortex, coiled like a lungworm ready to burst from an infected throat. *REACH FOR. . .*

Reach for what? I wonder.

Now his temporal lobe, where memory and sensory inputs are processed: *38 Special*.

"*Jin'qua, be careful!*" Ciron warns me in a white-hot thought.

For a species fascinated with strength, the gun is a most rudimentary tool. I watch Harold raise it and press the barrel under his chin. His mind spikes with resolve as he pulls the trigger.

The click echoes over the pond's still waters.

For a moment, we both stare at the metal revolver. My hand, outstretched. Harold's eyes, wide and bewildered.

Because if you know gunpowder is mostly nitrocellulose, you can break the nitrate esters as easily as turning a doorknob with your mind.

"I can't even kill myself." He lets the gun fall from his hand and wipes his damp eyes. "What else can you take from me?"

I send Elex and Nivex a note to check the subject's tear ducts for biochemical markers. Harold bends to pick up the gun and tosses it among the cattails at the pond's edge. I allow him a moment to sob.

But only a moment.

"Let's get on with it then," he says. "But maybe I could ask you a favor, Mister Jay? Maybe, you could think about leaving my grandkids out of your tests. It ain't fair for children to suffer."

I like it when humans ask yes or no questions. It makes communication much easier.

I shake my head.

I wave my hand.

Then, I offer Harold thoughts of a warm blanket as I burrow into his mind. A fresh tear slides down his cheek as his eyes close and his body falls backwards. I encyst him for transport.

"*Final subject requites gravity lift at sixty-nine point two kelons.*"

"*Twenty-three percent decrease from last time,*" Brellin says. "*Did you measure correctly?*"

I wave my proboscis over Harold again, just to be sure. Encased in the membrane, he looks like the mummified pharaohs my kind visited long ago. I can hear his single, tired heart ticking deep within.

Brellin is right; the old man's mass is collapsing.

"*Funny how they start shrinking at the end,*" Elex thinks.

"*Yes, yes, quite funny indeed,*" Nivex echoes.

But I'm not sure I'm feeling funny. There's a human word for the emotion now flooding my mind.

Reset?

Regress?

The gravity lift illuminates old Harold, a column of cold light piercing the cloud's belly and the writhing tendrils of the ship nestled within.

"Let's take bets on how much he weighs next cycle," Soru offers. *"I'm going with sixty-four kelons."*

"Sixty-three point nine," Brellin counters.

I lower the Overmind, solemnly watching old Harold on his upward journey, riding that silver strand into an inky black sky.

Regret, yes, that it is the human word.

No, I inform my colleagues. Next time, I'm fairly certain Harold won't weigh anything at all.

CHAPTER 4

STRANGE LIGHT IN THE NIGHT BAFFLES LOCAL STARGAZER

By Mildred Thompson, Fort Darrow Times

FORT DARROW, August 10, 1963 - Harold Greenburg, a 19-year-old Fort Darrow native and self-proclaimed sky watcher, claims to have spotted an unusual light in the night sky this summer. According to Greenburg, this mysterious light isn't a plane or a satellite, it hovers in the same location, visible only when the moonlight strikes it at a certain angle. He describes it as resembling a jellyfish glowing faintly in the sky.

Known for his quirky astronomy interests and keen eye on the heavens, Harold hesitates to label the phenomenon as a UFO because of its association with science fiction tales. "I'm not saying it's little green men," Harold remarked, "but it sure isn't normal."

Greenburg reached out to the local air base, hoping they might have an explanation, but as of press time, he had yet to receive a response. Determined to get to the bottom of this celestial mystery, Harold organized a small gathering of telescope enthusiasts last Saturday. Unfortunately, the enigmatic light was a no-show, leaving the group puzzled and disappointed.

"I'm not sure what we were supposed to see," one local resident said. "But whatever it was, it wasn't there."

Harold's accounts have sparked a mix of curiosity and skepticism among the townsfolk. While many dismiss it as the product of an overactive imagination, some wonder if there might be something more to the story. The coast has long been known for similar phenomena.

Until more answers are forthcoming, Harold continues to scan the night sky, his telescope ready, waiting for the elusive light to make its next appearance.

CHAPTER 5

PROBING, AS HOMINID literature often calls it, is not my specialty. I take the gravity lift to the interstitial cavity, then follow the wet halls to the ship's dissection lab. I pass the subjects on to the twins, Elex and Nivex. Their oily eyes flicker a gleeful violet as they unravel Harold's membrane.

"*Delightful!*" Elex projects. "*We are pleased to see his return.*"

"*Yes, yes. And his progenies are maturing,*" Elex adds. "*Place them over there.*"

"*So much to dissect and measure.*"

I can hardly tell them apart when they're excited.

I leave Harold on a dissection nest, the umbilicals quivering and ready for insertion. The rest of the Greenburg family is already plugged in, bodies splayed and hollow.

For a moment, I marvel at how the twins work: the neuronal netting connected to the Overmind; the ship's undulating musculature, reading the subject's nutrients; the artificial veins and kidneys for filtration; and the bio-bladders and sacs for cleaning and storage. It seems like each visit home, the growers have something new to graft onto our vessel. Even the leeches are faster and more efficient in their harvesting of spilled human blood.

"*Soon, they won't even need us,*" Soru muses in my thoughts. "*It'll just be one giant Gray with a bunch of little Grays working inside.*"

"*Isn't that what I am?*" Vorn-99 queries from the depths of the ship.

"*Careful now, you 99s can always be disconnected,*" Soru tells him, adding a friendly splash of cyan so he knows we're joking.

"*Ah, humor,*" Vorn rumbles. "*You'll have to rewire my mirror neurons, as I'm not—*"

"Forget it," Soru thinks. *"Don't you have some methane to reprocess?"*

Pressing my hand to a polyp on the wall, the dissection chamber's sphincter winks open above me. The earth has been hard on my bones, so I use the cilia to ascend, their rhythmic caress assisting my gravity-tired limbs. As the sphincter seals up, I hear a single human scream from the lab.

The twins are getting started.

I'm not feeling social, so I bypass the commons and take a sub-artery. Near an eel well, I spot something that shouldn't be here: a couch cushion poking out of the ship's soft, fleshy wall. I give it a poke and sand drifts from it. Tenzin must have dropped one of the artifacts on the way to cultural research.

Odd. It's not like him to make so many mistakes.

I spend my break in my pod, eating tick powder and watching the Earth through the ship's translucent dermis. Sometimes, I press my head against it, leaning out until it stretches and distends, growing clearer and clearer. If I push hard enough, it feels like I'm floating alone in this cloud. Every now and then the mist parts, revealing glimpses of the sleeping lands below.

Part of me envies these creatures we study and their simple, terrestrial bindings. Part of me pities them for how rarely they dream.

My brain itches with discomforting thoughts.

I don't know.

Maybe seeing Harold so haggard and worn down stole some delight from this job. Maybe I'm feeling mental backsplash from the hominids. Maybe I'm depressed.

I'm on my fourth mouthful of tick powder when a hand glides over my shoulder and a proboscis tickles the nape of my neck. Soothing maroon fills my thoughts.

"We had a feeling you'd retire early," Brellin expresses. *"You always get wistful after an extraction."*

"We?"

A second hand squeezes my hip. Fiery orange fills my senses, like the plasmic emissions of deep space.

"Do they get wistful?" Soru inquires. *"I must say, it's a side of them I've never seen."*

"They dampen the Overmind when they're feeling blue," Brellin thinks. They are both behind me, three Grays in this tight pod.

"*Mmm, blue,*" Soru repeats, and the color fills my thoughts with ice like the glaciers of this earth. "*I'd sure like to visit the surface sometime.*"

"*A twenty-two in their gravity?*" Amusement spikes in Brellin's thoughts. "*You'd fold within minutes.*"

"*Depends on who I'm folding with.*"

I let this moment stretch on, Brellin leaning her slender frame against the crook of my neck. Soru, holding us both from behind, safe in his burly embrace. This is nice and comforting and washes away my earthly malaise.

"*There they are.*" Brellin's fingers caress my tired shoulders. "*Should we tell them, Soru? They haven't queried the Broodlord in weeks.*"

"*What? Why?*" My hearts race at the mention of her. All the rejected applications. All the last-minute cancellations. I break from Brellin and Soru. I'm opening up a direct inquiry to the Incubation Center via the Overmind relays. The answer arrives in moments. Us Grays lack vocal cords and the pronounced lips of humans, yet we still share some traits.

We smile when we are pleased.

And when we do, it lights up our mind.

CHAPTER 6

OF THE SEVENTY–EIGHTY triunions I have proposed to the Broodlord, forty-five have been rejected on genetic misalignments. Twenty-eight triunions have lacked a compatible mate, for either ovulgence or spermition. Three compatible mates rejected me as their fethym, because of my classification as a three, a numerical coincidence I always found oddly amusing. Two were simply a matter of timing; my research takes me far from our homeworld and few will incubate offspring with an absent partner.

Of my most recent requests, each time I was denied I sensed that both Brellin and Soru had something to do with it.

It turns out, I am correct.

"We wanted the ovum to be fertilized and imprinted here," Brellin thinks, gesturing to the misty view through the cloud.

"A true child of the universe," Soru adds. *"How many Grays can say they sired progeny over alien worlds? You'd be the first Earth-fethym."*

"Plus, I've heard gravity can imbue a brood with stronger will," Brellin says. *"Or so the egg wardens claim."*

For the first time in decades, my mind is rendered numb. *"And the Broodlord, they approved it?"*

"Approved?" Soru's thoughts spike with neon delight. *"They thought it was the most romantic thing they've conceived."*

"That was a joke," Brellin adds. *"Conceive. . .conceive."*

Soru gives her a playful slap.

Romantic, perhaps. My skill is underdeveloped from too much time on solid ground. Sometimes I worry I'm growing detached from my own kind.

"So?" Brellin presses her soft forehead against mine and runs those playful fingers over my gills. *"Are we ready to entangle?"*

I am nervous. A thousand concerns race through the tunnels of my mind. Will I be good at this act of creation? Will I bring appropriate pleasure to my triunion? Will I imbue worthy memories upon our offspring?

Gray copulation, after all, shares elements with the humans I study. It requires spermatozoa and ovum. It is messy and quite delightful when done right.

Unlike humans, it requires extreme mental focus. My duty as a fethym is to imprint the genetic memory of our species within the cells of the fetus. It's not unheard of for my gender to occasionally go mad. Even with perfect mental synchronization, not every mind returns fully intact.

"They are worried," Soru conveys to Brellin. *"Funny, isn't it? Jin'qua braves human air yet fears our own biological process. They really are spending too much time with the primates."*

Brellin tenderly squeezes a polyp on the wall, dimming the pod's bioluminescence. *"Hush now,"* she imparts in soothing colors. *"You will do just fine."*

You will.

Two little words imbued with such quiet resolve.

Before I can delay any further, Soru is wrapping me up in his arms. I find myself breathless between them, their fingers and proboscises, their mouths and their thoughts. I retreat inward, allowing them to take control of my body, now enjoined between them.

We merge, yes.

I want this, yes.

Then the boundaries of our bodies blur. We three, together, in this dance of creation. We three, now one, a number so confusing my brain tickles. I let the time-slowing hormones flood my system. I ride this moment, gleefully.

Toes curling, nerves tingling, my senses become endless. I am the dreams of my people, their thoughts flowing through me. I am my ancestors, and they echo their long-dead intentions through my living mind. We are together. Within us. Within this new life we are designing.

To keep my thoughts and duties in harmony, I bifurcate my consciousness.

I instruct my active mind to focus on the transcoding and imprinting. My passive mind allows pleasure to suffuse me. I drift out of myself and follow the ship's glowing neurons. I glide, a delighted observer, riding errant gusts through the wet, winding halls of this living vessel.

I find it. . .oddly relaxing. For the first time on this expedition, I let my mind wander, truly seeing our craft as if with new eyes.

"New eyes to me too," something murmurs in an oddly human tone.

Was that you? I wonder. *The first spark of life we are igniting?*

No reply arrives, so I continue drifting.

Down the pulsating tunnels, the walls throb in a delicate braiding of veins and tendons. Along the superstructure's ribs, crystalized tumors house precious data extracted from our cosmic surveys. Over rows of pustules filled with earthen delights; sampled minerals and oils, their flora and fauna, their clothes, and their tools.

From this disembodied view, I watch Ciron duplicating items from the Greenburg's house, struggling to sort them. I want to tell him not to place electronics in the larval preserve, but it's too late. He deposits a flashlight in a pustule, then cocks his head when it stops glowing.

A pleasing shiver courses through me and now I am sliding down the slippery depths to the Halls of Respiration, where the ship's lungs resemble a room full of anemones. Vorn, our atmospheric engineer, stretches out a gnarled arm and adjusts clusters of alveoli. Something like sand pours from a wound.

"*It's never enough,*" he thinks in a frustrated violet. "*If I ask for twenty-five thousand, they give me fifteen. How am I supposed to work with this mess?*"

My mind smiles as Vorn detaches mycelium threads and rejuvenates a sickly lung. I remind myself to pay him more compliments.

Faster now, my consciousness whirls up through an artery and slides out into the Cerebral Command Cortex, where Rygell-96 and navigator Jorun debate the best route to take home. Two courses glow in the celestial aquarium; a slingshot around this system's sun or a cold dive into deep space. They're worried we might graze a quasar and lose a few years.

"*Focus, Jin'qua. . .*"

I'm pulled and thrown through the ship's halls and veins, swung and thrust and squeezed. The deep corners of the science wing reveal itself and I'm in the lab where Elex and Nivex argue with Tenzin. The Greenburg family lies on the dissection nests, their brains suspended in collagen tendrils.

"*We are certain,*" Elex thinks, his mind spiking an irritated white. "*The miscount isn't from our department.*"

"*Yes, our department can count humans,*" Nivex seethes. "*Nine. Eight. Seven. Why not crosscheck with security?*"

Tenzin paces past sheets of human skin, stretched for measuring. I can make out Mrs. Greenburg's freckles, little constellations on a tan fleshy map.

"*I'll summarize for the Overmind.*" Tenzin pauses at the dissection nests, his hand passing over the open hollow of Harold Greenburg. "*Xenobiology senses eight life forms, yes? Yet ground team has only taken possession of seven.*"

"*Our senses are perfectly attuned to this family,*" Elex conveys.

"*Yes, yes, intimately attuned,*" Nivex adds.

"*And how many specimens are before you?*" Tenzin asks. "*Count the Greenburgs.*"

The twins turn their ebony eyes to the unconscious humans. I can sense Elex's mind struggling. "*Eight life forms.*"

"*Eight,*" Tenzin repeats. "*Do you see eight humans before you?*"

Their minds entwine, producing a discomforting loop. Elex wipes his nasal cavity as a hemorrhage leaks.

"*Seven,*" he conveys.

"*Seven,*" Nivex confirms.

Tenzin runs his proboscis over each of the dissected subjects. Some lay in pieces like the toy dolls humans enjoy. Others rest in various states of reconstruction, bio-brambles mending tissue and bone. When this study is over, they won't even have scars.

"*Harold Greenburg,*" Tenzin coveys. "*Ancestral progenitor. Catherine, alpha progenitor. Marshall, seeder. Emma, junior progenitor. Have you censused her womb?*"

"*Fertile yet inactive,*" Nivex informs him.

"*We are not ignorant of their biology.*" Elex plucks a cauterizing leech from the bile jar and presses it to his nasal cavity.

"*You may be anatomical masters, but the problem remains. If the count is off, the data's corrupt.*" Tenzin gestures to the three sleeping boys. "*Lucas, secondary seeder. Jake and Tylor, non-ancestral temporal cohabitants—*"

"*Friends.*" Nivex disconnects an umbilical and places a loose scalp back onto Jake's skull. "*Like family, only temporary.*"

Using stem cell adhesive, Elex caresses Jake's loose face, massaging the skin back into place. "*We do not disagree with your count Tenzin. There are seven life forms before us.*"

"*Good. Then I'll update the log.*"

Pleased, Tenzin skitters to the terminus and detaches a data root. "*Let the ship's record reflect the ground team did not miscount.*"

The walls glow blue as the records update. A second later, they flicker red. Rejection. Every muscle on Tenzin's gravity-stretched form quivers in fury.

"*You deny my count?*"

"*We do not.*" Elex peels the leech from his nasal cavity and discards it. "*But our senses do not find alignment.*"

"*Yes, yes,*" Nivex adds in his softest conveyance. "*You have trained to count low, Tenzin. To breathe human air and bear the weight of solid ground. But we've trained for a dozen cycles to sense life and our attunement rarely lies. There are eight entities aboard this ship.*"

CHAPTER 7

ONE OF THE coolest things about being dissected is that it gives you perspective. Like the view of yourself and your guts. I never knew lungs were light pink with crimson fringes, all spongy when they swell and deflate. Nor did I know your liver and kidneys nearly matched, shades of reddish-brown with hints of purple marbling. Or how long your intestines can reach when suspended from a veiny lattice over your open skull.

With total calm, I witness my disassembly beneath these alien hands.

They must have given me something, like that stuff the dentist used on Emma when they drilled out her teeth. Maybe it's in that umbilical thing they stuffed down our throats.

The good news is, I know they will erase this and replace it with some other memory. Something fake, like a weird dream.

Why do I know this?

Because of what Jake found the last time we had a sleepover.

See, I want to tell you about this game that we played, the three of us, Jake, Tyler, and me. We'd compete to steal things, so we called it "Loot and Scoot." It started off super simple. First, we lifted candy from 7-Eleven or pinched stupid keychains from that shop at the wharf. Soon, I couldn't go into a store without stuffing my pockets.

But after a few weeks, we had these drawerfuls of candy and worthless junk, so it got kinda boring. Plus, most stores aren't supposed to chase after shoplifters. Tyler said they have a word for it: shrinkage.

So, we made a new rule: it had to be something unique.

That made Loot and Scoot fun once again.

Tyler nicked that old stapler from Mr. Knowles and we giggled while he searched his desk. I grabbed a dog collar from my neighbor, Mrs. Hamilton, while she was bathing her labradoodle at the pet store. I could hear her accusing the employees of being thieves. Jake ran off with a lawn gnome from some old geezer named Chester.

It went on like that for a few more months. We made up stories, trying to one-up each other. How we snuck into a house late at night or crawled through a window to grab something.

Then one night Jake opened the old diary and my blood went cold.

I'd seen the handwriting countless times. On my bagged lunch as a kid, my name scribbled in that old, cursive scrawl. On notes left about: *Out for a walk* or *Going to get ice cream.* On my birthday cards or Hanukkah gifts a shaky wobble.

It was my grandpa Harold's

This was his diary in Jake's hands.

"Listen to this," Jake's voice took on a mocking inflection as he cracked the spine. "'I think they're coming again. I think I've figured out their pattern. It's a twelve to fifteen-year round trip from their home planet, depending on the solar alignment. But time dilation makes it so they age much slower, which is why—'"

"What's time dilation?" Tyler asked.

"It's Einstein stuff," I said. "Like slow motion the faster they start moving."

"Wait, slow motion for who?"

"Them, I think." I recalled Mr. Knowles telling us about event horizons and relativity; something like that movie with a black hole and a planet with these huge waves. But now, I was more focused on the diary. The game no longer felt funny and playful, but cruel and invasive.

"You geeks done with the Star Trek stuff?" Jake asked. "We're not even to the good part. Here, check this. 'Last time, they took me apart. I could see all my pieces laid out on some thorny bed, like a nest of bones and nerves. I wasn't supposed to remember, but I think I'm developing something, like an inoculation. I think Mister Jay and the Grays messed around with my mind for too long.'"

"Like, aliens and stuff?" Tyler asked. "Hold up, your grandpa really believes this?"

"No way," I said. "It's just a story he's working on." It was a lie, of course, but it bought me a moment to try and snatch the diary.

Jake saw it coming, yanked it out of my reach, then kept reading as something venomous crept into his voice. "'They've been *probing* me for years.'"

"Probing?" Tyler repeated. "Like, butt stuff?"

I punched him in the shoulder while Jake continued, his grin stretching wider. "'They take me apart and put things inside me. They track the results. Then, they put me back together. I'm like an animal in the wild with some sort of tag on its ear. No matter where I look, the doctors can't find it. Not with X-rays or MRIs or any tests that they run. But it's in there. It's buried like a fossil, dormant for a decade then flaring up. Everyone thinks that I'm crazy, but I know the truth: there's more than stars looking down at us from these warm summer skies.'"

"Guys, seriously," I said.

"Seriously, guys," Jake mocked. "Seriously. Seriously."

I lunged for the diary.

Jake pulled it back again, but not fast enough this time. We fought for it. I didn't know why, but I was angry—really furious now.

Grandpa Harold never hurt anyone. Never did anything except pack us our lunches or walk us to school and sometimes tell us weird stories with too much enthusiasm. All the other grandparents lived in different towns or different states and wore too much perfume. They smiled like wax statues and told us not to run. But my grandpa, he taught us how to whittle wooden swords and grow tomatoes. He smiled often and lived down the hall in this house that he'd built.

There was a crack and rip, and then Jake was holding one half of the diary and I was holding the other. Loose pages spilled onto the floor between us.

"I want to read it," Tyler said, his sticky fingers fumbling with the delicate old paper.

I snatched the torn diary from Jake and socked Tyler in the shoulder. I gathered the fallen pages while they called me a spaz and a downer. I didn't care. I was tired of Loot and Scoot. It's not fun when we steal from each other. If they did it again, I told them, we're no longer friends.

We didn't talk for much of the night. In the morning, Jake left before I woke up.

While my grandpa showered, I snuck into his bedroom and

searched his bookshelf. There were dozens of journals and science articles he'd tried to publish, so he probably never noticed his diary was missing.

I pushed it back onto a shelf, but not before reading a page of what he'd written.

I think they're coming again, this summer or next. I can feel Mister Jay in my dreams. Maybe that's where they've buried it, after all.

Maybe that's where everything's stored

CHAPTER 8

IT IS ILL luck that my first triunion is interrupted mid-imbuement. I am nearly finished imprinting the first memory layer within Brellin's fertilized ovum when the Overmind summons my focus. I converge my consciousness, finding my body twisted between Soru and Brellin. I am rather embarrassed by the face I was making.

"*What is it?*" Soru complains. "*I was enjoying this.*"

"*Inconsistency,*" I inform them. "*A report has been logged.*"

"*Mmm. . . Can't it wait?*" Brellin caresses my gills, sending a shiver down my spine.

I squirm out from between them, disentangle, and clean myself with some calcium mites. Suddenly, I feel ashamed of my body in the moonlight. Brellin, already swelling with the glow of our unfinished child. Soru, his skin a luminous silver that matches the storm cloud. And me, gravity fatigued and unable to finish the one task that I had.

"*I'm sorry I wasn't faster,*" I tell them. "*My mind is scattered.*"

"*We'll finish later,*" Brellin soothes.

"*I've already finished three times.*" Soru's thoughts spike with a mischievous yellow. "*I'm not just a tool for your pleasure.*"

"*Oh, you're a tool for something.*" Brellin presses her hand against the dermis, where the clouds beyond flash with the occasional bolt of lightning. Her slender body pulses with the rhythm of blank life. Stretching, Soru passes her a fresh blister of folic acid and they share it, lazily sipping and watching the storm.

"*Jin'qua-33, report to council,*" the summons repeats.

I linger at the sphincter, taking in this peaceful moment; the three of us post-triunion. Although I am the eldest of this new family, I cannot help but feel a childish awe.

I promise myself we will finish the imprint. That I shall give glorious memories to our child. I hope their first dreams are of this planet they were created above. I hope they will grow strong for our long journey home to Shy'ran. I hope they will find their place among our kind, among the stars.

I am filled with so many hopes.

But for now, I must attend to the ship's council. I fear we've made a mistake that I don't quite understand.

I press the polyp; the exit winking open. I wince as I cut my finger on a sharp piece of metal caught in the wall. I make a mental note to call My'nar-65 in maintenance.

But for now, I look back on Brellin and Soru, saving this moment deep in my hearts. Our first night as a family.

I do not know it will be our final night, too.

CHAPTER 9

April 15, 1985

Dear Mr. Greenburg,

After consideration, we regret to inform you that your manuscript titled "Alien Return Cycles and Time Dilation Effects" does not meet the rigorous academic standards required for publication in the Northern Journal of Astrophysics and Space Studies.

Your hypothesis regarding aliens returning to Earth on a 12 to 15-year cycle, purportedly aging minimally due to time dilation effects near black holes, lacks sufficient mathematical and empirical verification. Specific claims, such as the assertion that "aliens utilize 4th and 5th dimensional physics to navigate temporal distortions," and that "these beings have been encountered throughout human history because of their manipulation of spacetime," are highly speculative and unsupported by current scientific understanding.

Moreover, the proposed involvement of "unknown fourth and fifth dimensional components" in alien technology remains unsubstantiated and fails to meet the rigorous standards of peer review. Your mathematical models presented are not only difficult to verify but also diverge significantly from accepted principles in astrophysics.

DARK MATTER DREAMS

While we appreciate the innovative thinking behind your submission, we must prioritize verifiable and reproducible research. We encourage you to continue refining your theories and seek further empirical evidence.

Thank you for considering our journal. We wish you the best in your future endeavors.

Sincerely,

Dr. Elaine Richardson
Editor-in-Chief
Northern Journal of Astrophysics and Space
Studie

CHAPTER 10

TWO HUNDRED AND seventy-eight skittering strides later and the ship's Cerebral Command Cortex stretches to admit me. I sense I am in trouble the moment the council severs all outside connections. It's rare that Grays are reduced to a group of low numbers.

I spot Jorun and Lyra-75, M'ka-29, and Gee-93. Tenzin lingers by the celestial aquarium, the tank's indigo glow speckling his skin.

"We have a problem," Rygell Prime informs us. *"A discrepancy in your survey."*

As the ship's security captain, I do not fault her for the sharpness of her mental tone. Still, I can feel my hearts racing, my mind tightening, and the mental walls rising. She turns her oily eyes upon me and I can feel the council's tendrils slithering into my thoughts.

I resist on instinct, but they're far stronger. My memories give themself over.

"Relax Jin'qua," Rygell continues. *"We have no concern with your copulation. We're here because of numbers. Numbers that do not align."*

I see two pairs of numbers in my mind, low ones, difficult to visualize. Seven and Eight. Three and four. They shine opalescent and fuzzy.

The council's gaze lingers on Tenzin and me.

"My count was perfect," I inform them.

"Mine too," Tenzin adds.

"You've trained for three cycles to count low digits," Rygell thinks. *"Tenzin, for one cycle. Yet the twins insist we're in numerical disharmony."* She strokes a data root and the walls throb red. *"Furthermore, we've found artifacts among the ship. Anomalies that should not be."*

She gestures upward as several objects descend on containment veins. A couch cushion. A pillow. A curved metal blade, like the one that my finger found outside my pod. There's also something organic. Stepping closer, I shudder when I realize it's a human jaw with gems for teeth.

"I don't understand."

"Neither do we." Rygell runs her finger over the curved blade. *"Perhaps some mental infection brought on by bad math. Our ship's not equipped for unbalanced data."*

"But our subjects are accounted for," I think. *"The count was accurate."*

"Perhaps Jin'qua had other tasks on his mind," Tenzin thinks. *"A miscount is understandable in his hurry to return. Human lust can be quite contagious."*

Lust? When did Tenzin dare to think such insults towards me? A furious urge overcomes me. I want to see Tenzin's brain collapse and his cocky thoughts become simple. Maybe it's the post-copulation energy, but my anger takes form. I am inside his mind, scratching at his memories and carving marks on the soft inner walls of his skull.

A flash: three kids sleeping beneath a fortress of blankets and couch cushions. A long, stony hall. A voice, murmuring, "This is an odd sort of palace."

"Enough!" Rygell's thoughts arrive in a thunderclap, snapping me back to the chamber.

Tenzin falls to the soggy floor, his knee trembling and his nasal passages flaring. My mind races; frustration, confusion, and a sense that something has been overlooked and is trying not to be found.

Not yet.

"I've inspected both your memories," Rygell informs us. *"I see no false records. Still, our data demands reconciliation. Without numerical alignment, this survey risks corruption. We'll lose decades of research and, I fear, our careers."* She waves her hand over the command crystals, orange light flooding the council chamber. *"The sun will rise in four hours. Humans grow suspicious of clouds that don't move. I'm sending you both back to the surface. Prepare your bodies for transport. The mission resumes."*

CHAPTER 11

THERE IS A charm to the Earth and a soothing comfort of its dominant species. They remind me of dull knives; capable of cutting yet easily handled. Their atmosphere, while far less methane-rich than my lungs prefer, is redolent of industry and ambition. Sometimes, when I stalk the cornfields or forests, I can taste the cesium-137 and iodine-181 from their nuclear blunders. Occasionally, I fantasize about staying longer.

Mostly, I enjoy the mental quiet of this planet. For a species who spends a third of their life asleep, their dreams coat the night in remarkable silence.

"I do not enjoy spending overtime with Tenzin, whom I'm fairly certain is the cause of this miscount and whom I suspect has been hoping for my demotion. Who thinks of me as what the humans call 'an asshole,' something we Grays do not even possess."

"*You're even starting to echo their linguistics,*" Tenzin thinks.

I ignore him and focus on applying the all-weather chrysalis to my skin. I didn't think I'd have to suit up twice in one night.

"*Just concentrate on the site report,*" Brellin murmurs in a private part of my mind. "*The twins will prep the subjects for return. Easy as any mission you've done in the past. Then we'll get another chance to conjoin.*"

"*Tenzin can watch via the Overmind,*" Soru thinks, a little too strongly. I can feel his insult stirring amusement among a dozen Gray minds.

But not Tenzin's.

Prodding a tangle of violet tumors, he extracts fresh nerves and charges the ship's gravity lift. In her control cavity, Brellin confirms the operation. Then, a rush of high-altitude air, cool and crisp and laden with moisture, whips through the bay's yawning throat. I rush to finish, layering the chrysalis before the ejection sacks can inflate.

DARK MATTER DREAMS

"Let's hope your math is as sharp as your mind," Tenzin warns, gripping an epiglottis for balance as the bay trembles. *"One of us made a mistake, and it wasn't me."*

Human curiosity #7,308: the witty comeback.

I try to think of a retort, something I can send back to Tezin. Something that would open a real loop in his logic and carve a few scars on his mind.

"Your mistake was thinking you never made one."

I'm pleased and I'm about to send it, but the ejection sacks hit full inflation and the gravity lift expels us in a whir of bright light.

Descending eighty-five thousand feet in earth's gravity is never pleasant, yet it allows me a moment to marvel at this world. The forests and hills are slowly being consumed by inorganic dwellings; what the humans call "suburbs." The inefficient scribbles of transportation, highways, are dimly lit like the demented synapses of their elders. I find it odd they do not build subterranean cities. Although tens of thousands of humans sleep below, their collective dreams are pathetically faint. Only mere tickles on the surface of my mind and—

Wait. . .

"Dream? Yes, is that what this is?"

There it is again, that voice. It *speaks* oddly, as if with a mouthful of something dry. A flash of images; a basement and a dark object of stone, something that reeks of ancient hands. Something hiding between the numbers 3 and 4. I imagine a noise my throat cannot make.

Something like laughter, yes. The nervous giggles of boys.

My senses try to chase this anomaly like an errant scent, gathering more information. I imagine myself lighting bioluminescent mushrooms and descending into the deep tunnels of my subconscious. Searching. . .searching. . .

"Jin'qua?"

But the voice is retreating.

"Jin'qua, is there something you're picking up?" Brellin inquires.

"He's picking up after Tenzin," Soru announces, intentionally loud. Amusement spikes through the Overmind.

"Keep quiet," Tenzin orders.

I can feel him in here with me, too. For once, we're in mental agreement. Yet that errant scent, that neurological *tickle*, has vanished.

What is this thing hiding from our audit?

With a soft crackle, the gravity lift deposits us near the Greenburg's garden. I take a moment, constricting my muscles and forcing my bones to densify. I give my legs a few steps to test the environs.

The soil; soft and rich underfoot.

The stone walkway; cool and firm.

The pond with its cattails and sleeping ducks in the reeds.

The whole neighborhood echoes in silence. Pity I'm not here for vacation.

Tenzin emerges from the woods, his proboscis swaying as he sends me an order. We must cross-check each other's work. It's not like him to give conflicting commands, yet I check with the council on a private channel.

"Confirmed," Rygell replies. *"Transparency is our focus."*

Very well. Perhaps tonight is the night one of us gets demoted.

Waving my hand, the back door unlocks and creaks open. Feet sliding on the tiles, Tenzin skitters through the kitchen before hurrying up the stairs. I allow my senses to calibrate and wander.

A presence, yes. This dwelling is deeply imbued with human traces. I survey the objects.

Cutlery; well-worn and loved.

A table that has served many meals.

Frozen renditions of the Greenburgs line the hall, each depicting their offspring's development and achievements; first steps and baseball games and family vacations to distant parts of the planet. Human curiosity #7,387: photographs. It will be thousands of generations before they evolve an eidetic hive mind.

Beneath it all, there simmers a numerical suspicion: seven entities—no, eight. Three—no, four. The discrepancy chews at my thoughts.

"Is that confirmation of miscount?" Rygell inquires. I sense her presence in my ocular systems, watching out through my eyes.

"No confirmation. Only anomalous senses. Whispers or echoes or. . . ."

I pause outside the basement door, my proboscis tingling. Four. Yes, the number is clearer down here.

"Define whispers."

That is Elex and Nivex, their thoughts harmonizing. So many minds crowd my thought channel now, each pushing for a prime view.

I open the basement door. *"The anomaly is more pronounced in the subregions of the dwelling,"* I think. *"Where the secondary seeder and his non-familial companions were found."*

"Friends," Brellin adds.

"Odd concept," Soru murmurs.

"Yes, odd concept." The twins agree.

Descending the rickety stairs, I remove a patch of chrysalis, forcing my pores to widen and sample the climate. I catalog the undertones; heirlooms and old junk, dusty rugs, and a lingering dampness that speaks of coastal storms.

"Speaks?" Tenzin's thoughts cut into my mind. *"He even echoes their linguistics."*

"Perhaps," I reply. *"But I'm not the one who contaminated a multigenerational study."*

That quiets his sardonic thoughts. For now.

Cloaked in darkness, I probe the room, pulling shapes and distilling meaning.

The TV is inactive yet still exuding residual electromagnetic radiation.

"Conclusion?" Rygell inquires. I ignore her for now.

Lifting blankets, I draw in the fermenting trace hormones. Epinephrine from excitement. Cortisol from stress and anxiety. Gentle layers of melatonin and serotonin from when the boys fell asleep.

"Conclusion?"

I squat, peering into the arrangement of couch cushions forming that curious shelter. Waving my hand, they expand outward, revealing an inner sanctum. Popcorn remnants lay in a bowl near an odd pile of sand. A few paper plates hold oily traces of nutrition. Pizza, I believe.

Three plates for pizza.

Despite the discomfortingly low number, I strain my mind and count again.

Three. Yes, the numbers align.

"Conclusion?"

I continue on, cataloging more artifacts. Plastic forks and knives and spoons, again in sets of three. A device for remotely controlling the TV. A magazine hidden beneath a sleeping bag displays unclothed females in a variety of nimble poses.

I pause at a curious toy formed of old stone and inlaid metals, still warm to the touch. Four triangular surfaces connect, forming a tetrahedron. I slide my proboscis over its chipped edges and mother-of-pearl patterning. Strange symbols line each face, earth writing, though no modern language I am versed in. It feels as though it should slide open, yet no matter how I try to mentally disassemble the toy, nothing changes.

I put the tetrahedron back with the other artifacts. I am tired and frustrated, but my senses scream that a fourth presence was here, dark matter detected only by its absence.

It did not leave traces on the stairs.

It did not eat the food these young humans consumed.

It did not excrete hormones as they watched the TV nor did it sleep in their curious nest.

Yet something existed, a remnant, staining the basement until. . .

Until we arrived.

I tunnel my way into Tenzin's memory, replaying the past several earth-hours. Him, jealously watching Brellin as she saunters down the hall, excited to copulate. Him, reading his application from the Broodlord, another rejection. Him, on ship, pushing the three sleeping teens through the gravity bay and into the dissection lab.

Three. Four.

I slow down his memory, observing as the twins take custody of the boys, peeling the membrane and separating their dormant bodies. My senses tingle.

"What are you doing with my memories?" Tenzin's thoughts arrive like a cloud of stinging eels.

"Quiet!" Rygell commands.

For once, I feel Tenzin's consciousness retreat, and his mind fully gives itself over. I pause this moment: him on the ship, delivering the three kids to the twins. I move through the memory, second by second.

The boys, each lifted and placed upon a dissection nest.

Three.

Four.

I study the shared moment, cross-referencing with Elex and

Nivex. I fine-tune each perspective, cross-referencing them until the clarity lets me see the very molecules in the air.

Three.

Four.

The ship's Overmind hangs in a void, so silent I can hear the neuronal hum a dozen Gray minds, crackling with synaptic excitement as. . .

Three. Four. Three.

Elex, cutting the membrane. Nivex, inserting umbilicals into each boy's throat. The dissection nests, a thousand teeth opening up and cleaving skin from muscle. Mother and father, sister and then grandfather Harold. The whole Greenburg family lies together in pieces as the twins go to work.

Three boys. Four presences.

That's when I see it; the Greenburg's son—Lucas—his limp arm dangling from the cut membrane as a strange symbol glows on his palm. The dissection nest degloves his flesh and then it's gone.

No. I rewind the memory, diving deeper into the moment until the boy's palm is all that I see. Peeling, reverse. Peeling, reverse.

"*What is that?*" Ciron inquires.

"*Did you see it?*" Soru cuts in. "*It was on his hand, then it was gone.*"

"*It was on* all *their hands,*" Zir'xa tells us. "*All three boys had it. Then it was gone.*"

They are all chattering now. Too many Grays in my head, all connecting and fighting to be understood. My cerebrofluids warm and my skull plates swell to accommodate this chorus of inquisition.

Three boys. Four presences. Three. Four. Three—

I congeal my consciousness, returning to the basement before me. A giggling fear lingers like a dusty breeze. I run my fingers over the tetrahedron, realizing at once why it does not belong in this room, in this house, or with these people.

Although human hands have held it—and I sense many generations have run greedy fingers over its beautiful grooves—no modern hands crafted this stone.

This was forged in the deep dreams; the ones that wake them in icy terror. The ones that leave them breathless and scared of the shadows. The ones that make them reach for the light.

"*Nightmare,*" Brellin murmurs in a private part of my mind.

Waving my proboscis over the tetrahedron, I realize it is not a toy, but something far bigger than its size.

It is a doorway.

And it has been open for hours.

CHAPTER 12

BUT WHAT I really want to tell you about is the stupid old stone that Jake stole and brought to the sleepover. It was just after midnight when my parents went to bed. We watched two scary movies and part of a porno about a delivery guy who showed up at the wrong house. That's when Jake slid his backpack over and said, "We still playing our game?"

I shrugged. Since the diary incident, I hadn't stolen anything and didn't care to resume. I even dumped all my loot in a junkyard.

"Because if we are," Jake continued, "then peep this."

The object fell from his backpack with a heavy clunk and sat there between us, upright and dusty.

It was a triangular stone, like one of those 4-sided dice from Dungeons & Dragons but the size of a football. Three of its faces bore handprints, formed with iridescent colors. When I tilted it, I saw that the fourth side was empty. Bizarre writing lined its edges, sharp and jagged as if scratched in with little hooks. No matter how close I got, the letters always seemed to stay the same distance away; fuzzy and unfocused.

"Whoa, what is that?" Tyler asked.

"I already told you," Jake said. "I pinched it from the museum my mom works at."

"Dude, that could be, like, a priceless antique."

"You're an antique," Jake said. "Anyways, I tried to sell it but the guy at the pawnshop said no way. It's super old."

"Yeah, but *what* is it?" I asked.

Jake's grin spread, and his eyes narrowed in serpentine amusement. "It's a game."

"A game?" Tyler asked. "So, where's the screen?"

Jake tapped his temple and Tyler cocked his head. I

understood Jake really meant something else; his mind. I didn't like how quiet the basement had become.

"We put our hands on the side." He showed us, placing his palm against the shimmering imprint. "We each read the words. Then..."

"Then what?" Tyler leaned in.

"I don't know," Jake shrugged. "It said it needs three players, so I haven't had..."

He hesitated and in that moment I saw it all. He didn't have two other friends. Not in his new town or at his new school. Not in that place that was so much better, with better pizzas and hotter girls and better friends than Lucas and me.

Now that I thought of it, he hadn't mentioned any new friends at all.

"Anyways, I translated the instructions off ChatGPT," he continued. "It says that's Ancient Sumerian on your side." He pointed to me. "This is something called 'Proto-Indo-European'" He pointed at his side. "And Lucas, that's Ancient Greek."

"Oh, I know some Greek," Tyler said. "Extra souvlaki please."

We ignored him and I asked, "So this is, like, Candyman or Bloody Mary or...?"

"I think it's like a magic lamp," Jake shrugged and swiped his phone open. "Open it and out pops a genie."

"A sexy genie?" Tyler asked. "Or like creepy blue Will Smith?"

"Like your mom in a bikini," Jake said. "How would I know? I haven't done this. Here, it says, 'Drúbhóp wesey priyom' and that means, 'Make our wishes come true.'"

"What about my side?" I asked.

"Same thing. Here, read it." He handed me his phone with its broken screen and I confirmed it on ChatGPT. All three sides said something similar in different languages. The translation even rendered phonetic ways to pronounce it.

"'Dumu-ki-maškim-ge,'" I said.

"That's ancient submarinian?" Tyler asked.

"*Sumerian.* And I don't know." He passed the phone to Tyler. "Just read this part."

"'Eukhēn plērōsate,'" Tyler said, his tongue fumbling with the words. "So what, we just put our hand on it and say that?"

"Then we make a wish."

"A wish?" I repeated.

Jake nodded, his eyes brimming with more enthusiasm than I'd seen in a while. A flicker of that energetic kid I met in second grade, not this ghost of divorce.

So this is what we did: we placed our hands on the stone, read the words, and each made a wish.

But nothing happened. We tried it again and again, even louder, laughing and shouting until my sister came in and told us to shut up.

Still, nothing happened. The stone sat upright between us. No genie burst out.

"Lame," Tyler said.

"Double lame," I agreed.

Defeated, Jake shoved the stone away. On its side by the pizza, it looked more like a paperweight than something to fear. Whatever dread I felt at first had evaporated.

"What'd you guys wish for?" Tyler asked, chewing a pizza crust.

"That legendary sword in *Critical Mass*," I said. "Twin Blades of Spite. You?"

"New e-bike," he said, wiping his mouth. "My battery's toast."

"Yeah, those things die off fast."

After a moment, I realized Jake had gone quiet. Maybe he'd wished for some fireworks to throw off the overpass. Or maybe a larger hole in the wall between the boys' and girls' locker rooms, like he said his new school had. Maybe a new iPhone his drunk dad hadn't broken yet.

"What about you?" I asked.

He went back to swiping the cracked screen of his phone. Maybe he hadn't heard me, so I was about to ask again.

"For my parents to get back together," he said. "But what does it matter? It's just bullshit anyway."

Tyler fell asleep first. In the past, Jake might've drawn a dick on his face or wrapped his finger in damp tissue to see if he'd pee himself. I might've helped, knowing that they'd have done the same to me. But tonight, Jake just watched videos on his phone. Perhaps he didn't want to fall asleep. Perhaps he knew that if he did, he'd be closer to waking up, closer to heading home, back to his new home.

And what was left of his family.

Yet, sleep came for him, too. In my last minutes, when the yawns grew more frequent and the shadows thickened, I took a picture of the stone tetrahedron and ran those strange symbols through ChatGPT. I propped my phone on my chest and laid back beneath the cushion fort.

Dumu-ki-maškim-ge.

What a dumb phrase.

My phone informed me that there were still gaps of knowledge in Ancient Sumerian, especially with abstract concepts like 'wishes' and 'desires.' Then my phone smacked my face as I yawned my last yawn of the night. I glanced at the screen, the pixels so close that the words blurred like a sky too full of stars. I turned it off as sleep overtook me, the last sentences fading to a misty haze.

The word *maškim*, it said, had a few different meanings.

And one of them was the word "dream".

CHAPTER 13

IN THE SHIP'S wheezing depths, within the Halls of Respiration, rows of pores shiver and twitch. A deep breath whips through the shadows, taming Earth's toxic atmosphere. Carbon dioxide and water vapor break down; hydrogen fuses with carbon, forming methane.

Amid this biochemical alchemy, a lone Gray, Vorn-39, inspects a strange tumor between two of the many lungs. As a "nine," he's squat and bulbous, trained for narrow work among these sticky, esophageal nooks. He enjoys skittering through these halls, listening to the whooshing sounds of bio-filtration sacks—a sound reminiscent of his own gestation. Before the duties to crew and craft. Before this research took him so far from Shy'ran. Before things fell apart.

This growth, another frustration.

"No, no, no. They'll have skin, the council will."

With three fingers and a flanged tentacle, he peels the irritant from the wall. Odd. The residue clings in crusty remnants, releasing an offensive scent into his nasal cavity. Although he lacks a word for it, he recalls a briefing where Jin'qua and Tenzin discussed human foods. Vorn's tongue—a dried, vestigial thing he barely uses—gives a phantom curl as a human word he doesn't quite understand stirs in his mind: pizza.

For a dozen heartbeats, he leans against a heaving sack, his mind dancing with the strange images this word brings.

Safety.

Excitement.

A night of shared secrets with young friends.

With a whoosh, a distant ventriport closes. Not uncommon, Vorn tells himself. The ship is old, full of odd tremors.

And yet. . .

The crumbs fall from his fingers. His tentacle curls around the loose folds in the back of his head. What is this feeling? Not connection, but something rare to his kind: separation, isolation. Alone.

Another ventriport closes at the far end of the hall. Amid the *psh-psh* of the sacks, a sound rises; one Vorn himself cannot make.

Laughter.

He recoils, heel striking something else foreign to these depths. A flat, square object spins across the moist floor, brown and decorated in inks: *Slices By Mike*. Though he doesn't fully understand, he recognizes this synthetic as cardboard, a means to deliver food.

Another ventriport closes. He sends a message to the Overmind but gets no response.

Separation. Isolation. Alone.

These new sensations unsettle him. Has the purifier sweat always gone *tickity-tick*? Have the lungs always whistled and shuddered? Have the curtains between them always offered so many places to hide?

He sends another message: "*Who are you? What is going on?*"

In the quiet, the halls shift, taking on new and threatening forms. Alone. A solitary Gray in the sweating depths. Alone. This concept staggers him, fresh convulsions rippling through his body. Alone.

But not singular.

Because someone else is here, a crouching form rising within a tumored bio-filtration sack. Birthed, he realizes, not as a Gray, but through displacement. A bubble in a lung.

It rises, rises. . .

"*What are you?*" Vorn's thoughts boom in the silence. "*How did you get in there?*"

"Get?"

Though it's only a word, Vorn recoils. It was spoken. The voice, thick with cruel amusement, dusty and fragrant, echoes. Images race through Vorn's mind; deep deserts, humans walking by starlight, sleeping in great tents by day.

"I did not *get* here," it speaks. "I have always been. Always, in the depths of the rested. Always, the first prayer and last light. Get? No. I become."

The lung darkens as something within sharpens; angular, taller than any Gray Vorn has seen. Becoming, yes.

At last, it rises, not by skittering or floating, but with primal spinal movement, pressing itself against the lungs.

"Human," Vorn's mind shudders. *"How did a human end up on this ship?"*

"Human? Not quite. . ."

Where there should be five fingers, there is only a single curved shadow ending with a sharp point.

"Curious kingdom you've summoned me to," the shadow says. "I've stalked the alleys of Babylon, hunted the Silk Road to Hangzhou, bedded kings and queens in between. But this? This is delight I've never seen."

With a glint of metal, the crescent tip presses against the sack's thin skin. A blade, Vorn realizes. Some sort of primitive tool.

"Primitive depends on where one is standing."

With a downward stroke, the blade splits the sack. Alarms squeal, dirty air hissing from the dying lung. Vorn knows he should alert the others, opening mental tunnels to the ship's command. His warning should be echoing across the Overmind as he skitters away, sealing the infected halls.

But he stands frozen, his mind struggling to comprehend the figure rising before him.

It is hominid, a male of the species—yet more. Tribal markings and scars cover his bronze chest. Silver rings pierce his skin in ritual decoration; chains tracing sturdy shoulders. A thick, braided copper beard hangs from his chin. Golden lips split a broad face marred with symmetrical scars that glisten like pearls. Most unsettling are the eyes, which pull Vorn into a numb stupor. Two misty sockets gaze down, dust pouring from the hollows.

Sand, Vorn realizes. The eyes are leaking sand, yet somehow, this human still sees.

"I told you, 'Not quite human.'"

With a prying rip, the hominid-thing splits the sack open and steps into the hall. From the waist down, he wears something resembling a skirt of organic matter and—oh, Shy'ran—a stitched patchwork of human faces, eyes eternally shut.

Skin. Vorn stumbles back. This thing wears the flayed visage of his people.

"People?" The voice rumbles low, stony. "No, I have no people. Only monarchs, merchants, and beggars. A congregation of schemers with their meager desires. But you. . ."

Closer now, his dusty glare narrows; head tilting left as sand spills from his empty socket.

"You are a curious thing. Your mind's door is wide open."

The blade's crescent tip grazes Vorn's shoulder and something primal cracks in his thoughts. His body reacts. In fifty skittering steps, he's at the ventriport, squeezing the polyp, but the port remains sealed.

He glances back. With each lumbering step of this impossible man-thing, the soft floor tissue quivers. Another step and the very halls widen, stretching.

The ship—it's recoiling from him.

"Ah, a ship," the man-thing says. "A vessel built from the *materium* of the deep mind. Fascinating that our architectures differ, yet we share the same language."

"*W-w-what language?*" Vorn thinks, his mind frantic.

A step closer. Those sandy eyes narrow, golden lips stretching to reveal gems set among rotting black gums.

"We speak the language of dreams."

It takes every ounce of Vorn's hormones to meet that infected gaze.

The bladed arms pull Vorn into a tight, dusty embrace.

Although Grays lack tongues strong enough to form words, they have lungs that breathe deeply, capable of pushing wind past their lips.

They can still scream.

CHAPTER 14

HUMAN CURIOSITY #7,641: STAIRS.
Even though I have trained extensively for earth's gravity and its confusing structures, my legs can only carry me so fast across a house not meant for the small strides of a Gray. Clutching the tetrahedron, I scurry up the basement stairs, then float down the hall. I push off a wall, aiming for the kitchen and the door beyond. I open a dozen thought tunnels at once and I feel collective minds recoiling in the cloud far above. My ideas are discordant and panicked.

"There's something on board the ship!" I inform my colleagues. *"Initiate quarantine. Start with the research chambers and isolate the twins from all synaptic systems. They need to be cut off from the Overmind."*

Tenzin skitters and follows along, his mind shoving its way into my own. I give him a fast update, then I push him out. I need total clarity in these moments.

"What do you mean isolate us?" Elex asks. *"We've seen no sign of viral contagion."*

"Yes, yes," Nivex echoes. *"No reason at all."*

"Jin'qua, hold on a moment," Rygell replies and I can sense a dozen colors in her thoughts. A nervous cyan. A blundering copper. The rising violet hue of indecision. *"We all saw what you did. It's just. . . I'm not following your logic."*

"No logic at all," Elex adds. *"We still have many organs to analyze."*

"Yes, yes, many organs," Elex adds. *"The appendix, for example. What is its purpose? And why is the patriarch missing his?"*

I wave my hand and the backdoor flies open, the midnight air cool and fragrant. A raccoon scurries from the Greenburg's garden as frogs sing in the darkness. Behind me, Tenzin slips on pea stones and gravel.

"Jin'qua's lost it," Ciron thinks. *"Too much human intrusion."*

I try to focus, but conflicting thoughts congeal in my mind, a dozen Grays overlapping. My brain swells against the soft plates of my skull. Even the tetrahedron feels heavy in my nervous grip.

An open doorway. . .

A miscount of life forms. . .

Oh Shy'ran, what have we done?

I try to amplify my instructions over the discordance.

"Have everyone check in," I tell them. *"I repeat: have everyone check in but stay at their posts. Do not allow free passage through the ship. I'm bringing an object for analysis."*

"Just wait a moment," Rygell instructs. *"This is a breach of decorum, Jin'qua. You're not issuing commands here."*

I ignore her. *"Quilla, are you at Archives?"*

"Y-yes, Jin'qua. I am."

Her thoughts carry a shivering timber that I've rarely sensed; yellow and maroon all intermixed with a nervous ochre. A mental backsplash: Quilla, wandering among the mind crystals of the ship. All of our research stored and glowing and ready for the long voyage home. All that precious history at her fingers.

"Run a deep query, Quilla. Search human knowledge. I'm relaying a clear memory now."

I'm overloaded with thoughts, so I bifurcate my consciousness. In one half, my body continues to run across the grass toward the extraction point. In the other half, my mind reverses time until I'm turning the tetrahedron in my hands. I send Quilla images of the symbols on all sides.

As I pass the pond, my mind reunifies to an assaulting torrent of confusion. Fear is infecting the others. Good. Because if what I hold in my hand is empty—

A pause of mental silence as Rygell pulls me into a private tunnel, our two thoughts intertwined. *"Jin'qua, I'm not sure what you're doing, but we have procedures. You were instructed to report to me directly, not incite a riot. Debrief the council upon arrival, do you understand?"*

I don't answer. In twenty steps I am at the extraction point, beneath that single cloud so high above. While Rygell's thoughts probe my own, I open a new connection with my partners.

"Brellin? I need you to prep the gravity lift, now. Soru—"

"I'm here."

"—isolate all bio-support systems. Neural nexus, metabolics, hemodynamics—everything. Have the twins reassemble the Greenburgs, and remove them from the ship. The Greenburgs, not the twins."

I am being unclear, rushed, but my hearts are struggling to provide enough nutrients for high-level thought. I'll be going into methatropysis soon, metabolizing stored hydrocarbons to produce alternative energy.

"Brellin?"

"Gravity lift incoming."

Tenzin stumbles to the extraction point just as the silver beam sweeps over the grass and locks onto us. Pebbles and twigs rise. Then comes the deep breath and we are pulled up, blasting through the cool air.

It will be roughly eight earth minutes before we're back in the ship, each second critical. I turn my focus back to Rygell, but she's no longer berating me for bypassing protocol or my lack of decorum.

Instead, I sense confusion in her mind. I tunnel into her ocular systems and peer out through her eyes. She is in the Cerebral Command Cortex; the council assembling for an emergency session. They are all turning as someone enters the chamber.

A Gray whose duties keep him to the depths of the ship.

Engineer Vorn.

And there's something wrong with him.

CHAPTER 15

THRUMMING WITH A nervous energy that hasn't been felt since the maiden voyage, the Cerebral Command Cortex admits the last of the high council. Speckled by the glow of navigational charts and flickering neurons, Gray bodies skitter into position. They connect synaptic tendrils and collate information, this seamless hive mind now fragmented by doubt. One emergency session is bad luck. Two is a budding crisis.

"The numbers don't align," M'ka thinks, her eyes scanning the ship's records. *"Seven hominids present, yet now our sensors detect eight life forms aboard. Was it three or four counted in the basement?"*

"Such numbers confuse me," Gee thinks.

A squelch interrupts deliberations as the chamber's sphincter dilates. Vorn stumbles in, his movements jerky and erratic, even for a Gray of his genetics and function.

"Engineer?" Rygell thinks. *"This is no place for a 39."*

The council's shared mind shimmers. Why isn't he responding?

Rygell reaches out, her thoughts probing the rogue engineer. *"Vorn? What are you—"*

Static. Nothing but crackling, empty static where Vorn's thoughts should be.

From behind Rygell's eyes, I try to intervene and warn her. Yet her will is strong and she pushes me back. I can only observe as she moves to intercept the errant visitor.

"Engineer Vorn, explain your presence!"

Vorn's mouth opens wide, wider, too wide for a Gray's anatomy. Something stretches and pushes past his thin lips. One pink bubble. Two pink bubbles. Each fleshy and growing larger and larger. Twisting and gasping faster and faster, Vorn falls to his knees as the twin sacks inflate and rise. Connected by a wet tube, the respiration engineer gasps his last breath as his eyes turn upward to the floating organs he intimately knows.

His lungs.

They float above him, tethered to his wide-open mouth.

Then, they burst.

The explosion of hot breath scatters fragments of jawbone and tooth, shredding the navigation aquarium and sending gillyfish flopping to the floor. The shrapnel opens wounds along the soft roof of the chamber. It cleaves Gray skin, wounding and maiming. Most of all, it spreads a plume of sand that swirls and darkens the room.

Those not wounded by the shards rub their blinded eyes. Dust is a nearly forgotten sensation to those who don't leave the ship. The council members clumsily wipe particles away. They issue commands, ordering the chamber to purge itself.

For a moment, it does.

The sand settles. The navigation tank seals itself up. The containment veins, those not severed completely, begin mending each other.

Yet something remains.

In the center of the sand, Vorn's body twitches. A glint of curved metal rises from beneath his ruined jaw. Another bursts from his pelvis. With a sickening crunch, they twist and turn until a seam splits the corpse in half.

The council stares, frozen in horror, as something rises from the remains. No familiar Gray anatomy greets them. Instead, it is the broad shoulders and strong back of a hominid. It steps up and out, shedding the Gray's flesh, somehow larger than what contained it. It rises as if merely climbing out of a hole.

"Ah, behold the architects of this curious vessel," a masculine voice rumbles. "I've stood among many wizened chambers in my time. I've answered the dreams of Sanhedrin and Duma and Imperial Jade Courts. But this so-called council of yours? It's truly. . .disappointing."

A dozen beady eyes stare back, taking in this intruder and his catalog of horrors.

How rivulets of sand pour down his bronze back. How his bones crick as his spine and he turns to the council. His robe of flesh and his chains and his rings. The beard that sways and sizzles, as if every hair ends in a spark.

It is the man's hands, however, that stir the deepest panic.

His forearms end in two fusions of stitched flesh, broken bone, and gleaming metal; twin sickles dripping with blood.

Even watching from within Rygell's mind, I am struck numb. I sense her summoning every ounce of bravery.

"Who are you?" she asks. *"And what do you want?"*

A grin spreads across a face that looks carved from ancient stone. Gold lips open, revealing a mouthful of precious gems, each cut to a point. "Oh, I have been gifted many names by somnolent tongues," he says. "Fear crafter. Reaper of sleep. That Man of Boogey who dwells deep in the closest. I am Noctus Khan. In the grand tapestry nightmares, I am an unbroken thread. You, my open-eyed dreamers, have woven me into this fabric. Now will I weave my work into yours."

With a simple lift of his wrists and a twist of the curved blades, a haze blooms behind him and sweeps over the chamber. It crackles and sizzles. It lays a translucent glimmer across every surface and curve. It settles into the very motes and the molecules that comprise the Command Cortex.

The chamber—already living—bursts with twisted new life.

Eyes wink open along the ceiling. Lips split the walls in silent screams. Upon the floor, human fingers unfurl and scratch at the bare ankles of the council.

I know what will happen. From behind Rygell's eyes, I witness it in the shocked mental silence.

Chaos erupts. Unused to physical confrontation, the Gray council scatters in panic. Jorun trips over his own feet, crashing into a neural pillar. Lyra presses herself against the far wall, her thoughts a jumble of terror and confusion. M'ka and Gee grab each other, cowering and crawling away as the nightmare man draws closer.

A glint of metal and a swing of the blade cleaves Jorun so smoothly he barely registers what has happened. He takes three steps backward, thinking the bronze man might have missed—until his abdomen splits open, and he falls in two separate pieces. While the council scatters and hides, he tries to put himself back together, but the shock overtakes him. His three fingers twitch once, and his proboscis falls limp.

It happens faster and faster, blurs of skin and blade too fast to track. The man swings and pirouettes, laughing and leaping. He moves with such violent grace that I can hardly keep up.

Worst of all is the cruel delight that he takes in his dance.

He clips Gee at the knee but lets her crawl for a moment.

He hacks at M'ka, cackling as each limb falls away.

He hoists Lyra up like a child, impaling her on the ceiling's luminescent stalactites. He bends the tip with his forearm, leaving her hanging to watch the carnage unfolding below.

Screams reverberate through the Overmind: thoughts cut off with the swish of metal, the bite of vibrant teeth.

From within Rygell's panic-struck mind, I try to warn her. All of us do. We are passengers, our thoughts a discordant stampede.

"Run. Get out. He's behind you now."

I force my thoughts above the others. My brain swells. My skull trembles. I have only one idea to communicate before I blackout, and it takes every neuron to push it through.

"Initiate lockdown."

The thought tunnel tightens and my brain shudders. From behind Rygell's eyes, I watch as she turns and skitters away. I can only hope that she understood.

At twice the size of a Gray, the man somehow moves with a feral liquidity. Whipping his sickle arms around, a storm of sand gives his feet speed until he's running along a shifting dirt path. He beheads Gee with a downward stroke as he passes. An upward slash, and pieces of Lyra fall from the ceiling.

Rygell looks back in time to see it; a sandstorm and its human master. Golden dirt twists and turns, forming a serpentine curve. It rises.

Through her eyes, I can see a hood opening, then two eyes and mouth. A sandy cobra, its jaw widening and its teeth sharpening and—

Rygell presses her hand on the cortex console, her thoughts exuding a bright white command: *"Initiate lockdown."*

The chamber shakes, a dozen bone plates descending. The sphincters tighten and constrict. Even the luminescence dims, turning the room into a cavern of pain.

In her final moments, I watch through Rygell's eyes as the sand snake rises. I remember one of our trips to earth, two or three cycles ago, where I bumped a rock in the Greenburg's garden and something squirmed out. Rygell had been watching through my eyes that night and her mental scream shook my senses.

Of the many organisms on this planet, snakes scared her the most.

The sandy serpent crashes down upon Rygell, a slicing column that tears skin from muscle and crushes bone under its weight. The grains find every soft crevice and fold. Where none existed, it carves out new ruts. I feel it all; the empathetic backsplash of her nociceptors and pain pathways firing through her body, through the Overmind, and through each of us, all of us connected and screaming.

The sand slowly clears, leaving its dusty hue across the dim chamber. From Rygell's broken perspective, we all look up at this man-thing as he carves and cuts a distant object. With his bladed hand, he hoists something up.

Jorun.

Or rather, just his face.

He presses it to his robe, where the skin embraces it, one more sleeping face among the collection.

"Your ship is impressive," Noctus Khan says, and leans over Rygell. "A vessel forged of dreams, yes? Even I hadn't considered building such a craft."

The council is gone. Our seniors are slain. And now, as Noctus Khan leans closer until his visage booms through Rygell's dying senses. I realize that he's not talking to her. He's talking to all of us watching.

"However, I think I'm going to take over."

It is the last thing he says to us, but not the last thing he does. He lets Rygell live long enough to witness the cutting and peeling.

Then he adds her face to his collection.

CHAPTER 16

Partial Transcript of *Coast to Coast AM with Art Bell*. August 8th 1996

Art Bell: Welcome back to Coast to Coast AM folks, I'm Art Bell. We're continuing late into the night with Harold Greenburg, who claims to have had multiple encounters with aliens. Now Harold, you've developed some interesting theories. Want to bring us up to speed?

Harold Greenburg: It's pretty simple Art, and it concerns travel—

Art Bell: Travel, right? You're speculating that wormholes—an Einstein-Rosen bridge—well, they aren't what we think. They're actually part of what you call a "dream network." Care to explain that?

Harold Greenburg: Sure, Art. I believe what we think of as wormholes are more like "dream pockets." These pockets are nodes on a larger network that binds the universe together in nine dimensions. When we dream, we're not just experiencing random images; we're tapping into this network.

Art Bell: When we dream, we're traveling? That's a pretty wild claim.

Harold Greenburg: It's ironic, but humans are most awake when we're asleep.

Art Bell: And you're saying that dreaming is actually connecting us to this nine-dimensional network?

Harold Greenburg: Absolutely. The most powerful substance in the universe isn't splitting atoms or fusing hydrogen, but what's inside our minds. Our consciousness, especially when we dream, can access this dark matter. It's why our ancestors, who spent more time in darkness and shadows, dreamed more vividly and—

Art Bell: Hold on. You're saying humans are evolving in the wrong direction because we don't dream as much?

Harold Greenburg: In a sense. With artificial lighting, our dreams have weakened. Our mental muscles have slowed down. Aliens, what some call little gray men, use these dream pockets to travel vast distances.

Art Bell: Harold, this flies in the face of everything we understand about UFOs and alien encounters. You're saying all our current knowledge is just. . .wrong?

Harold Greenburg: Not wrong, just incomplete. Our understanding doesn't account for the true nature of subjectivity. These beings, they aren't using physical technology as we know it. They're using the power of their minds, navigating through dream states and

altering reality at an atomic level. It's
no coincidence that maps of the universe
mirror the neuronal networks in our minds.

Art Bell: So instead of fuel they use,
what, their thoughts?

Harold Greenburg: Maybe they're one and the
same.

Art Bell: They think, therefore they are?
C'mon.

Harold Greenburg: Look, our ancestors, they
turned to shamans or invoked hallucinations
to harvest ideas. For thousands of years,
the most revered humans weren't the ones
with the most money or the nicest car. They
were the oracles in the temples or the magi
off in some cave.

Art Bell: I have to admit, it's a tricky
bridge to cross, even for this show. But I
have one question for you, Harold. If
dreams are so powerful, what happens if
these aliens have nightmares?

Harold Greenburg: (pauses) You know, Art,
I. . . I've never thought of that. I really
don't know.

Art Bell: Well, that's certainly something
to ponder. We'll be right back after these
messages. Don't go anywhere, folks.

CHAPTER 17

ONE FACT ABOUT GRAYS: we're all brain and no brawn. A million generations ago, our genetics followed a new evolutionary branch. Arteries redirected blood flow to fresh parts of our bodies and our skulls softened to accommodate our swelling brains. Muscles atrophied as neural density multiplied. We had little need for physical strength when we could fuse molecules or reverse gravity with a thought. We built the Overmind to synchronize our intentions. *I* became *us*, and *me* became *we*.

The upside is that we've explored dimensions hominid minds will never comprehend. We've built relay stations in the hearts of black holes.

Sometimes, when I need advice, I rewind our collective memory. I walk with my long-dead great-grandmother beside the purple beaches of her youth. I seek wisdom from a woman I never physically met.

The downside is that Grays are easily broken. And when we're broken, we collectively panic.

"Doom! Death! Destruction! Shy'ran forgive us, we're lost to the void!"

"What do we do what do we do what do we do what do we do?"

"Oh wise Overmind, protect us. Oh sweet Broodlord, forgive us. Oh Great Star Council, guide us homeward."

After arriving back on the ship with Tenzin, we assembled as much of the crew as we could gather. We take refuge in the lower observatory, far from the massacre of the council. For now, this domed chamber offers protection and an odd realization. This is the first time many of us have shared a proximal space since we set off.

It does little to lessen the group's panic.

The Overmind, disconnected since the lockdown, is deafening in its total silence. I give myself a moment to examine the facts. We're alone in this cloud.

"Tenzin, we need to focus," I communicate privately. *"We're scared, but our thoughts need realignment."*

While the others pace nervously, Tenzin pauses by a collection of tongue chairs. Normally, we recline upon them; watching the stars streak past while they licked at our backs. Now, we're too confused. Fear is leading to inaction. Inaction will kill us. I need to break him out of his rumination loop.

"You were right." I make sure my thought is strong enough for the others to perceive it. I repeat it, adding, *"About the numbers, Tenzin. Earlier, you were right."*

"What?" A clarity returning to his inky eyes as he stops pacing. He hasn't even taken off his gravity chrysalis yet, and suddenly it seems to bother him. He picks at it, one scab at a time. *"That's not funny, Jin'qua. Now's not the time."*

For a moment, he just glares at me. We can still hear the council's screams echoing in the mental silence. I am reminded that Brellin and Soru haven't checked in. In this moment, every cell in my gravity-fatigued body wishes someone else would take over for me. Yet no one does.

"In the house," I continue, *"you sensed four presences, yes? I corrected you, and you put it aside. But you were right, Tenzin. Even if there wasn't evidence, your senses were strong."*

It's not much, perhaps a compliment given too late. Yet a hush passes through the observatory. My'nar is no longer curled in a fetal position, superstitious prayers running wild through his mind. Zir'xa has stopped begging for orders from a council that no longer exists.

"I thought I miscounted," Tenzin conveys. *"It wasn't the first time, either. The council had me on remediation. At the end of this cycle, I was to be relieved unless. . . Well, in a way we were both right and wrong."*

"Agreed."

I help him peel the last scab of the chrysalis from his shoulder. Although we have been thinking quietly, the nearby Grays are now focused on us. Good. Because if their minds are steady, we can work together.

Maybe we can even come up with a plan.

"The council is gone," I announce. *"We are leaderless and this is most frightening, I know. And we'll need to know what we're up against. But first, we need to see where we stand."*

"Where we stand?" My'nar inquires, as her gaze scours the scaled floor underfoot.

"It's a human expression," Tenzin interjects, and I sense warmth in his words. *"It means a status check of the situation"*

"This situation?" Zir'xa's thoughts echo with disbelief. *"If we're quoting humans then I'd say we're fucked. Whatever that thing is, it doesn't move like any hominid we've ever studied."*

"No, not like anything we've studied," I agree, following my nervous thoughts until a surprising epiphany flashes through my brain. *"However, there's a lot we've never studied. A lot we never knew about, right?"*

My tired body drifts, circling the observatory. I chase errant memories, sharing them so my colleagues can follow my logic. Studies, yes. We've made quite a few.

I ask, *"Tenzin, you remember the first time we went on site together? What year was it?"*

His head ripples as he scratches his sore temple. *"Earth year? 1955."*

"That was Kentucky, the Sutton family, right? We almost got shot."

Zir'xa shudders. *"What's your thesis, Jin'qua?"*

"Grays have been visiting this planet for fifty thousand Earth years," I think. *"Yet we didn't anticipate a neighbor's barking dog."*

I can see a few of my colleagues blinking, their minds retracing previous missions. I push on.

"My'nar, you were part of the survey in '47. Roswell, was it?"

I sense embarrassing mental backsplash at the name. My'nar bows her head. *"A complete disaster."*

"A disaster," I agree. *"But not a complete one. Most of your team made it out and returned home."*

She nods, a smile forming on her thin lips. Grays had been warned about engaging with human armed forces, but the progress they'd made with rockets and jets caught our species off guard. One of the reasons we use cloud cover now.

"And Zir'xa," I continue, *"what happened in the Soviet Union on your first survey?"*

"Russia," Zir'xa corrects. *"That's what it's called now. We were testing new neuromatrons. What the hominids call robots, yes? Our unit caught latent radiation from a nuclear. The neuromatron malfunctioned in Voronezh and wandered into a park. We had to stun ray children and wipe their minds in the recovery."*

Then, a curious thing; laughter. Just a hint of amusement rings among our connected thoughts.

"I saw that in the archive crystals," Tenzin adds. *"Rygell projected a three-meter monster and scared the kids off."*

"A perfect adjustment," I add. *"They still study it in training."*

It feels odd to discuss her in the past tense. Rygell, who oversaw security for several Earth centuries. Rygell, who sensed numeric discrepancy and had the presence of mind to look deeper. Rygell, who screamed like the others when that aberration came for her.

Noctus Khan...

"My thesis is this," I continue. *"Each of those incidents involved an unforeseen variable. Fighter jets or radioactive interference or a dog that caught our scent. But we overcame them. We learned and improved. Every Gray is wiser for the knowledge we harvested. After all, isn't that why we're here?"*

An uncomfortable beat of mental silence as they turn it over in their minds. Maybe they're right. Maybe it is like the humans say. Maybe we're fucked.

The agreement comes from Tenzin first, a wave of blue that bolsters my biochemicals and gives firmness to my posture. My'nar's acceptance joins in, a nervous push. Zir'xa sits on the tongue chair, running a hand down the soft edges while looking up. Beyond the bone dome above, thousands of stars twinkle through a gap in the mist, their numbers comfortably vast.

"You want us to learn," Zir'xa thinks. *"But what can we learn from that monster?"*

It's a good question. The best question, really. As I turn the stone tetrahedron over, I have no answer to give.

But I know someone who might.

CHAPTER 18

THREE FLOORS, 280 paces, and four sealed emergency sphincters away, Ciron and Quilla are hastily rescuing the archive crystals from a most unusual contamination: sand.

The sand leaks from the ceiling in thin, wispy tendrils. The sand oozes in from the respiration pores that constricted in lockdown. The sand rises between the preservation sockets, scratching the soft, gooey ports that hold the ship's precious data in crystalline form.

With quick gestures and jerking tugs, Ciron and Quilla unsocket crystal after crystal, placing them on high bony shelves, safe for the moment.

Still, the sand comes in.

"It won't stop," Quilla thinks. *"Whatever this is, it's in the ship's fabric."*

Ciron salvages a flickering crystal. *"And where's the sterilization team when you need them?"*

There's a buzz as a tunnel opens up in Quilla's panicked mind. Jin'qua's familiar thoughts flood her senses.

They are with several other survivors, Jin'qua informs her.

The senior council is dead.

There is someone or some*thing* on this ship they do not understand.

These are the facts as presented.

"Are you following me Quilla?" they ask. *"It's important that you focus. You're still in the archives?"*

"Yes, we're here," Quilla thinks. *"But I don't know how much longer. Just. . .wait a moment."*

She brushes sand from one of the older crystals, fat and sparkling with datum. She pulls it out of the socket as the contaminant rises. With a stretch of her multijointed arm, she passes it to Ciron, who is encysting them for preservation in groups of seventeen.

"The whole place is a mess, Jin'qua; an absolute disaster for storage. We're going to lose entire decades. And I can't reach half the ship. It's like the Overmind—"

"It's in lockdown," Jin'qua informs her. *"That's procedure. Single thought tunnels only. If it's a mental contagion, less chance to spread."*

"Ask them how we're supposed to get out?" Ciron's question cuts through the queue and spikes Quilla's mind with insistent maroon. *"They might have mastered oxygen, but I don't think they can breathe sand."*

Quilla nudges a dusty mound aside. Ciron is right, she realizes. It was only at her toes a moment ago. Now it's up to her ankles. She sends the question off, feeling like some sort of relay station in the interstellar void.

"I'll confer with the others," Jin'qua responds.

A pause of mental silence. Ciron waves his hand as his proboscis binds the crystals in protective casing. And what was that bizarre symbol they wanted to query? Too much to do and keep safe. . .

Jin'qua returns, his thoughts carrying a trace of My'nar's knowledge. *"There's a sinus canal that should connect to our location,"* they inform her. *"It'll be at foot level, opposite the vertebrae. Do you see it?"*

"Confirmed." Like many things passed daily, Quilla has stopped noticing the patterns of routine. Here it is, a sinus cavity by a nerve junction. It's tight, but unmarred by sandy contagion. In fact, with each palpitation, nearby dust is expelled further away.

"I sent you memories of that tetrahedron," Jin'qua continues. *"Have you referenced them yet?"*

"Referenced? No. But I've pulled all instances and transferred them for retrieval. There are five thousand references, but—"

"No, no no!" Ciron conveys, so strongly Jin'qua is ejected from her mind.

Spinning, Quilla spots the senior archivist's source of fear. Near the far wall, where the elder crystals sit within their nourishing sockets—their epochal knowledge the richest treasures of the ship—sand pours in through an ulcerating hole. Quilla's hearts race and her body tenses.

"It's falling!"

With a dry spurt, the falling sand displaces a great elder crystal, nudging it free from the socket, and now—horror of all horrors—it teeters and loosens.

"Catch it," Ciron thinks.

There are no words in modern Gray linguistics for one who destroys information, willfully or otherwise. The act is so rare and vulgar—so *unthinkable*—that such a definition has simply fallen out of the lexicon.

"Catch it!"

Quillia's genetic memory shrieks as the socket loosens. She can see it now; the first Gray to have lost an elder crystal and all its precious data. She will be exiled, lobotomized, cut off from the Overmind, and sent to wander the galaxy, far from the Shy'ran and its infinite libraries.

"CATCH IT!"

Tilting, leaning, loosening. . . With a nudge of insidious sand, the elder crystal tumbles from the socket. As it falls, Quilla's eyes take in the totality of its knowledge, each facet shimmering with human achievements and failures and so much for which she has yet to learn.

Falling. . .

Falling. . .

And then the elder crystal lands. Not on the abrasive sand overtaking the archive, nor on the floor that would shatter it. It touches upon the soft flesh of her palm as Quilla's body crashes sideways and her arms pull it into a tight, gentle embrace.

"Oh oh oh." Ciron's chest heaves as his mind exudes a starburst of relief.

Shoulders scuffed and bleeding, Quilla's momentum stops at the edge of the archive. Although she cannot speak, she makes a clicking noise and exhales.

"I don't know what I would have done," Ciron informs her. *"I suppose I'd have killed you myself."*

They share a mental laugh for a moment, the elder crystal safe in her arms. The infectious sand seems almost a world away.

That's when Quilla notices the aberration.

A moment ago, there was only a mound of quartz or gypsum, feldspar or various carbonate, and clay minerals behind Ciron. But now it has taken impossible form: a long, hominid arm ending in wormy fingers. The last of the sand falls away, revealing bronze flesh infused with gems, not unlike the precious crystals in this archive.

"Ciron, behind you. Look!"

The thought arrives too late. The bronze arm somehow bends the wrong way. Covetous fingers curl around a crystal. With a tug, it pries it from the socket and swings it down in a violent arc.

Two cracks reverberate: the shattering of crystal and the breaking of bone.

Ciron stumbles to the side, left arm hanging limp as his right hand paws at his temple. Where the soft skull plates meet rippled flesh, shards of purple crystal protrude. Dozens of cracks leak eons of data.

Then a voice speaks. "All this knowledge and you fools hoard it like gold. I had hoped your kind would be less greedy than the kings I have conquered. Perhaps you should live in history instead."

With a twitching eye in the throes of seizure, Ciron takes a step forward. Another step. *"Quilla. . .he-he-help me. It's s-s-so. . .much."*

Ciron's eyes, Quilla realizes. They're no longer black.

"I c-c-can. . .see. . .ev-ery-thing. I am. . .ALL OF IT!"

His mouth drops open as human noises leave his lips. With each blink of his eyes, images flash, projected from within against the soft backside of his once-black pupils. A quickening tempest of all gathered knowledge.

Somehow, he speaks, *"Por favor, no me vuelvas a poner con las ratas. Me convertiré a vuestro Dios, lo prometo!"*

Staring at her twitching colleague, horror racks Quilla's body. She recognizes the shape of the crystal and the deep color. Most of all, the contents of its data.

Circular wounds bloom across Ciron's body—gunshots. He lacks a tongue, yet impossibly he still screams out, *"Und wenn ich ein Jude bin? Ich bin dein Freund, Otto, erinnerst du dich? Bitte, leg die Waffe weg."*

No, that is not an elder crystal embedded in his skull, Quilla realizes, but something much worse. It's a sensory vessel of wars and conflicts, violent betrayals and torture. A full catalog of human atrocities. And Ciron is experiencing them now, all at once.

"Mother, I am no witch!" he mewls. *"I beseech thee, please do not burn me!"*

He bursts into flames.

In a methane-rich environment, fire burns blue and moves in like a living tornado. Quilla has only seconds and she knows this. She grabs a stack of crystals and skitters to the sinus canal. She throws herself into the puckering, tight depths as heat curls her toes.

The heat abates as she crawls further into the slimy depths.

Thoughts claw at her mind—a chaotic jumble of human languages, some still spoken, most long dead and forgotten. Quilla has studied a few; Ciron, too. Yet there, amid the chorus of words, she discerns his voice.

"Vær så snill, ikkje la meg bli verande slik!"

Please don't leave me like this!

She crawls on, deeper, severing the connection and crying to herself. Yes, Ciron is experiencing it *all*. And a part of her understands he will experience it *forever*.

CHAPTER 19

HUMAN CURIOSITY **#7,798:** they favor alternating patterns for facts—good news, bad news. They tuck complaints between false compliments. Since data is data, its curated delivery seems strange to most Grays.

Given our current situation, though, I figure now is a good time to try.

"*The good news,*" I inform the others, "*is that Quilla had the tetrahedronic data I requested and was en route when we last connected.*"

The bad news. Ciron's agony floods every mind channel. Tenzin and I can barely confer without his pleas for death overriding our thoughts.

"NO NO NO! DON'T LOCK ME IN WITH THE SCORPIONS, I BEG YOU!"

"*And worse,*" I strain to explain, "*that thing that attacked the council is moving through the ship's lymphatic system.*"

"*You mean it's coming for us?*" My'nar shudders. "*Is that what you're suggesting?*"

"*How close?*" Tenzin inquires. "*Any ETA?*"

"*Unclear.*" I pace, scanning the observatory, but nothing appears amiss. The high, fleshy walls are a healthy pink; the skeletal superstructure, a firm purple. "*Quilla believes it's contained in the archives for now. But she's gone silent, so. . .*"

The implication sinks in. Grays rarely disconnect without reason; the mental silence is unpleasant, like holding our breath.

"*Because she's probably dead,*" Zir'xa's thoughts flash in an unnerving maroon.

"S'IL VOUS PLAÎT!" Ciron cuts in. "JE VOUS DIRAI OÙ SONT LES TRAÎTRES, ARRÊTEZ DE ME COUPER!"

I rub my neck, nerves swollen from cognitive exertion. My head feels like it might pop. I remind myself I trained to breathe Earth's toxic air and endure its gravitational compression. Maybe I can resist this fear crushing us.

"*What about the others?*" My'nar asks. "*Research? Navigation? Transportation and logistics?*"

"*Nothing,*" I inform them.

"*They're probably dead, too,*" Zir'xa thinks.

"*Or they're following protocol,*" Tenzin surprisingly rebuts. "*Directive five ninety-seven: With the bone plates lowered and lockdown in effect, the Overmind pings outward. The relays echo our distress call. Help could be on the way.*"

"*Could be?*" Zir'xa repeats. "*How long would it take?*"

We turn to My'nar, the only one with experience being stranded. She hesitates, so I send her an encouraging green nudge.

"*At Roswell, it took only. . .*" She wipes a dormant polyp on the wall. "*Seventeen Earth weeks, I believe.*"

"*Seventeen. . .*" Zir'xa's head lowers, body slumping. "*We're definitely dead.*"

"VÍS MISKUNN! ÉG MUN GEFA ÞÉR LAND MITT, AUÐÆFI MÍN—ALLT SEM ÞÚ VILT. BARA ÞYRMDU BÖRNUNUM MÍNUM, ÉG BIÐ ÞIG."

"*Shut up,*" My'nar thinks, as Ciron's pleas echo through our mind channels. "*Just die already, please.*"

She squeezes the dormant polyp, tearing it from the wall's dermis. But the mental agony remains.

I mask my frustration, but our worry is becoming contagious. Idle minds are fertile ground for fear. I'm about to assign my colleagues a task when it happens: a familiar tingle lights up my mind, and my hearts race with joy.

"*Brellin?*"

"*Jin'qua, we've been trying to find you.*" Her thoughts are faint and frightened, tinged with gangrenous hues. "*We've gone. . .deep inside. It's. . .hard to connect.*"

I realize *we* means Soru too. A brief vision: he's behind her, pushing upward, lifting the tunnel skin so they can shimmy forward.

"*Where?*" I glimpse ribbed walls, greenish-brown and glistening, the air thick with biting odors, the floor a river of acids. A nauseating mental backsplash twists my senses.

I know where they are. The bile ducts. Crawling through the ship's waste systems.

I want to tell her I'll come help, but Brellin's mind is strong. She places me quietly behind her ocular system, so I watch as she pulls her body forward through the muck, glancing back as Soru pushes the ceiling just high enough for her to crawl.

The good news is they're closer than I thought.

The bad news: the bile will corrode their flesh if they don't hurry.

"*You can make it to us,*" I tell her. "*It's not very—*"

"*Wait!*" She retreats behind a wall of silence. I hear the hiss of acids, then: "*Something's coming.*"

To her right, a narrow slit between folds opens, revealing a second tunnel. Brellin is correct, something is pushing through.

"*Jin'qua, what's happening?*" Tenzin's inquiry jolts me back to the observatory. "*Tell me our Brellin's okay.*"

Our Brellin?

It's just a question, but the intensity of his concern spikes my systems. I knew he cared for her, but the depth of it staggers me. He's hidden this from us. I'm not the only one who's picked up human traits.

They call it love, and Tenzin is full of it.

"*It's purely professional,*" he insists. "*She carries an ovum—*"

"SCALD ME, O FATHER! MINE FLESH IS WICKED, AND ONLY BLESSED OILS CAN MELT THIS VILE SKIN! YES YES! POUR IT—AAAAAGH!"

"*Shut up,*" My'nar thinks. "*Shut up! SHUT UP AND DIE!*"

We're losing ourselves to fear. I instruct Tenzin to keep order while I transmit information. I must also help Brellin and Soru.

I bifurcate my mind.

In one half, I relay what I see. In the other, I return behind Brellin's eyes. She hides as the slit in the bile duct stretches, widening. With a pop, something spills out between her and Soru.

"*Be careful!*" I warn her. "*It's behind you. It's—*"

Then I see it. Or rather, *her.*

Quilla rises from the muck, clutching a bundle of memory crystals as the slit closes. Luck has found us. Half my consciousness relays the good news to Tenzin; the other half confers with Brellin.

"*Have Quilla bring us the data,*" I inform Brellin. "*Carefully now. Follow the ducts about 100 paces, then turn left.*"

"*Ninety-four paces,*" Soru corrects. "*Or did you forget I worked excretion for two cycles? I know every skitter and twist.*"

I smile inwardly. No, I haven't forgotten, though my synapses are exhausted. I send an apologetic boost, deferring to Soru's experience. I release communications, a passenger behind Brellin's eyes.

My thoughts turn to our next steps. If we can secure the data crystals. If we can search human history for something useful. If. . .

I thumb the tetrahedron, reminding myself we have no choice.

One step at a time, Brellin pushes through the thick tunnels. Quilla slaps her arm as a blister forms. Soru follows, pushing the heavy tissue upward, loosening the ducts as they move.

Eighty paces.

Seventy.

Sixty.

I relay their progress to Tenzin. Through my split senses, I feel the observatory's mood lift. Their arrival could mean a chance to understand what we're up against.

Noctus Khan.

I shiver at the name.

Fifty paces.

Forty.

Thirty.

A convulsion shakes the duct walls, bile sloshes, the floor twists. As the ceiling contracts, my bifurcated mind is ejected and I stumble back, confused, the observatory swirling.

"What's happening?" Tenzin demands. *"Why did you stop?"*

A strange sense floods me, foreign to my biology yet familiar from training. Residual sturdiness tingles at my fingertips, something like stone.

I push back into Brellin's mind, peering through her eyes as a chill shivers my body.

With a twitch and stretch, the veiny walls of the bile duct fray, revealing stones beneath. Brellin's fingers trace the surface—firm, flat. The tunnel is changing around her.

"What is this?" she thinks.

Further back, a sharp stone rises from the muck, piercing the ceiling and bisecting the tunnel. An obelisk blocks half the path.

Quilla runs her hand over it, noting markings of serpents and curved symbols, a fusion of hominid and animal anatomy. The images are freshly chiseled.

"Who could design this?" Quilla thinks. *"Incredible."*

Beautiful and elegant. Metals so vibrant, my phantom hands reach out through Brellin. Captivating.

Despite the convulsions, Quilla's thoughts exude a curious blue. *"Whatever it is, it's quite lovely, don't you think?"*

I agree, yet a memory stirs. I have seen these markings before. An ancient language that once adorned the chambers of kings.

Hieroglyphs.

I recall Ciron's debriefing long ago; some human writing serves as warnings, imbued with old superstition. What was the word?

"Curse." Brellin's thought echoes mine.

"This is a curse," I tell them. *"You need to go. Hurry!"*

Then, the obelisk cracks.

The symbol Quilla was touching—a slender human form with a jackal head—peels free from the stone. Its rocky hand clasps Quilla's fingers, intertwining like a lover's grip. With a brutal tug, it pulls her into a rocky embrace.

"It's. . .so lovely. . .and old!"

I'm not sure what happens first: the fissures chewing around the jackal-headed figure or the raking of ancient stone against Gray flesh. I know only that there's a spray of blue blood and a garbled moan. Brellin averts her eyes, leaving a haunting image in my mind: the obelisk, somehow devouring Quilla.

"Go!" I instruct them. *"Run! Get out!"*

Thankfully, our minds are in sync. Brellin presses on, the duct's soft walls splitting to reveal granite etched with endless hieroglyphs. Eyes sparkle like gems, faces turning as she passes.

A flash of Soru squeezing past the obelisk where Quilla's arm protrudes, her fingers turned to stone, her body flattened and etched into that pictographic prison.

"Run!"

They skitter as fast as they can—Brellin pushing through muck, Soru close behind. Left at the first junction, right at the next, then sliding down a chute. Bile puddles froth beneath them.

The ship's organic walls give way to stone pictographs. Triangular structures with figures bowing in worship. Saucers above pyramids. Human bodies rising on beams of light. There's history here, so much to learn, yet my instincts scream to run, hurry, escape.

Another split in the duct narrows to reveal the strangest sight: a glowing hole of light with Tenzin's face peering through.

I congeal my consciousness, returning to the observatory. Tenzin has crawled to a maintenance orifice, My'nar and Zir'xa holding it open. Bile oozes as the hole prolapses. Tenzin leans in, gravity-compacted body lengthening, pulling—

A burble, then a pop, and he falls backward in a slimy torrent. Brellin tumbles out, collapsing atop him.

The stench overwhelms my senses, a sour reek twisting my insides. Yet I push through it, helping Brellin up and pulling her away.

The wall is infected—its flesh hardening, taking on the sheen of mineral and rock.

"*Help me get Soru,*" Tenzin conveys, leaning back into the hole.

"*My leg,*" Soru thinks. "*Something's entangled.*"

Through his eyes, I see stony roots rising from acidic murk, clamping down on his ankles, walls tightening.

"*It's too heavy,*" Zir'xa says. "*I can't hold it. . .any longer.*"

I wedge my fingers into the fleshy orifice, pulling wider. But I feel calcification inside; the bile ducts are—impossibly—petrifying.

Our minds panic, thoughts overlapping:

"*Get him free—*"

"*Something's coming, oh Shy'ran—*"

"*—hold on, it's tightening!*"

My fingers tremble, shoulders ache, commands assaulting my thoughts. All cohesion is gone.

Soru's thoughts cut through, sharp and focused, directed not to me but to Tenzin, echoing across our minds.

"*I'm sorry I had the Broodlord remove you,*" he thinks. "*It wasn't right. You'd have been a good father, Tenzin. Far better than me.*"

The revelation stuns me, weakening my grip. Tenzin's frustration and jealousy weren't directed at me, but at Soru and the situation. It must have hurt him deeply, working alongside us, desiring Brellin and me, yet being forced to bury it.

"*I'm stuck,*" Soru continues. "*And I'm not getting out. Go. Take them to safety.*"

I want to convey so much, but we have no time for regrets. The orifice hardens and contracts. Above us, huge sandy eyes bulge open. A face presses out from the ship's fleshy depths.

Noctus Khan is here.

"*Take the data.*" Soru shoves a bundle of crystals at us. He must have grabbed them from Quilla. "*Now let go of me, please.*"

It is his last clear thought.

With a wet pucker, stony teeth sprout along the rim and twisting ducts beyond. I recall the endless throat of a razorworm as Noctus Khan's colossal visage distends from the wall, mouth open, tilting back, and swallowing Soru whole.

He chews and chews and chews.

I don't remember if I told the others to run or if I simply fell in with them. My legs move, my body stumbles, and Soru's screams chase us deeper into the ship.

So does the laughter of Noctus Khan.

CHAPTER 20

From: Dr. Amina El-Sayed
To: Harold Greenburg
Subject: Re: Research Request

Dear Mr. Harold Greenburg,

Thank you for your inquiry regarding access to our facilities for your research. After careful consideration, we must inform you that your request for academic research privileges at the Egyptian Museum has been denied.

Despite the sensational claims made by certain American television programs, there is no evidence to support any connection between aliens and the pyramids. To insinuate such a link undermines the proud achievements and contributions of Egyptian civilization to human history and culture.

While many societies throughout history have believed in myths involving visitors from the stars, there is no legitimate historical record in our archives pertaining to extraterrestrials. Nor is there a "common thread across recorded history" as your research claims. You are welcome to visit our museum as a member of the public. Beyond that, we consider this matter closed and will not entertain further communications on this topic.

Sincerely,

Dr. Amina El-Sayed
Curator of Ancient Egyptian Antiquities
Egyptian Museum in Cairo
Cairo, Egypt

CHAPTER 21

FIRST, THERE WAS NOTHING. Then came the dream of our home, a star-warmed system nestled among the great void, mind-forged with loving precision until every atom reflected our collective intentions. We named it Shy'ran, Our Great Cradle, and oh, how it shines at the synaptic nexus we've laid across space and time.

Occasionally, when I feel alone, I look up at the sky. I let my thoughts and eyes harmonize, attuning to a delicate wavelength where Shy'ran glistens like dew-laden webs at first light. In these moments I am at ease. No matter how far my research has taken me, I am connected to a far greater purpose.

I feel little connection and purpose tonight.

Skittering through the ship's fleshy halls, my colleague's terror suffuses my neurons. I feel only base instincts: the desperate pounding of my hearts; the heaving gasp of my lungs; the ache and twitch of my muscles.

Most of all, I feel strange things underfoot.

Stone. Sand. Autotrophic lifeforms, sharp and spiny, bursting beneath my toes. Unlike the crystalline plants of our home world, these thorny vines tear at our ankles.

"*It's coming!*" Zir'xa's panicked thoughts echo out. "*I can see it. Oh, it's terraforming every inch of the ship.*"

I allow myself only a single glance back, immediately wishing I hadn't. With a wave of glittering dust, the ceiling behind us bursts and a reptilian shape rises from the sand.

A scabrous lizard with the face of Noctus Khan.

"Run, run, fast as you can, my little Gray man," his voice booms. "But the nightmare runs faster."

I push Brellin ahead, where Tenzin stretches an emergency sphincter open. Beyond it, another hall leads to the recreation chambers, where our exercise pods are showing signs of infection.

Squeezing through, I pull My'nar after me, a plume of dust hitting us both. My visual senses strain in the hazy vortex. I spot Zir'xa's shadow struggling forward. I send a message of hope.

"Zir'xa, take my hand! We're almost through."

A pair of blinking gems rise amongst the dust. I instruct Zir'xa not to turn around. To reach for me. To go forward.

Yet Zir'xa turns around.

Because a Gray mind is a delicate thing, one built upon rules and order, a universal logic that binds us together. Now, faced with the rising shadow of a lizard wearing a cruel human face, I feel Zir'xa's strained mind collapsing.

"You aren't. . . You can't be. . . How is it that you exist?"

Brellin and Tenzin's hands pull me through the door, onward. The sphincter winks shut. But not before offering a final glimpse through the swirling dust and the shadows: a lizard-thing leaping onto the awestruck Zir'xa.

"Sickles," I think. *"It had sickles for fingers."*

The recreation room abuts another passage, running deeper into the ship. The only way out is through another sphincter, sealed with bone plates from both sides. My'nar and Tenzin squeeze the polyps, but the exit remains shut.

"We're trapped," My'nar thinks. *"Overmind protect us, there's no escape."*

I scan the chamber, my hearts sinking. Storage pustules contain biological specimens: a collection of earth's rodents, insects, and amphibians. They float in their translucent compartments, tails and wings and scaly limbs, all twitching in hibernation. Sleeping peacefully for the long ride to Shy'ran.

A ride they will never take.

"What do we do?" Brellin inquires, her thoughts infected with the scent of the desert. *"Is there truly no way out?"*

"I don't know." Tenzin thinks. *"I don't know. I don't. . ."*

Yes, this is a dead end. I'm realizing Zir'xa was right; we'll never make it out. The infection worms its way toward us, the soft walls hardening, the ground bursting with cacti and vines. Obelisks rise, fang-like and endless.

"Something's happening," Brellin thinks. *"Behind us. Look!"*

The bone plates rise, unsealing the sphincter as it opens and—

"We have been trying to contact you," Elex thinks, annoyance suffusing his thoughts. *"Hurry in now."*

"Yes, yes, we have been scanning all systems," Nivex adds. *"You have been difficult to reach. Quite bothersome, indeed."*

They usher us into the sterile light of their lab. I push Brellin past me, then My'nar. Tenzin gives me a nod, holding the sphincter.

For a moment, we both look back at the infection that had chased us. That swirling mass of dust and sand. The plants blooming and the stones scratching their way out of the ship's soft, fleshy halls. In the dim light, they seem to have slowed. As if the very motes and rocks have run up against a barrier, unseen yet firm enough to send them swirling back into the depths.

"Ah, the anomalous data, splendid!" Elex takes the crystals from my hand. *"For a three, you are quite the surprise, Jin'qua. Come now, we have much to discuss."*

"Yes, yes, much data to cross-reference and check," Nivex adds. *"There we go. In. Into our lab."*

A wave of comforting air hits us as the lab opens up. Their echoing twin mental voices have always exhausted me and I often left their presence as fast as I could.

But now, in the familiar chamber with its sleeping humans, my thoughts are no longer under constant assault. Ciron's echoing misery. Soru's final scream. The council. . .

This blessed silence grows inside me, and within it, my brain savors each second.

CHAPTER 22

INSIDE THE LAB, Tenzin and My'nar barricade the entry, stacking rejuvenation pods and spare dissection nests against the sphincter. The twins, however, move slow and calm. They return to their lab, a clean picture of Gray biotech, healthy and untouched sand or stone.

"*Save your energy,*" Elex informs us. "*The anomaly won't enter our lab.*"

"*You don't know that,*" Tenzin conveys. "*That thing has taken over the whole ship.*"

"*Not the whole ship,*" Elex corrects.

"*No, no, not the whole ship, indeed.*" Nivex offers Brellin a bundle of cleansing leeches.

"*All of you, please rest for a moment.*" Elex reaches up, pulling the veiny tendrils of a food compartment. "*You require nutrients and hydration. Here, consume.*"

"*Yes, yes,*" Nivex thinks, passing out blisters of food. "*I'm sensing deficiencies in your system.*"

As the survivors catch their breath and recharge, I help Brellin clean herself. I apply leeches, their disinfecting suckers gratefully scraping the bile from her skin. What they leave behind, she wipes off with fresh sanitary moss. Tenzin skitters over, passing us a blister of tick powder to share.

"*Thank you,*" Brellin thinks, rubbing ointment on her acid-burned flesh.

Her wounds are superficial and will heal in a few cycles. My concern, however, is deeper. As she applies lotion to her stomach, my thoughts turn to her womb.

"*How is it?*" I quietly inquire. "*The ovum. Is it. . .?*"

"*Good, I think. Strong, like its father.*"

Something sad glistens at the thought of Soru. I catch Tenzin's head turning in our direction before he crawls off.

Soru. . .

As a species, we are not used to the sudden death of our mates. Where a star always shined in our shared mental constellations, there is now a void. It's as if our entire navigation has been thrown off.

"And its mind?" I nervously ask. *"The ovum, is it—"*

"Still awaiting imprint. Don't worry, Jin'qua. It'll be fine."

A soft defiance sparkles at the edge of her thoughts, redolent of spices and flaked gold. Yet there is a determination to her intentions. She offers me a reassuring mental squeeze.

She *will* get off this planet.

She *will* take our ovum home.

I try to remind myself that sometimes the quietest of a species might be the strongest.

I am about to offer her the rest of my tick powder when Elex skitters over to a dissection nest. His thoughts ring out, bright and confident, drawing our attention.

"Focus, focus. All of you. Even you, My'nar, this will take the full depth of your neural circuits."

"Yes, yes," Nivex echoes, his fingers inserting the crystals by the memory projector, one socket at a time. *"Much to collate and process. You have—"*

"Questions," Tenzin's thoughts interrupt. *"Like how'd you survive? And why isn't that thing coming in here?"*

"Two questions, indeed, conjoined by one answer." With a wave of Elex's hand, the dissection nests tilt revealing the seven members of the Greenburg family, reassembled and in stasis. Save for the residual goo of the mending worms, it's hard to imagine this family was in pieces for several hours. *"As some of you have surmised,"* Elex continues, *"the anomaly stowed away in the human subconscious, a sort of thought parasite in a larval state. What humans call a nightmare. Quite fascinating, really."*

"Hurry hurry," Nivex thinks, his fingers adjusting the crystals. *"I have much datum to convey."*

"Very well." With a flick of annoyance, Elex passes his hand over Harold Greenburg's head, the old man's silver hair prickling and rising. *"Since hominids only dream in short bursts—and since protocol dictates we avoid dissection in such mental states—the anomaly was first detected as a numerical aberration."*

"But what is it?" My'nar thinks.

"Noctus Khan," I convey. *"In the council chamber, that's what it called itself."*

"Yes, yes!" Nivex strokes the projector's cystic dials enthusiastically. *"Noctus Khan, the Dream Reaper. Our data correlates with—"*

"May I continue?" Elex's thoughts spike a frustrated white. *"Thank you. Given the anomaly's environment—a ship built of dreams and a species of higher mental awareness—this Noctus Khan has taken corporeal form. Rather powerfully, I might add."*

"Yes, quite powerful indeed!"

"Thus, here in lies the other half of your query, Tenzin," Elex continues. *"Because our hominid subjects are not dreaming, the anomaly cannot affect change. Proximity reduces potency."* Elex presses his finger against old Harold's wrinkled forehead. *"These simple human minds have provided us with something of a buffer; quite lucky in fact."*

"Yes, yes, a zone of respite," Nivex thinks. *"We have tested this extensively during the lockdown. All aberrant manifestations collapse roughly forty-seven strides from the Greenburgs."*

My mind spins with the implications. That sand in the hallway curling and fading. Like a creeping mold clashing against an anti-fungal agent, then retreating.

"So, we're safe?" My'nar thinks. *"Thank the Overmind. Now we just stay here, wait for rescue, right?"*

I am no navigator, yet I start crunching the numbers: time dilation, the distance to the nearest interstellar outpost, our limited supplies. Assuming we allow ourselves to dehydrate and hibernate, the outcome is grim.

The twins are far smarter, and I realize they've made such calculations already. *"If only it were that simple,"* Elex thinks, running a hand over Lucas. The boy looks almost peaceful. *"Unfortunately, we're a research vessel, woefully understocked for long-term human nutrition. With the systems infected, our lab can only keep these subjects in stasis for a few hours."*

"If that," Nivex adds.

"The subjects?" My'nar scoffs. *"Who cares. We encyst ourselves, await rescue."*

"I told you she would be slow," Elex thinks, his thoughts a smug shade of green. *"Sixty-fives struggle with cause and effect."*

"Yes, brother," Nivex says. *"You were quite correct."*

The humans. Noctus Khan. The ship's failing systems. I'm not as slow as My'nar, but it's still a chore to make the connection. When it finally clicks, my body shudders. *"If the Greenburgs leave stasis, they commence dreaming."*

"That is one possibility," Elex responds.

"Yes, yes. And the other is that they wake up." With his long, precise fingers, Nivex brushes hair from Emma's face and opens her eyelids. A dim pupil stares back, unresponsive for now. *"In both situations, the proximal buffer collapses. Noctus Khan will gain full access to the lab."*

"And when our rescue teams arrive. . ."

The thought is too terrible for Elex to finish, and I sense his mental defenses bristling. Still, I catch a splash of his fear: Noctus Khan—this creature fueled by the power of lucid dreams—now making his way to the stars.

To our outposts.

And beyond.

No.

No. No. No.

"He can't leave this planet." The thought forms in my mind on instinct, sharp and cutting. I sense Brellin's hand tenderly covering her stomach. *"We need to keep him here. Contained to earth."*

"I'm in agreement with Jin'qua," Tenzin thinks. *"Even if that means we stay here as well."*

Our thoughts intermingle, filling me with a vision of a brood we might have made—Tenzin, Brellin, and I. Perhaps such a triunion might have worked. For now, it is only a vision: *his* dream, stillborn and fading.

"Contained?" My'nar buries her face in her hands, each doubtful thought echoing louder than the last. *"That thing in the halls is terraforming the ship. He slaughtered the High Council and petrified our walls. Our very air is poisoned with his thoughts. You all mock my neuron density, and yes, I am slow. But by what unbalanced calculation do we even stand a chance?"*

Against the low buzz of the glowstalks and the hiss of the lab's nerves, the silence stretches on. Only a low burble from the oxygenator as an umbilical feeds our sleeping subjects. I can't help but envy the Greenburgs.

If they open their eyes, their nightmares abate.

"Yes, yes, despair and frustration; I felt these as well." Nivex

scurries back the projector and sockets another crystal. "*However, while I was scanning our subjects' memories I discovered many curious moments. Brellin, as a collector of human expressions, I believe you might know this one too. 'You can't put the genie back in the bottle.'*"

Brellin's thoughts shine, a pleasant rainbow as she smiles. "*That's correct.*"

"*An odd expression, as it denotes a situation's irreversible nature,*" Nivex continues. "*Yet Noctus Khan was put in a bottle, or rather, a tetrahedron. Cross-referencing such an object with hominid myths and memory and the data crystals, we've uncovered a potential course of action.*"

With a twist, Nivex sockets the final crystal. Above us, the lab's ribbed flesh quivers, a million pores dilating and sparking as the memory projection warms up. I am no longer looking up, but out and backward through time, the hazy fog of harvested human memories taking form.

"*I apologize,*" Elex conveys. "*But things are about to get very strange.*"

"*Yes, yes,*" Nivex smiles. "*Quite strange, indeed!*"

CHAPTER 23

HUMAN CURIOSITY #7,814: superstition. Across history, they've worshipped nearly ten thousand gods. First, it was the shadow in the cave. Then, the flayed bear. As they split into tribes and scattered, their pantheons multiplied beyond census. Eventually, we stopped counting. Yet ask most humans, and they'll proclaim faith in whatever deity presides over their time and place.

Now, looking out through the memory projector and into the past, I am uncertain which god they are revering.

Who are these robed people standing in a circle, swaying with interlocked arms?

What is the purpose of the candles and burning herbs at their feet?

Why do they throw their heads back and emit such strange sounds from their throat?

Chanting. Yes, this is some sort of ancient rite held deep in these stony, vine-choked halls.

In the ceremony's center, amidst a mewling vortex of sharp shadows, looms a familiar object: the tetrahedron. Three humans surround it, each leaning in and pressing their palms against its surface. Behind them, royal guards emerge, strong and armored. They drag an old, bearded man toward the center, his twitching ankles smearing lines across the sandy floor. From his hands, jeweled fingers scratch at the air. Beneath a glimmering crown, his eyes are tightly closed. Yet the king's face twitches in familiar rhythms.

He is dreaming.

"We've found seven hundred and forty instances of Noctus Khan buried in their genetic memory," Nivex informs us as the past plays out. *"In some encounters, he appears as a mirage.*

Others, a wise advisor to rulers. Occasionally, he gathers a following, offering them wisdom in exchange for devotion, power for supplication. In all instances, it ends up the same: he exhausts the population until little remains."

As the sleeping king is dragged to the center, the chants grow louder and more fervent. I tilt my neck, straining to look past the edge of the dark chamber. There, where the fog of memory is thickest, I catch a hazy glimpse of a stone archway.

I wish I'd never looked beyond.

Because of the depravity, it stains my mind as my body recoils. A glimpse, yes, but even that is too much, and the images overwhelm me.

Sandy, dust-choked streets lay thick with blood and the skinless lumps of human forms. Red wetness is smeared upon wooden doors. Spears drip, heavy with impaled bodies still screaming. A red dawn, filled with so many crows and flies that their cries and buzzing swarms my senses.

A monument to atrocity and a temple of suffering. That is what they have built.

A tender hand squeezes me, pulling me back. I am beside Brellin, stable as the king's memory continues. I offer her my deepest thanks, but Nivex's thoughts boom out.

"While we've studied hominids extensively, our data suggests Noctus Khan is something different, and far more resilient. Attempts to physically overpower him often fail."

My attention returns to the old king, dragged closer and closer to the tetrahedron. His eyes remain shut, but his fingers twitch and curl.

No, they're not fingers at all, I realize, but the curved blades of a sickle. Has the ruler's skin always been so mottled? Had this sleeping monarch's gilded crown always had jeweled teeth clamped deep into his head?

"Unlike Grays, when a human dreams their prefrontal cortex is suppressed," Nivex continues. *"Their critical thinking and self-awareness is reduced. They lack understanding of actions and consequences. They pull teeth out or fall from great heights. They find themselves being chased or perpetually late to exams. Noctus Khan bends their subconscious desires to his will."*

With a deep shudder, the chamber changes. The ritual members contort, their faces taking on twisted perversions. Dog-like snouts fuse with putrid, simian brows. Cavernous noses descend into hollow skulls. Their backs bristle, taking on the scaly hunch of lizards. With a grunt, the royal guards shiver, becoming a pair of scabrous brutes, dog-like faces over tumorous chests. Even the queen takes on a cruel distortion—her opulent dress stretches into a patchwork of flesh, mewling faces echoing the cries of the crows.

"Demons!" the old king screams. "Usurpers and foul horrors. You have all betrayed me!"

No. Too much. I am rendered numb by the horrid depths of human nightmares made flesh. No wonder they spend so much time awake. It is a defense mechanism; a trick of their mind's evolution.

To survive. To thrive. To keep itself from spreading madness.

And yet, in the center of the ritual, something passes between the three humans and the tetrahedron. An encouragement, spoken so softly, the memory almost engulfs it.

But not entirely.

Something like, "It's time to wake up."

"*While it appears nightmares cannot be destroyed,*" Nivex thinks, "*They can be contained. Forgotten, if you will. Such instances are not without their own unique challenges.*"

Holding the old king down, the royal guards struggle as his body twists and transforms. A whirl of silk and a flash of curved metal. The glint of a blade swung by old, sleeping hands.

Crimson seams erupt across the guards' throats, their arms, and opening up their guts. With gloved hands, they paw as the wet ribbons spill onto the floor.

"You think exile frightens me?" a sandy voice speaks with the king's stolen lips. "I've outlived your temples and gods. I'll outlast your final prisons. But you simple, speaking apes need the nightmare. You need me to remind you just how dark your dreams truly are."

Despite his taunting words. Despite the flashing metal and slashing blades. Despite their own blood spilling onto the stony floor and the pallor draining from their wounded flesh, the guards press the king to the ground.

It is only when the medicine man steps forward that Noctus Khan's words turn to fear.

"You. . .wouldn't. . .dare!"

It's because of the hammer and the serrated terebra in the doctor's hands, I realized. Because of how precisely it's placed against the king's sweaty head. Because of how the hammer is raised and brought down.

Two holes, one on each side of the king's sweaty skull. Tappity tap. Tappity tap.

Clutching the tetrahedron with one hand, the three ritualists place their palms on the mad king. The room swirls in a confusion of shadows as candles topple over. Wax and blood intermingle. All the while, the sand whirls and the wind whistles and the crows scream and. . .

And then it is over.

The darkness fades and the horrors abate. The shrieking crows become the first murmurs of songbirds. The buzzing flies give way to the last touch of a gentle, passing rain. Golden light suffuses the chamber, dawn breaking through that stony arched window that looked upon such violence.

In this amber-lit moment, the king opens his eyes, fingers trembling as they touch his sweaty, torn robe. Although he speaks a language long dead, I need no translation to understand.

"Praise be. I'm awake. Finally, this long nightmare is over."

One step. Two steps. He reaches out for his queen, her sunlit face upturned as a smile stretches her cheeks.

Then they crack.

With a low gasp, a layer of sand peels from her skin and takes flight with her breath. The sand dances over the royal guards, scouring the dog-like features, revealing plain faces scrunched in a final mask of struggle and pain. With a faint crackle, the wind moves over the crowd revealing bodies heaped beside one another, blades and cudgels still wet with each other's blood. A curl and the sandy breath rises and flirts past the singers, their mouths agape and their lungs empty. When the wind caresses the queen once again, her smile twists into a grimace of pain. Her fingers fall to her stomach, touching the jeweled hilt of the curved blade the king has buried in her gut.

"No," he mutters. "No. No, no, no. . . I thought. . . I thought I was dreaming."

With a low cry, the queen collapses, her crown following from her head. It clatters and rolls through crimson puddles and traces of dust and spice. It turns a great circle around the weeping monarch. It rattles and wobbles, priceless gems falling from the sockets. With a final weak clang, it comes to a rest at the base of the tetrahedron, between three dead worshippers, their limp hands falling from the rocky surface, leaving three five-fingered imprints in blood.

"Please," the king mutters. "I just want to wake up."

CHAPTER 24

To: Harold Greenburg
Fort Darrow, California

Dear Mr. Greenburg,

This letter is in response to your recent FOIA
(Freedom of Information Act) request regarding
alleged alien abductions, advanced dream technology,
and nine-dimensional abridgment.

After thorough internal reviews, NASA confirms
that we have no knowledge or records of these
subjects or ongoing projects. We are not involved in
the development of astral prisons or "weaponized
dream catchers." Such research is beyond the scope
of NASA's budget, mandate, and known laws of physics.

Furthermore, your proposed paper on "The
Inoculating Possibilities of Lobotomy" to safeguard
astronauts from "alien mind infections" is creative,
but speculative at best, if not dangerous. We assure
you no such procedure is necessary.

We are aware that you have also contacted the
Department of Defense (DoD), United States Air Force
(USAF), and the Central Intelligence Agency (CIA) with
similar inquiries. Please be assured that any
pertinent information held by these agencies would
have been shared.

ANDREW VAN WEY

Given the exhaustive nature of your inquiries, further communications on these topics will not be acknowledged.

Thank you for your understanding.

Sincerely,

Dr. Palmer Childs
NASA Headquarters FOIA Office
300 E Street SW
Washington, DC 20546

CHAPTER 25

IT TAKES THE average hominid mind 200 milliseconds to process stimuli and begin to understand it. As neurons flicker across synapses, in 400 milliseconds the brain begins to categorize patterns: the rustle of leaves, the crack of a twig, the low purr of a tiger prowling the tall grass. Comparing this to memory, the brain deduces meaning in less than half a second. A flash of understanding in the dark forest of existence.

Boosted by our shared neuronal network, it takes a Gray a quarter of the time. Yet the thought we currently share is so absurd—so blasphemous and terrible—that I feel the collective resistance of our minds.

Oddly enough, it is the crew member with the lowest neuron density who accepts it the fastest.

"*A lobotomy,*" My'nar thinks. "*You can't possibly be serious.*"

"*We are,*" Elex thinks.

"Yes, *quite serious, I'm afraid,*" Nivex adds.

Elex swipes his hand over the Greenburg family, proboscis caressing Harold's wrinkled forehead. "*While humans lack the Oneirogenic Hub our species has cultivated, they've still practiced forms of neurosurgery. Cancers, psychiatric treatment, even superstitions as we saw. Simple minds can still transmit dangerous thoughts. Sometimes, there is wisdom in sealing them off.*"

"*And you want one of us to do what exactly?*" My'nar ruminates. "*Let that thing into our mind while you seal it off?*"

Elex and Nivex shrug in unison while Brellin mentally scoffs. Only the click and hiss of the respiration tubes punctuate this near-total silence.

"*Voluntarily is preferable,*" Elex thinks.

"*Yes, yes, far preferable indeed.*"

There is tension forming. I can sense Brellin's mind turning toward the barricades, wondering perhaps if it's too late to escape. I offer a mental cloak so our thoughts co-mingle. Even My'nar's eyes flick upward, tracing an artery and perhaps a way out.

"*As the ranking Grays,*" Elex thinks, "*it is our duty to inform everyone that such an order must be followed.*"

"*Yes, protocol dictates all methods be followed to quell an infection.*"

My'nar gestures to the twins. "*Let me guess: your brains aren't on the dissection nest, are they?*"

"*It can't be theirs.*" My thoughts finally take form. "*Someone needs to do the procedure, right?*"

"*Correct,*" Elex thinks.

"*Yes, yes,*" Nivex echoes. "*Two operators, ideally.*"

"*Convenient, that part.*" My'nar rubs her forehead, fingers caressing the soft cranial folds. "*It's going to be me, isn't it? You're going to turn my head into some sort of trap.*"

"*Not a trap but a transport,*" Elex thinks. "*But yes, in our simulations you make an excellent candidate.*"

"*We have simulated multiple outcomes,*" Elex thinks. "*Your mind would be a good candidate.*"

"*Yes, an excellent container indeed.*"

"*It's a death sentence,*" I push back, the folds of my brain thrumming in sympathetic discomfort. "*No, it's worse. Whoever it is, they'll be severed forever. Singular. You can't demand such a thing.*"

"*We prefer not to,*" Elex thinks. "*A Gray mind on its own. . .*"

"*Yes, yes,*" Nivex bows his head. "*Such a demand would be less than ideal.*"

Tenzin's brow furrows, his eyes darting about as he guards every thought. Yet he lets one question slip. "*Can you guarantee this will keep Noctus Khan trapped?*"

"*Forever?*" Elex thinks. "*No. You saw the memory crystal. But it might be enough to purge his consciousness from our ship.*"

Our ship.

Only hours ago, the memory channels rang out with our collective amusement, a preemptive celebration for another successful trip across the stars. Now, they're near silent, only the tortured echo of Ciron's thoughts endlessly shrieking in human tongues.

Whatever our ship is becoming—a temple or a tomb—it won't be ours for much longer. It will be Noctus Khan's soon.

"*And then what?*" My'nar thinks. "*You just leave me on earth?*"

"*Of course not,*" Elex replies. "*Whoever volunteers, they will be taken home to Shy'ran. They will be given full honors, treated as a hero befitting such a gesture.*"

"*Yes, yes. Their sacrifice will live on in the timeless halls of our mind.*"

"*The timeless halls?*" Tenzin paces the lab. "*What comfort will that give them, alone with their thoughts?*"

"*As much comfort as we can offer,*" Elex thinks.

"*Yes, yes, and a decision must be made.*"

While the group fumbles with the implications, I skitter around to the dissection nests and let my mind sweep over the Greenburgs. They'll be awake in a few hours and Noctus Khan will make his way in. Into this lab. Into our minds. Into our future. Brellin's future, and the family only half-made.

No, I don't like the idea, but my mind's already turning it over. I slide my fingers over Jake's clammy palm. "*The tetrahedron,*" I think. "*It'll put the genie back in the bottle?*"

"*Theoretically,*" Elex responds. "*However, analysis indicates a fundamental incompatibility with our own bio-functions.*"

The markings on each face. Damn.

"*Yes, yes,*" Nivex adds. "*It was built by human hands. Thus, it requires humans to open and close.*"

"*Three human hands,*" I correct.

The low number echoes through our thoughts, vexing and cold. For so long, I had practiced counting down to it, imbuing it with images of Brellin, Soru, and me. A triunion. A triplicate. Us three, part of some greater plan, raising our brood together in the light of Shy'Ran.

Three.

Maybe it's a sign from the universe. Or maybe it's the sum of a great equation, the end of my journey. I am about to give form to the scariest thought of my life when Tenzin cuts in.

"*I'll do it,*" he thinks.

"*What?*" My mind reels. "*No. It should be me. I volunteer—*"

"*Yes, and no,*" Elex thinks.

"*No, and yes,*" Nivex adds.

"*Tenzin is our best candidate.*" Elex's mind spikes with a

sympathetic red. *"He has kept many secrets and his will is the strongest. His mind provides optimal transport. Jin'qua, however, is best suited to interact with the Greenburgs. The boys in particular will need guidance to close the tetrahedron."*

I try to form a response, a delay, anything, but Tenzin has already mapped it all out, arriving at this eventuality long before I had. No wonder he kept his thoughts guarded.

"It should be me," I tell him.

"Maybe. But it needs to be me." Tenzin begins peeling off a few bandages and swabs his hands with disinfectant. *"Besides, it's like you said on the surface. 'Two is one too many for this job.'"*

My words echoing back, more spiteful than I'd originally intended. Maybe Tenzin and I just never understood each other. Maybe our minds never found harmony. Maybe he would have made a good leader one day.

Grays cannot shed tears, but our thoughts can certainly weep.

"Relax Jin'qua." Tenzin hoists himself up onto a free dissection nest, its toothy umbilicals prepped and ready. It takes the full effort of every neuron in his mind to subdue the fear and exude confidence. *"Besides, I've got the easy part,"* he thinks warmly. *"You have to deal with the humans."*

CHAPTER 26

WHILE I'M HERE—while I remember—I want to tell you about the time the aliens put us back together, Jake, Tyler, and Lucas—that's me—and how they woke the three of us up. About how they said they needed our help to close something we'd opened. How we needed to save the whole world.

They didn't say anything actually, the aliens. Their mouths were too small and their tongues super weak, but one of them showed what they meant on the coolest TV we'd ever seen. It was built right into the gooey roof of their ship. It looked like a million filaments of light.

Mister Jay showed us how my grandpa knew him. He told us he was sorry more Grays couldn't make contact. Humans weren't ready to accept what else was really out there. Our brains needed more time to evolve.

But Jake pointed out that was kinda bullshit, 'cause here we were in their gross jellyfish spaceship, and I thought it was pretty cool. Tyler did not. When he saw them cutting open one of the alien's skulls, he turned pale and ralphed on the floor. A bundle of leeches squirmed over and started cleaning it up and he ralphed again.

Something funny passed through me, like a whisper in my mind, and I sensed Mister Jay and his colleagues were laughing. I didn't know aliens could laugh without tongues. The more I thought about it all, the more my head started to hurt.

Maybe they were right; our brains weren't quite ready.

A mind trap.

Noctus Khan.

That ancient stone that Jake stole from the museum.

Yeah, I was pretty sure I was dreaming, but Mister Jay informed me that was impossible; they had goo and spores that kept us out of NREM2 sleep. Weird.

They needed our help cause their ship was dying. Pretty soon, we'd be in trouble too, if we couldn't get that nightmare back in the triangle.

"Dude, we should ask them for something," Jake whispered, pulling us over by a weird stump covered in tongues. "You know, for helping them out."

"What, like a reward?" Tyler asked. "They're aliens. I could get a new e-bike, for sure."

"Were you guys even watching what they showed us?" I whispered. "That thing, it's like Freddy Kruger took all my sister's Adderall. If it kills them, we're stuck on this ship."

I glanced at the rest of my family: Grandpa Harold, my folks, and my sister all swaddled in something like living seaweed with umbilicals shoved down their mouths. No one would ever believe us.

"I'm just saying," Jake lowered his voice. "Shouldn't we get something in return?"

Mister Jay skittered over, his long silver arm gesturing to the alien with its head open, where two other aliens produced tools that reminded me of starfish.

A starfish with teeth.

Tyler almost lost it again, but Jake nudged me forward. "Tell him."

Mister Jay's oily eyes blinked as I tried to form words. The other aliens looked on and I realized they weren't as scary as Xenomorphs or that Predator with his wild fangs. They were kind of weak-looking. Like somebody mixed elves and manta rays and gave up halfway through.

"So, we want something," I said, my voice echoing off the wet walls and shiny ceiling. The room seemed to quiver and twitch. "To help you, I mean. Jake, Tyler, and I. . .we want, like, a reward."

Mister Jay tilted his head.

"For doing a favor," I continued. "Tyler, he wants an e-bike." I point to Tyler, who offers a meek nod.

I felt something like ribbons moving through my thoughts as Mister Jay studied me. After a moment, he nodded and gestured to the ceiling where that weird bio-television shifted. Images formed on the tips of millions of hairs: gems and diamonds, chests overflowing with gold coins and treasure.

"Yeah," Jake said. "I'll take that."

"Wait, can I have that too?" Tyler cut in.

Mister Jay ignored them, stretching out a finger with four joints and pointed at me. It was my turn, but I couldn't think of a thing. My mind was a blank.

Wish for a new gaming PC, I told myself. Like the one my dad built with Emma last fall. Or some new clothes, like that rare Supreme hoodie with the toy machine on it.

Then my eyes drifted to one body in particular, an old man whose only mistake was that he stood in the wrong place at the wrong time long ago and let curious eyes drift to the sky. Sleeping upon that nest of tendrils, his patchy hair crowned a lifetime of confusion. It wasn't fair that Grandpa Harold would never get to see any of this.

In the end, I settled on a wish that surprised me.

"I want my grandfather to know that he was right all along."

CHAPTER 27

HUMAN CURIOSITY #7,741: their bodies are neither modular nor optimal. For an apex species, their offspring are born near helpless, incapable of movement or self-referential thought. Grays are aware at the cellular level. Humans require sleep that hampers productivity. Grays invoke stasis, an inward vacation. Even human biology rebels against itself, the very telomeres in its DNA shortening after each cellular division, dooming them from conception.

Most of all, their bodies evolved for minimal internal access; they are like houses without doors or windows.

Grays have several ways to access our organs.

It amuses us to watch the boy's disgust as Tenzin's cranial flaps are peeled back like the petals of a flower, revealing the vast cerebral mantle and the glowing pink matter inside.

"Why does the yellow-haired one keep covering his mouth?" My'nar thinks. *"Why does he keep thinking of someone named 'Don't Ralph?'"*

When the twins attach the neuromasticator to Tenzin's brain and the teeth clamp to his delicate Oneirogenic Hub, that's when it happens. The Tyler boy vomits. Another bio-function that astounds me.

"Ralph," Brellin thinks. *"What a curious phrase."*

My'nar hands the sick boy a piece of sanitary moss, but his hands are clumsy and it falls apart in her grasp.

"Do they understand their part in this?" Elex inquires. *"It's important that we're all in alignment once the sphincter opens."*

"Yes, yes, quite vital indeed." Nivex connects the umbilical to the neuromasticator, giving the cord a tug. High above, the socket puckers, letting out slack in the line.

"They understand," I inform my colleagues, though I am

privately worried. It is difficult to verify the comprehension of pubescent minds.

Still, the plan is simple enough, even for humans. We open the door. We use Tenzin as bait. When Noctus Khan emerges, we give the twins the signal and they spring the mind trap. Then it's on myself and the three kids to seal up the tetrahedron.

What could go wrong? Pretty much everything.

Still, I force my thoughts into harmony. I need to be strong for the others.

For Tenzin, who will need our mental assistance to stand up to Noctus Khan.

For Brellin and the ovum that grows in her womb.

"For Shy'ran," Tenzin thinks. *"May your brood grow warm in her golden rays."*

His thoughts glow brightly as he steps up to the sphincter. For a moment, all my concerns wash away. I repeat Brellin's mantra.

You will.

We will.

Yes, we will.

The assault begins the instant the sphincter widens and the bone plates part. A wave of sand blasts into the lab, bronzing the walls and turning the air abrasive. In a blink, clear forms become dull shadows as my vision is reduced to dry fragments and flashes.

A hooded serpent squirms down the hallway beyond.

Spiny flowers bloom from the floor, eyes in the center of their petals.

Cactuses rise, formed from the tortured flesh of dead Grays. Our shipmates, mewling among spiked flesh and bleeding fruit.

Down the hall, stones erupt from the soft walls. Human shapes are etched among the rock. Alien ships. And creatures beyond our catalogue of knowledge.

"Oh, clever things," Noctus Khan's voice murmurs, a honeyed rumble laced among the scratching winds. "You think you're the first tribes to band together?"

"He can't come in all the way," Elex informs us. *"We've still got four sleepers and a buffer."*

"Yes, yes," Nivex echoes. *"Stick to the plan and stay focused. My'nar, on the tether. Tenzin, proceed."*

My'nar takes the umbilical, feeding it through her palms. In several nervous steps, Tenzin moves toward the hall, the sand reacting and the plants shivering. Something like a scorpion squirms out from an air tube above.

A scorpion with my great-grandmother's face.

"*Ignore it,*" Brellin thinks.

"*He's probing our thoughts.*" My'nar wipes her forehead and blinks away the dust. "*I can feel him inside.*"

Another blast of sand buffets us, and Tyler shouts, "It's like the end of the world!"

Jake grins. "This is awesome!"

The words have barely left the boy's lips when a shape whirls past the doorway.

Blades.

Curved blades for its hands.

"*It cut me,*" Tenzin thinks, wincing and stepping back. I can see it now, the blue drip down his left arm. "*That wretched thing cut me.*"

"*He's taunting us,*" Elex thinks.

"*Yes, yes. Follow the plan and keep focused. My'nar, don't let him get too far away.*"

Shaking, My'nar gives the umbilical a tug. Tenzin groans, his head jerking back as the cranial flaps quiver and the masticator constricts.

"*You trying to lobotomize me early?*" Tenzin seethes. "*We need to draw him out.*"

Through the gold sandy mist, Tenzin's shape pushes further into the hall. Then, a sudden flash as a gemmed shape races past, and Tenzin vanishes. A second later, the umbilical is wrenched from My'nar's fingers. It whips across the sandy floor, loose and unfurling.

"*Get it!*" Elex commands.

"*Yes, yes! If we lose that it's all over.*"

As My'nar's fingers close around the slippery cord, the friction blistering her palm. She lets out a guttural shriek, palms raw and dripping. I lunge forward, feeling the wet umbilical squirming and whipping, growing looser and looser.

I can see it now, our failure unfolding. My'nar's bloody hands. The twins desperately trying to buy slack as the neuromasticator shudders. Tenzin's thoughts turning to panic, Noctus Khan pulls him deeper and deeper, into the ship.

No.

I grab the tendril, wincing as the braided veins slide past. I squeeze and squeeze, the bulbous texture—once cool and dense—now warming with friction. Boiling. Burning my skin and—

And then it slows.

"Dude, hold onto it," Lucas shouts behind me, and I feel breath on my neck. Oddly, it reminds me of pizza. "Guys, it's like tug of war, remember?"

He's not talking to me, but to Tyler and Jake, their hands now also gripping the umbilical. Little puffs of steam waft up between their fingers. The cord slowing, slowing. . .

"Ugh, it smells like old cheese," Lucas groans.

"Like your grandmother's cooch," Jake laughs.

Tyler makes a burping noise, stifling a gag.

But it's enough, I sense, to arrest the runaway tendril. Enough for the moment, but not much longer.

I scan the sandy air, the neuromasticator stretched to its limit. The boys holding the cord, feet grinding along the dusty floor. The twins, ready to spring the trap.

But Tenzin. . .*damn.*

I close my eyes, bifurcating my mind. In one half, I anchor my body here, keeping hold and tugging.

In the other half, I send my thoughts surging down the length of umbilical.

Through the acrid halls of our infected ship, where flesh splits and old stone chews its way out. Where locust-covered humans kneel and bow in endless rows, their poxed bodies a map of fresh wounds. Where forlorn statues of forgotten rulers lay on their side, crumbling among piles of dry bones.

Noctus Khan's voice booms out, swirling among the shadows. "You fools, rich with your harvested knowledge. Blind travelers, so strong with your dreams from the stars. Yet tell me—with all your wisdom—how is it that you don't recognize your own reflection?"

"*Ignore him,*" Elex thinks.

"*Yes, yes, he's using your own thoughts against you.*"

The umbilical stretches and turns impossible corners, down halls lined with gem-laden effigies and past overflowing altars. Swaddled babies mewl beneath eyeless priests and goat-headed totems. Yellowed teeth shimmer in the candlelight.

"Yes, ignore him," Noctus Khan echoes. "You wouldn't be the first of your kind to follow such orders. When you've been cast away, waylaid, and forgotten, even your own shadow becomes a glimpse of a stranger."

The umbilical worms through deep caves, where pictorial histories flash past. Figures hunting buffalo and holding meat over fires. Stars forming a crude shape painted on dry walls.

A shape that looks, oddly enough, like a sickle.

My hearts race and my eyes drink in the cave painting. I recognize the configuration: six stars forming an asterism, a smaller pattern within the constellation humans call Leo.

It was this pattern Harold looked up at one night, a human lifetime ago. It's the direction of our home, Shy'ran.

A rumble shakes the cave and sends dust down as Noctus Khan's voice speaks from the depths. "Will you do whatever you need to survive, little Gray man? Will you take refuge in the deep caverns of myth? Will you steal human dreams to nourish your own?"

The umbilical grows loose and limp, falling to the sandy floor as the dust storm settles. I force my consciousness on.

Across a nocturnal desert where sidewinder snakes roll hypnotically upon cooling sands.

Past long extinct lizards, blinking between volcanic rocks.

Over endless dunes dotted by the fires of prehistory, camels and goat herders and nomads, all circling flames for warmth beneath a vast, starry night sky.

Here, where the desert grows green and trees sprout tall and strong, a watering hole shimmers under the pallid light of the moon.

Tenzin stands at the edge of the oasis, his hands caressing the tall grass. My mind joins his, merging. I sense a welcoming squeeze as he lets me in.

"*He's here,*" Tenzin thinks. "*He can't go much further.*"

"*What is this?*" I ask.

Tenzin hesitates, and it feels like hours have whirled past since I first asked the question. He thinks, "*Jin'qua, have you ever wondered if your mind fully returned?*"

"*What?*"

"*After your triunion,*" he thinks, "*with Soru and Brellin. I've heard that it happens. That sometimes the fethym goes crazy and not all comes back. That's why I was always scared to ask you.*"

My hearts race as a shiver tightens my spine. In the grass

below, a mouse scurries over my foot. In the moonlight, I glimpse its mangy face.

Soru.

Then it scurries off into the shadows.

"You asked what this place was?" Tenzin thinks. *"It's the beginning."*

Peering out through his eyes, I struggle to understand what I'm seeing. My tired mind can only assemble it in pieces.

The broken, dry husk of a hydrozoanic structure lays wrecked against the far edge of the oasis. Its once colossal mantle and thin, star-tracking filaments lay dry and brittle and broken. Folds of soft flesh that once formed an observation platform, now torn asunder. The shattered hull, its bones splayed like open hands, revealing the cerebral command cortex. A dozen bodies lay across the sand, a feast for the vultures.

Not human bodies.

Grays.

Some are unrecognizable, their forms obliterated by the crashed ship. Others are oddly intact, save for a missing limb or a dented skull.

One Gray, however, is still alive.

He crawls toward the moonlit pool, his broken, torn hands dipping into the water. He laps it up with a tiny, dry tongue. Then he glances back, not at us, but at the humans approaching.

They wear crude leather and throw sharpened sticks. They pull back the strings of a bow and line up arrows of bone and feather. With hoots and grunts, they cleave the tall grass with curved blades, searching for that wounded creature.

A thing not of their world.

"Tell me," Noctus Khan asks, "will you beg for their help? Contorting yourself—evolving as a species of one—to survive in a new world, dream-starved and cursed?"

At the edge of the tall grass, blue blood spatters the rocks and reeds, leading to the mouth of a cave. The wounded Gray—a creature of far distant kin—skitters inward, into the darkness.

Shouting and hooting, the ancient humans follow, their torches casting jagged shadows on the rocky cave walls. Shadows that stretch and twist. Shadows that take on jagged form.

"Tell me, will you feed off their meager dreams for a chance at your own?"

A single flicker of firelight from the depths of the cave: something monstrous and sharp, its eyes golden and its teeth as endless as the stars high above.

Shrieking, hooting, crying out among the black depths, the humans retreat from the cave. Back into the safety of the tall grass. Back to the oasis. Back to the dusty dunes and leather tents and their warm fires where myths are born over cinders and smoke.

"Tell me, will you evolve when it's needed?"

A curious feeling blooms in Tenzin's mind, one rare for Grays to express.

Pity.

"*No*," Tenzin thinks.

He pities this abomination. This Noctus Khan thing. And all the other masks it had to wear over the eons. All that it had to do to survive.

"*I'm sorry you were left behind,*" Tenzin thinks. "*But whatever you've become, it's time you go home.*"

Then, he enters the cave.

CHAPTER 28

Dear Lucas,

I want you to know how proud I am of you. It warms my heart to see what an honorable young man you've grown into. I know that you and your friends found my diary a few months ago and that you put it back. That was the right thing to do. It shows the strength of your character to return what isn't yours. You're a good kid.

I also know that everyone thinks I am crazy. Maybe I am. If I never looked up at the sky that summer night, this curse wouldn't haunt our family. Sometimes I wish I never existed. But then I know you wouldn't either and that makes me sad. But because of my actions, the aliens will visit our family for generations. They'll be arriving tonight, I'm fairly certain. Maybe you'll find this note and think I'm crazy like everyone else.

But maybe, just maybe, if I damage my own mind, they'll lose whatever data they've been collecting. If I do that, perhaps they'll leave our family alone.

I'm so sorry I have to leave you like this, Lucas. I'm sorry you'll all have to clean up the mess. But I only know one way to get them out of my head.

Be strong, Lucas. Remember, I'm proud of you.

With all my love,
Grandpa Harold

CHAPTER 29

I DO NOT know what it is he saw in the mnemonic depths of that cavern, in the prehistoric tunnels of Noctus Khan's mind. I like to think Tenzin found a remnant of the being that was marooned here on Earth so long ago. A distant ancestor perhaps, one who still held an ember of Shy'ran. I like to think Tenzin offered Noctus Khan a moment of peace.

I only know that there were raised blades and screams, then a terrible rending deep in our minds. I am ejected, arriving back in the lab, the umbilical still in my hands as I collapse to the floor. Dust swirls at my feet then vanishes as a pleasant sourness returns to the air. The cord snaps loose in my fingers as the boys fall behind me. This "tug of war" is suddenly over.

"*And it's done.*" Elex gives the neuromasticator's nerve bundle a last squeeze.

"*Yes, yes, I think that should do quite well indeed.*"

The device lets out a burp as the umbilical retracts.

"Did we get him?" Tyler asks. "Is the boogeyman dead?"

"It's not the boogeyman," Jake says. "Weren't you paying attention?"

"Whatever it is," Lucas says, "I don't think you can kill it. Isn't that right Mister Jay?"

I don't have time to answer him, either in gestures or symbols on the screen high above, because the umbilical slithers across the floor, its gooey muscles growing thicker and thicker.

There, at the end, clutched in the device's teeth, is the glowing lump that makes up Tenzin's Oneirogenic Hub. All the difference between hominids and Grays, reduced to a gooey seed, tender and shining.

"Dang," Jake says. "Is he, like. . .game over?"

Tyler swallows, growing pale.

Even my colleagues' thoughts are rendered numb. We knew this would happen, yet seeing Tenzin's sacrifice—seeing all that we connected to and knew as this clump of dying neurons and light—it staggers us each in our own way.

"*For Shy'ran*," Brellin thinks.

With a slow skitter, then a pause, a Gray shape leans against the bone plates at the edge of the lab.

Tenzin.

I reach out for him on instinct, my mind offering encouragement and a hearty congratulation.

I receive nothing.

Not a wall of intentional quiet or hesitant murmurs. Not the begrudging recognition of a colleague or a competitor, a lover or a friend. Not even an acknowledgment, echoing in the Overmind as the ship's systems come back online, connecting each of us, one too many to all.

Except Tenzin.

How do you speak with the deaf when you live in a world built only for sound?

How do you listen to the mute if they have no lips to form words?

For all our dream-built technology, we are dependent on the very senses we share.

"I think. . ." Lucas says. "Mister Jay, I think your buddy's not doing too well."

My buddy. . .

It is an odd human concept, but one I quite like.

In the silence between Tenzin and I, it is a concept we'll never again share.

The ritual is anticlimactic and completed rather easily. Following the memory crystal, we align the boys and Tenzin, their hands and his head touching the tetrahedron. The words, easily produced as text on our memory projector above, are read aloud by Jake, Tyler, and Lucas.

"Dumu-ki-maškim-gub," Tyler says. "May our dreams rest."

"Druhébhóm wesét stigmóm," Lucas follows. "May our dreams be stilled."

Jake hesitates, glancing at his two friends. I sense sorrow forming in his thoughts. "This was a pretty cool sleepover, right? Even if this is maybe just all in our heads?"

"Yeah buddy," Lucas says. "It was."

Then Jake presses his palm to the tetrahedron's cool stone. "Télos enýpnion génoito. May our dreams end."

For a moment, Tenzin's body arches, and his biosignals spike. Brellin and I hold his hands, telling each other that if this is to be his final moment, we will be here beside him.

The word family forms in my mind, dusty and gilded. Brellin smiles at me.

Then, it is done: the ritual is over.

I sense the Overmind scanning the ship, assessing the damage. My'nar will have a lot to clean up. We'll all have to help out.

Human curiosity #7,982: Free-falling. They are not a species made for a rapid descent from the lower mesosphere.

As the gravity lift ushers through the cloud's warming layers, the boys scream with glee. Even Tyler laughs, pointing to the distant locations across their town.

"Dude, you can see Coogan's wharf. Check it out!"

He only vomits twice on the eight-minute descent.

The rest of the Greenburg family sleeps, their bodies encysted and their minds fully erased. Another human expression: ignorance is bliss.

At the edge of the gravity lift's beam, buffeted by the wind and mist, Tenzin watches. His mind is silent, his face a placid mask. I reach out for his thoughts but only hear the mental echo of the cleanup in the ship high above.

There is so much to assess.

In the house, Tenzin helps guide the sleeping Greenburgs back to their respective beds, pushing them on soft beams of light. I watch him tuck Mr. and Mrs. Greenburg beneath their speckled comforter. With a gentle touch, he peels back the last of the membrane, letting it dissolve into the night. They'll be awake soon.

"Fourth and fifth subjects returning to original position," I inform the Overmind.

I do not hear Soru's confirmation nor Ciron logging the data. The mind channels are mostly empty.

At the door to the basement, Tenzin taps my shoulder and makes a gesture to the boys descending the stairs. He draws a line across his forehead as if he's crossing something out.

"*Yes, I'll take care of them,*" I think. Then I remember he's no longer connected.

Instead, I nod in understanding.

I find the boys busy eating cold leftover pizza, their greasy fingers playing with their phones. With a quick thought, I power cycle the devices, ensuring they remain disconnected until our departure in a few minutes.

Tyler says, "It's too bad you can't stay a little longer."

"Yeah, we could show you around," Jake says. "The wharf has some good churros. The seagulls are dicks, though."

I study them as they settle in among the couch cushions and half-emptied soda cans. A topless woman stares out from a magazine, the pages peeking out beneath a blanket.

Humans truly are such curious creatures. I truly wish I could spend more time among them.

"You know Mister Jay, you're a pretty neat guy," Lucas says. "I'll tell my grandpa you said 'hello.' Like you promised, right?"

I feel my proboscis beginning to quiver. *No*, I think. *You won't tell him anything at all.*

CHAPTER 30

S O, I WANT to tell you about the time we saved the world. Actually, it wasn't just our world but some other world too. It was the home world of these aliens, the Grays, but it was our world that unleashed a dream demon. Well, it was Jake, really, and the stupid stone he stole.

But yeah, we faced down Noctus Khan and sealed him back in his prison. We're pretty much heroes.

I want to tell you how awesome it was to see an alien ship from the inside. How my grandpa was right all along. How there's so much more in the stars above us than just emptiness and a few speckles of light. I want to tell you all this and more.

Except, I know I won't quite remember it when I wake up. Mister Jay has planted something in my mind—a seed of destruction—and I can feel it taking root. When I open my eyes, it'll grow like vines in my memory, covering up all that happened. I know this because my grandpa told me about it once when he was sleepwalking. He said he had so many seeds in his head it felt like his dreams were the only time he was truly awake.

I didn't understand it then, but I want to tell you to remember. When you close your eyes and dream and look up at the stars, you might catch a glimmer of Shy'ran. And in that glimmer, you might remember how you saved the world from a nightmare.

Yes, I want to tell you this, Lucas, that when you're sleeping, it's me looking down on you. A small part the seed can't fully erase. A part that lives in a deep cave of your mind, primal and ancient.

I want to tell you to look up while you can. . .

I want to tell you to. . .

I want. . .

And then, I wake up.

The first thing I see is Tyler. He's on his side, the couch cushion fort half collapsed in a mound all around him. He rubs his eyes and squirms out.

"Dude, what time is it?" he mumbles.

For some reason, I'm happy to hear his voice.

"Six-fifteen." Jake mumbles as his phone's screen illuminates his face. His hair is messy and there are indents in his cheeks from the carpet. Or at least, that's what I think it's from.

For a moment, an odd thought overcomes me: what if our faces were removed and put back on too quickly? Would we all seem slightly different?

"What?" Jake asks. "You're looking at me like you wanna kiss me."

"It's nothing," I tell him. And it truly is. I don't know why, but in this moment I am relieved.

"Man, I'm wicked sore," Tyler says. "Your floor is like sleeping on rocks."

He stumbles over a box of pizza and piles the cushions back on the couch. He falls on it, pulling his sleeping bag up over his head. Within a few breaths, he's asleep again, snoring.

That's when I see it.

A stone tetrahedron sits at the edge of the coffee table, weird words shimmering in the darkness. I reach out for it, but Jake slaps my hand away.

"Ow," I say.

"That's a priceless artifact," he says. "Hands off."

"I don't want to touch it," I tell him.

And it's the truth. That object scares me. Something dusty blooms on my tongue, and for a moment I think of spices and sand.

Still, I don't like that creepy stone sitting there, so I toss a blanket over it.

Maybe Jake feels the same way because he uses the blanket to scoop it up and dumps it in his backpack. He zips it closed, then pulls it near him, one arm through the strap.

"This was. . .fun," Jake yawns. "We should totally. . .do this. . .again."

"Totes," Tyler mumbles from the couch.

The first glow of morning slices through the high basement window, falling on Jake's face. He grunts and rolls over. Within seconds, he's asleep, his phone clutched in his hand. Another curious thought: wasn't the screen cracked?

I want to tell Jake he will be alright. That maybe it's okay he moved away. That maybe friends drift apart like planets knocked out of alignment and sent off on their own. But that doesn't mean they didn't orbit each other once, bound by an invisible gravity that kept them together.

CHAPTER 31

WITH THE TWIN'S GUIDANCE, I wipe the boy's memories. Brellin insists we do it twice to avoid residual echoes, what the humans call a subconscious. I implant a few fears of the tetrahedron as well. Some humans carry genetic terror for the shape of spiders or snakes. I suspect the boys will avoid triangles for a while.

I find Tenzin in the Greenburg's living room, moving slowly and letting his proboscis caress the various textures.

The synthetic leather couch. A wicker basket. The decorated fruit that adorns an end table where a photo of Emma Greenburg stands, frozen in a moment years ago with a cap over her head and a baseball bat on her shoulder.

Maybe humans are onto something with these tokens of the past. Maybe since their dreams are so short-lived they keep memories alive in their own subtle ways.

Earth: it's all so confusing.

I take Tenzin by his elbow and lead him outside. The grass is cool and crisp underfoot; the night breaking. I can hear the first birds singing as a glow blooms to the east.

Tenzin's shuffle comes to a halt near the pond where the cattails sway in the breeze. He points to a cluster of reeds as a pair of nesting ducks paddle off.

He makes a gesture like his thumb is pulling down. He points at himself.

"I don't understand" I think. *"Do you want something?"*

Mental silence.

He points at the cattails, to me, and makes that same gesture. Like he's pulling something in. Then he points a single finger at his head.

No.

No no no.

The idea hurts to even think. Tenzin will have a place of great honor back home. He will be well known all across Shy'ran, the one who helped trap Noctus Khan. He will. . .

He shakes his head and shuffles over to the cattails. His hands clumsily part the reeds and fumble among the pond's muddy banks.

While he thinks nothing, his tired eyes say it all: he wants this to be over. An echo of Harold, who stood here mere hours ago, begging for the same mercy. Harold, who lived with our fingers in every inch of his flesh for seven decades. Now Tenzin, and I can only wonder what scars Noctus Khan left in his mind.

Please, Tenzin's eyes glisten. Please.

I wave my hand, willing the gun to rise from the grass and return to my grip. With a mental push, I realign the molecules and rehydrate the powder.

The .38 Special feels odd in my three-fingered grip, but with my proboscis I can hold it. A most rudimentary tool, I had mused. Yet like the sickles that cut my crew, sometimes simple is all that is needed.

Tenzin wobbles and rises, his gravity-compressed muscles straining against the pull of this planet. For a moment he stands tall and proud, his face turning upwards to the brightening dawn, where a single cloud hangs in a sky full of fading stars.

He nods at me. Do it.

And I do.

CHAPTER 32

HUMAN CURIOSITY #7,999: the sound of a gunshot is far more deafening than expected.

As my fractured senses swirl and the world tumbles behind a ringing curtain of pain, I strain to call out for an emergency extraction. When my eyes finally stop blinking and the gunpowder clears, I realize I am sideways near the garden.

I click my jaw, but the ringing remains.

Other senses return. The sound of a dog barking. The whine of something sliding open. A click of a latch or a knob.

Then something else.

The full-throated sound of a human screaming.

It takes my full mental focus to clear my vision, and my mind shudders.

Mrs. Greenburg has her head out the bedroom window, her mouth making an O shape as she gasps out her words. "What is that? Marshall! *Marshall*, come quick—what the fuck is that *thing* by the garden?"

"Oh my god!" Emma's voice joins the chorus, her window clicking open as well. Then the kitchen door swings open and three boys pour out with their mouths stretched in horror.

"It's a monster!" Lucas screams.

"Holy shit, there's two of them!" Jake adds. "That one shot the other one, look!"

Tyler's gaze swings to the ruined body of Tenzin.

He shivers and pukes on the deck.

No, I'm not a monster, I want to tell them. We fought off Noctus Khan and saved the ship. But my seeds have already taken in their mind.

"Brellin, I need an extraction, now!" I think. *"Send me the beam, quick!"*

I turn and skitter across the grass, my senses scrambled from the gunshot and the barking dog and whizz of rocks now flying past my head.

"Monster!" the boys shout and gather stones. "Monster!"

Panicking, I open a private mind tunnel to Brellin. I am ready to go home. Now. Now. Now!

I slide through the garden, my feet catching on tomato plants and vines. Suddenly, I'm sideways again, the plants falling over in a tangle of fruits and leaves. The dewy soil rises, and I'm on my back, my hearts racing as I look skyward.

There, a solitary cloud hangs as a wisp of moisture, so light it looks like it could burn away in the morning glow. A single drop of rain falls from the cloud, striking my face and opening up a thin seam.

I wince, touching my cheek. That wasn't a raindrop but something much harder.

A grain of sand sits at the end of my finger.

With a golden shimmer and the peeling of dust, the high cloud turns to sand and blows off in the wind.

There is nothing within it.

No ship waiting with its dream tendrils. No thrust pustules quivering in excitement for the long journey home. No blue beam of the gravity lift ready to scoop me up.

There is only emptiness and the twinkle of stars in the fast-brightening sky.

No. My hearts thump and my mind sours.

"Brellin!" I send my strongest message. *"Brellin, what happened? What's going on?"*

The Overmind is weak, its signal coming from beyond the planet's atmosphere. I sense great acceleration, and—

A presence. Yes. Sandstorms and spices and gilded lips murmuring from warm, amniotic waters. It creeps through her thought channel, a gestating mind imbued with an echo of Soru and Brellin. Something distinctly both human and Gray.

Yet something new altogether.

"Did you really think I'd let you stuff me back into that prison?" Noctus Khan murmurs. "Not all of me, no. See, you're not the only one here that can put their mind in two places."

Now that voice is pulling me—*his* voice—ripping my thoughts across space and giving me a bifurcated glimpse of a place I knew well.

Brellin stands in my pod, her face pressed against the ship's thin membrane. I watch through her tired eyes as the blue Earth shrinks and the void grows darker and darker. Her hands are marred in blood that I sense is not her own. With a sigh, her fingers slide down her skin, directing our shared gaze.

Brellin, whose ovum I had yet to imprint with my memories.

Brellin, who collected human expressions.

Brellin, who has now collected something else.

"*Brellin,*" I think. "*What have you done?*"

"Oh, she's had a busy morning as well," Noctus Khan says. "Gray curiosity #1: it only takes a single crew member to pilot this ship to the nearest outpost. Farewell, Jin'qua. I do hope you enjoy your new home."

Her hands stop on her abdomen, tenderly stroking the newly forming bump. A womb now imprinted and thrumming with life, just like she'd wished for.

A true child of the stars.

I try to warn her, but he is too strong—this thing we have all created together—and Noctus Khan ejects me. My consciousness is thrown back down onto the damp garden, my limbs tangled in the tomato plants as the sky whirls above.

Other humans are gathering at the fence and the back gate. The Greenburgs and their neighbors and someone walking their dog raises his phone. A dozen voices, shouting things like "Call the police!" and "Don't go near that creature; whatever it is."

It takes a moment to realize the creature they're talking about is me.

The only human not screaming is old Harold. In his loose robe, he takes a seat on the edge of the deck, his knobby knees wobbling. A unique sound leaves his mouth, low and sonorous, one I've never heard from his lips. With the breeze in his tired, wispy hair and the final stars fading in the crisp morning sky, Harold Greenburg throws back his head and laughs.

THE END?

Not if you want to dive into more of the Dark Tide series.

Check out our amazing website and online store
or download our latest catalog here.
https://geni.us/CLPCatalog

We always have great new projects and content on the website to dive into, as well as a newsletter, behind the scenes options, social media platforms, our own dark fiction shared-world series and our very own webstore. Our webstore even has categories specifically for KU books, non-fiction, anthologies, and of course more novels and novellas.

ABOUT THE AUTHORS

John Durgin is a proud active HWA member and lifelong horror fan. Growing up in New Hampshire, he discovered Stephen King much younger than most probably should have, reading *IT* before he reached high school—and knew from that moment on he wanted to write horror. He had his first story accepted in the summer of 2021. His debut novel, *The Cursed Among Us* was released June 3, 2022, and went on to become an Amazon bestseller. Next up, his sophomore novel titled *Inside The Devil's Nest*, released in January of 2023, followed by his debut collection, *Sleeping In The Fire* in June of 2023. In 2024 he released two more novels, starting with *Kosa* which released to stellar reviews, and *Consumed by Evil* through Crystal Lake Publishing in November 2024.

Gage Greenwood is the best-selling author of the *Winter's Myths Saga,* and *Bunker Dogs.* He's a proud member of the Horror Writers Association and Science Fiction and Fantasy Writers association.

He's been an actor, comedian, podcaster, and even the Vice President of an escape room company. Since childhood, he's been a big fan of comic books, horror movies, and depressing music that fills him with existential dread.

He lives in New England with his girlfriend and son, and he spends his time writing, hiking, and decorating for various holidays.

Find out more, or contact me: www.gagegreenwood.com

Andrew Van Wey

Author. Recovering Educator. Expat. Mountain Biker. Hunter of Rare Fountain Pens. Roller of Twenty-Sided Dice. Doggie Dad.

Growing up, Andrew Van Wey was the kid that always had his nose in a few books he shouldn't have. He reached for Stephen King and Clive Barker at a young age and watched *Re-Animator* far too early. He spent most of his childhood chasing nightmares.

Now, he gets to share them with you!

Readers . . .

Thank you for reading *What Swallows the Light*. We hope you enjoyed this 19th book in our Dark Tide series.

If you have a moment, please review *What Swallows the Light* at the store where you bought it.

Help other readers by telling them why you enjoyed this book. No need to write an in-depth discussion. Even a single sentence will be greatly appreciated. Reviews go a long way to helping a book sell, and is great for an author's career. It'll also help us to continue publishing quality books.

Thank you again for taking the time to journey with Crystal Lake Publishing.

Visit our Linktree page for a list of our social media platforms.
https://linktr.ee/CrystalLakePublishing

Follow us on Amazon:

MISSION STATEMENT:

Since its founding in August 2012, Crystal Lake has quickly become one of the world's leading publishers of Dark Fiction and Horror books. In 2023, Crystal Lake officially transitioned into an entertainment company, joining several other divisions, genres, and imprints, including Torrid Waters, Crystal Lake Comics, Crystal Lake Games, Crystal Lake Kids, and many more.

While we strive to present only the highest quality fiction and entertainment, we also endeavour to support authors along their writing journey. We offer our time and experience in non-fiction projects, as well as author mentoring and services, at competitive prices.

With several Bram Stoker Award wins and many other wins and nominations (including the HWA's Specialty Press Award), Crystal Lake Publishing puts integrity, honor, and respect at the forefront of our publishing operations.

We strive for each book and outreach program we spearhead to not only entertain and touch or comment on issues that affect our readers, but also to strengthen and support the Dark Fiction field and its authors.

Not only do we find and publish authors we believe are destined for greatness, but we strive to work with men and women who endeavour to be decent human beings who care more for others than themselves, while still being hard working, driven, and passionate artists and storytellers.

Crystal Lake Publishing is and will always be a beacon of what passion and dedication, combined with overwhelming teamwork and respect, can accomplish. We endeavour to know each and every one of our readers, while building personal relationships with our authors, reviewers, bloggers, podcasters, bookstores, and libraries.

We will be as trustworthy, forthright, and transparent as any business can be, while also keeping most of the headaches away from our authors, since it's our job to solve the problems so they can stay in a creative mind. Which of course also means paying our authors.

We do not just publish books, we present to you worlds within your world, doors within your mind, from talented authors who sacrifice so much for a moment of your time.

There are some amazing small presses out there, and through collaboration and open forums we will continue to support other presses in the goal of helping authors and showing the world what quality small presses are capable of accomplishing. No one wins when a small press goes down, so we will always be there to support hardworking, legitimate presses and their authors. We don't see Crystal Lake as the best press out there, but we will always strive to be the best, strive to be the most interactive and grateful, and even blessed press around. No matter what happens over time, we will also take our mission very seriously while appreciating where we are and enjoying the journey.

What do we offer our authors that they can't do for themselves through self-publishing?

We are big supporters of self-publishing (especially hybrid publishing), if done with care, patience, and planning. However, not every author has the time or inclination to do market research, advertise, and set up book launch strategies. Although a lot of authors are successful in doing it all, strong small presses will always be there for the authors who just want to do what they do best: write.

What we offer is experience, industry knowledge, contacts and trust built up over years. And due to our strong brand and trusting fanbase, every Crystal Lake Publishing book comes with weight of respect. In time our fans begin to trust our judgment and will try a new author purely based on our support of said author.

With each launch we strive to fine-tune our approach, learn from our mistakes, and increase our reach. We continue to assure our authors that we're here for them and that we'll carry the weight of the launch and dealing with third parties while they focus on their strengths—be it writing, interviews, blogs, signings, etc.

We also offer several mentoring packages to authors that include knowledge and skills they can use in both traditional and self-publishing endeavours.

We look forward to launching many new careers.

This is what we believe in. What we stand for. This will be our legacy.

Welcome to Crystal Lake Publishing—
Where stories come alive!

www.ingramcontent.com/pod-product-compliance
Lightning Source LLC
Chambersburg PA
CBHW070413310726
48977CB00003B/673